FROM YOU TO ME

K.A.HOLT

SCHOLASTIC PRESS/NEW YORK

Library of Congress Cataloging-in-Publication Data

Names: Holt, K. A., author.
Title: From you to me / K.A. Holt.

Description: First edition. | New York, NY : Scholastic Press, 2018. |
Summary: On the first day of eighth grade Amelia finds a letter that her older sister Clara wrote to herself before she drowned, and it contains a list of the things Clara planned to do in her own eighth grade year—so Amelia, with the help of her best friend Taylor, resolves to complete the list, in the hope that it will bring some closure and ease her still raw emotions.

Identifiers: LCCN 2017042922 (print) | LCCN 2017047166 (ebook) | ISBN 9781338193312 | ISBN 9781338193305 (hardcover) | ISBN 9781338193329 (pbk.)
Subjects: LCSH: Bereavement—Juvenile fiction. | Grief—Juvenile fiction. | Sisters—Juvenile fiction. | Families—Juvenile fiction. | Best friends—Juvenile fiction. | CYAC: Grief—Fiction. | Sisters—Fiction. | Family life—Fiction. | Best friends—Fiction. | Friendship—Fiction.

Classification: LCC PZ7.H7402 (ebook) | LCC PZ7.H7402 Fr 2018 (print) | DDC 813.6 [Fic] —dc23
LC record available at https://lccn.loc.gov/2017042922

10 9 8 7 6 5 4 3 2 1   18 19 20 21 22

Printed in the U.S.A.   23
First edition, June 2018
Book design by Baily Crawford

Dorothy Parker once said, "This wasn't just plain terrible, this was fancy terrible. This was terrible with raisins in it." This book is for anyone who has experienced terrible with raisins in it. It's a fancy terrible fist bump, from me to you.

CHAPTER ONE

TAYLOR SLAPS HER HAND ON her hip, the smack echoing through my bedroom. "I look good in these pants."

"You are a loony toon, Taylor." I hop into my matching pair, yanking up the zipper.

"Well, then I am a loony tune *who looks good in these pants.*" We stare at ourselves in the full-length mirror on the back of my bedroom door, lost in our own thoughts for a minute. When did Taylor get taller than me? I move my palm in a straight line from the top of my head and it bangs into her forehead. Taylor laughs.

"Okay, then." I lean over and grab a black T-shirt from the pile of clothes we've been trying on since seven a.m. I pull it over my head and say, "We're going to walk down those halls and every mouth in

Hemingway Middle School will gape open like that singing fish in your dad's office."

Taylor pulls an identical shirt over her head and tucks it into the identical black jeans she's trying on.

"I mean, you know what Beyoncé says."

Taylor raises her eyebrows in a mock questioning look. "Who run the world?"

"Girls."

"No, but *who* run the world?"

"GIRLS!"

We admire ourselves some more. All black. Yes. This will show the school that we mean business. This will tell everybody that summer is over and Amelia and Taylor are ready to take over the world. Top-dog eighth graders, that's who we are.

Taylor twists her long curls and spins them up to the top of her head. "I look like Sandy. Not even close to Beyoncé."

We start singing "You're the One That I Want" from *Grease*, both pretending to be Sandy from the end of the movie, when she's had her black leather transformation.

"You girls about done in there?" The annoyed voice calls over a loud knock on the door. "You don't want to be late on the first day!" Mom was a little grouchy about having to wake up so early to let Taylor in this morning. But then, thankfully, she realized the importance of getting our first day of school outfits *juuust* right.

"Almost done!" Taylor giggles.

We do some last-minute shirt tucking and walk out of my room and past my mother, whose face always looks pained these days. Mom hands us both breakfast bars and we grab our schoolbags. Taylor whispers, "Who run the world?"

I smile and hope that all the joking and singing has worked as some kind of magical camouflage. If I act happy, I will be happy. If I tell myself I'm happy, I will be happy.

I will be happy.

I will be happy.

CHAPTER TWO

SOMETIMES WHEN WE DRIVE BY the lake, I think I can hear it growling. Is that crazy? I see the dark stillness of it spread out along the horizon and I wonder if maybe under that peaceful surface is the whole body of a monster. Its head is turned up to face the sky, its mouth is wide wide wide open like that one time I watched a rat snake eat a baby possum. The monster is waiting quietly, patiently, for its next meal. I press my ear against the window of Old Betsy and I hear the rattling of her rusty doors and the whining of her all-weather wheels, but I also hear something else. Something low, almost more of a feeling than a sound.

The lake is hungry . . .

It's been three years since its last meal . . .

"Amelia." Mom's golden eyes, her tiger eyes, dart up to the rearview mirror, catching a glimpse of me in the back seat. "Amelia. Are you okay?"

I don't answer. Taylor looks me over and seems to decide that I'm probably okay. She catches Mom's eye in the mirror and nods ever so slightly.

Mom's eyes dart back up to the rearview mirror and catch my gaze for just a second. My own tiger eyes—identical versions of hers, with the golden sparkle, the flecks of green, the rim of brown—try to tell her what I'm feeling. They try to explain about the monster under the lake.

"I'll be late to the General Store today, maybe four thirty. I told Mrs. Grant, and she said that was fine. Will you be okay?"

I nod. Taylor's grandma has been giving me extra cheese on my grilled cheeses at the General Store soda fountain for three full years now. She makes me milk shakes and lets me pick out a handful of penny candy anytime I want. It sounds amazing, like a birthday wish come true. But I'd trade all the cheese in the world to have Clara back.

Even now. Even when it's not supposed to hurt every single day.

My eyes brim with tears but the annoyance of almost crying, *again*, seems to shut them down, thankfully. Taylor reaches over and squeezes my hand really quick.

Old Betsy grunts and wheezes her way around the rotary in the center of town. Instead of a stoplight, there's a huge fountain in the middle of the road that everyone has to drive around. A lot of days I think I feel like the fountain must feel. Everyone staring at it, wondering why it doesn't work. It looks totally fine on the outside, maybe a few cracks but nothing that's a big deal. But on the inside, something is definitely wrong. No matter how many experts and repairmen the town hires, no one can figure out why the fountain won't spray water anymore. It's been broken for thirty years because of some dumb prank, and it's like the prank just broke the fountain's heart.

My heart understands. Except that instead of NOT being able to spew water into the sky, I can't seem to stop spewing water from my eyes. None of the experts can fix me either. And believe me, a lot have tried.

Mom steers Old Betsy into the school drop-off lane and I thank the Universe that my water-spewing eyes seem dry right now. My heart is about to explode, but that I can handle.

That no one can see.

"Have a good day, sweetie," Mom says as Taylor shoves open the heavy car door and jumps to the curb.

You know those videos that are speeded up super fast? The ones showing a leaf falling from a tree, drying up, curling, and turning to dust in a matter of seconds? That's how I feel when Mom calls anyone—especially Taylor—"sweetie." But these days, pretty much anything that comes out of Mom's mouth makes me want to either crawl in a hole or run away as fast as I can (which is not very fast, but still). I can't exactly figure out why anything she does makes me want to leap out of my skin, but there you go.

Just another unfortunate mystery orbiting Amelia Peabody.

I kick open the car door and grab my nearly empty messenger bag.

"I love you!" Mom calls after me.

I want to call over my shoulder, "I love you, too!" but I don't. I mean, as far as last words go, *I love you* is pretty good. Yet . . . there's this part of me, a huge part, that wants to believe I can keep her safe by not saying anything at all. You can't get into a fiery car crash, you can't get struck by lightning, you can't trip and fall and break your neck, you can't be swallowed by the lake, if there are no last words. Right?

Taylor and I walk toward the big live oak tree in front of the school. I don't look back at Mom, even though I hear Old Betsy wheezing, even though I hear the car behind her gently honking. I hold my hand up over my head, a wave, even though I don't turn around. And finally, Old Betsy harrumphs out of the drop-off line and Mom is safe.

"Who run the world?" Taylor knocks her shoulder into mine and grins.

"Girls!" I grin back.

The bell rings and we both take a deep breath. We link arms and walk up the stairs through the heavy doors. My chin is high, but my heart is pounding. I try to ignore it. Usually all eyes are on me because I'm the poor girl with the dead sister. But now all eyes are on me because I WANT all eyes on me. No one feels sorry for Sandy in *Grease*. No one feels sorry for Beyoncé. Surely, my face only looks pale because of the tight black T-shirt. Definitely not because I'm afraid someone will call my bluff and realize I'm still the girl with the dead sister, the one who can't be trusted to speak out loud in class because she might burst into tears.

No. I'm the new Amelia. They're staring at me because they know I mean business. They know eighth grade is mine for the taking.

Well, mine for the taking after I peel my face from the edge of the doorway.

"Amelia!" Taylor's hands are over her mouth as she does a poor job of stifling her laughter. "Um. Watch out."

Perfect. Arriving in homeroom with a crease down the middle of my forehead was exactly what I had planned. Sigh.

Instead of milling around and talking about summer vacation, everyone in the classroom wanders from desk to desk scanning papers, with shrieks and moans and laughs filling the room.

"Wha—" I look to Mrs. Henderson, our new homeroom teacher. *New* meaning for eighth grade. Mrs. Henderson herself has been on the earth since the asteroid killed the dinosaurs.

"On each desk is a letter. Remember the ones Mrs. Werther had you write on your first day of sixth grade? Well, now it's time to find your letter and see what you've accomplished."

Mrs. Werther is even older than Mrs. Henderson. She was one of the aliens that rode in on the asteroid.

Taylor and I start to scan the desks, too. Taylor calls out, "Found mine!" and she sinks into her chair looking like she's ready to burst into terrified laughter. I walk up and down each aisle, not finding my name. The late bell echoes through the room and Mrs. Henderson shuts the classroom door. I'm starting to freak out. Where's my letter?

A desk toward the back of the classroom is empty, so I hurry over there. Surely, that has to be mine.

Dear Most Beautiful Queen of the Universe (snort).

I suck in my breath, running my hands over the impressions made by the pen and smoothing the letter flat on the desk.

NO.

No way.

Dear Self,

You have made it to sixth grade, no thanks to that seriously goofy little sister of yours and her obsession with trying to steal clothes from your closet. Hello, scaring me to death this morning when all I wanted was a clean shirt. GAH.

Holy Beyoncé. This is Clara's letter!

Without realizing what I'm doing, I drop into the chair attached to the desk. I hold up the letter and it shakes in my hands like my body thinks it's made of plutonium.

Mrs. Werther said to write something to yourself that would be inspiring when you read it on the first day of eighth grade. So. Hmm.

How about: Congratulations on making all your dreams come true! Making some of your dreams come true? Making at least a couple of them true? Remembering to just dream in the first place?

Well, in case you haven't made all of your dreams come true, here are some things I really hope you HAVE accomplished. And if you haven't... get after it, girl. Next year is high school! OMG.

1) Be nicer to Mom and Amelia. (Why is it easier to be nice to Dad? Try to not let

Mom and Amelia annoy you so much.
Remember, you love them. So much.)
2) Get on the softball team. (You're good.
Everyone says you're good. Always
remember... you're good.)
3) Ask Billy to a dance. (OMG. Billy. Sigh.)
4) Throw an awesome birthday party on the
lake. (Invite everyone, make sure the boat
is working, have enough ice cream for the
whole town, make sure everyone knows
it's YOU, Most Beautiful Queen of the
Universe, in charge.)
5) Plan the most epic eighth-grade prank ever.
(But do a better job than Dad did for his
prank—don't break the FOUNTAIN. Wow,
Dad, way to take it to the next level.)
   Seems doable, right? I mean, you ARE the
Most Beautiful Queen of the Universe. Anything
can happen.
   Good luck surviving middle school!
Love,
Yourself

I hear Clara's voice as I read the letter over and over.
It's as if she is leaning behind me and whispering in

my ear. Hot, embarrassing tears threaten to overflow down my cheeks.

I'm supposed to be tough and strong this year. How can I be tough and strong with Clara whispering in my ear about all the things she never got to do? And even worse . . . the one thing she did get to do: the birthday party at the lake.

The day the monster awoke. The day that was the end of everything.

"Amelia? Are you okay?" Mrs. Henderson's voice breaks through the clouds and mist of grief, and my head flies up to face my teacher. I grip the plutonium letter and want nothing more than to bolt from my desk, run home, and never come back to school. Ever.

"I'm—I'm fine," I manage to whisper. Taylor shoots me a look from across the room. If you have to say, "I'm fine," usually you are definitely not fine. This is something the two of us discuss a lot.

After an agonizingly slow nine-million-hour home-room, where all sounds and instructions seem to be coming through a tunnel a million miles away, where my head seems to be floating over my body, where I clutch the plutonium letter to my chest, afraid to breathe too deeply because I might combust into a cloud of atoms, the bell for first period rings. Everyone stumbles out of their desks and moves to the doorway. Taylor is by my side in about 2.7 seconds.

She kneels next to my desk, putting a hand on my arm. "Amelia. What is it?" I can't say anything. I can't move. She gingerly reaches over and pulls the now crumpled letter from my grip. As soon as she reads the top of the page, her hand flies to her mouth. She looks up at me, her eyebrows crinkling in an angry V shape.

"Do you think someone did this on purpose? To upset you? Who would do that?" Her eyes cast around the room, but everyone else is gone.

I like that Taylor always wants to protect me, but I don't think this was some mean trick. "I'm pretty sure Mrs. Henderson just saw the last name and got things mixed up. It's a miracle she's even still teaching. She's got to be at least one hundred and fifty years old. It had to have been an accident."

"Or some kind of divine intervention." Taylor's eyes are huge and her eyebrows now make wide arcs on her forehead. "Maybe this is the Universe's way of telling you you're on the right track—eighth grade really is the time for you to take over the world."

"What do you mean?" I sniff and realize there are tears spilling down my cheeks. That's me now: The Girl Who Doesn't Even Know When She's Crying.

Taylor glances down at the letter and then looks back up at me. "I mean, maybe you can do some of these things Clara has listed. You want to break out of your shell, right? What if you follow her lead?"

I reach over and take the letter from her, running my fingers over the handwriting on the paper. I can see where Clara's pen stopped for a minute while she must have been thinking about what to say next. I can see how her writing got messier when she was excited. I feel the grooves in the paper where she pressed her pen hard, making sure her words hit the page just right. It's like a little piece of her is here with me, after all this time. Something new, things I didn't know about her. Who is Billy? What does she mean about Dad being one of the kids who broke the fountain? I thought I knew everything about her, but here's this sudden peek into a girl I didn't really know.

"That'd be cool, wouldn't it?" Taylor presses. "You showing everyone that you're tough by following Clara's lead? I'd do it with you." Taylor gives me a hopeful smile.

I know it's probably been so hard for her, being friends with the Crying Girl, having to soothe me and help me on the days when everything just seems lost. That's why she's dressed in these ridiculous black clothes with me, why she wants me to see this as a sign—because if I can be normal again, then she can be normal again.

Maybe Clara's ghost is trying to tell me to be a better friend.

I don't know, though. Find this Billy kid and ask him out? Join the softball team? What would Beyoncé do?

"I think this is a terrible idea," I say.

Taylor claps her hands together and grins as she stands up. "We're doing it, then. AWESOME." I shake my head. Taylor is good at a lot of things, but not getting her way isn't one of them. She reaches down and helps me out of my seat. The classroom is filling with students for the next class.

"Come on, we're going to be late." Taylor drags me out into the hallway, pulling my schedule from my backpack, looking at my classes, and steering me toward algebra.

Is this crazy? This is crazy.

I don't actually want anything on Clara's list. If I'm honest with myself, I don't want to be wearing these black clothes. Do I even *want* to be queen of the eighth grade?

I think about my comfy bed. I think about pulling the covers over my head and just staying there, forever, like Dad almost did when Clara died.

I trip over my shoelace and Taylor catches me just before I sprawl out in the hallway.

"We might have to brainstorm a little about that softball thing," she says through a laugh.

This really is a terrible idea.

CHAPTER THREE

"EXTRA CHEESE?" MRS. GRANT'S SHARP stare bores holes in me and I wonder what secrets are leaking out.

"Yes, please," I say, looking down at the countertop. There are sparkly green flecks in the Formica. The Grants are very proud that the General Store hasn't been redesigned since it was built by Taylor's great-grandmother way back in the 1950s. It's like walking into a time warp, with the counter area for milk shakes and hamburgers, and the pharmacy in the back. How many places can you go get lunch, candy, toilet paper, and your allergy medicine all at the same time? Not many.

Mrs. Grant is flipping my grilled cheese on the griddle behind the counter. Her silvery hair is bunched up on top of her head, but the swirls of curls refuse to stay tied down and spring out all around her face and neck. I don't know how old she is, but she's never seemed like a grandma to me. She doesn't say a lot, but her eyes are these, like, magical black orbs that can apparently see into people's souls. Folks will sit at the counter and spill all their problems and ailments, and Mrs. Grant will listen intently and then offer a sandwich or a milk shake or a steaming order of hand-cut fries that seem to miraculously solve everyone's problems. At least for a few minutes.

I have more than a few minutes today, with Mom running late. I have no idea what her job is now that she's a "part-time city consultant" instead of the city manager, but whatever it is means that she's late a lot, and wears heels a lot. Not much different than before, really, except now when she's late, it means four thirty instead of eight thirty.

Taylor is upstairs in the apartment she lives in with her parents and grandma. She didn't say so, but I could tell she was ready to get out of the all-black clothes and put on one of her summery dresses. Taylor is a huge fan of flowy and flowery. I am so not, but I don't begrudge her. Just like she doesn't begrudge me my Chuck Taylor sneakers and constant stream of beat-up T-shirts.

I think my mom wishes I would dress more like Taylor, more like how Clara dressed, but she never says so out loud (unless you count deep sighs when I come downstairs dressed for the day).

17

"Let me know what you think." Mrs. Grant flips the grilled cheese onto a plate and pushes it toward me. She pumps a big squirt of vanilla syrup into a glass, scoops in some ice, and fills the rest with Coke from the hose thing connected to the big soda cylinders under the counter. I don't know why Cokes taste so much better here than anywhere else, but boy, do they. She gives the vanilla Coke a spin as she slides it to me, a smile sliding onto her face as well. She wipes her hands on the towel that always hangs from the front pocket on her apron.

"So," she says, her elbows on the counter, and her chin in her hands. "How is eighth grade so far?"

I take a bite of the sandwich and can't help the moan that escapes my lips. I catch a string of melted cheese dangling from my chin. "What is that? Cheddar, Havarti, and . . . did you put a sour apple in this?"

Mrs. Grant's eyes twinkle. "You're avoiding my question," she says. "Tell me about your first day." She winks and whispers, "Just a couple of thin slices of a Granny Smith apple. I know how you feel about tart things. If you like it, I'll make it a daily special and you can help me name it."

Naming the daily specials is a fun exercise in just the right puns. Taylor is really good at coming up with great ones. *Don't Go Bacon My Heart* was one of her best (BLT with extra B). And *Another One Bites the*

Crust was her idea for the French toast special. My suggestions are getting better. *I'm Kind of a Big Dill* tuna salad is one I'm proud of.

I take another bite and talk around the slight crunch. "It was mostly okay." I think about the letter, and about not saying anything about it. But there's something about those piercing eyes. They reach inside of me and I can't help but spill.

Taylor walks through the curtain in the back that hides the stairs leading up to the apartment. Her dog, Ratface, is right at her feet, hopping around like a squirrel. I'm not sure you're supposed to have a dog in a general store, but no one has ever said anything. Ratface is basically an unpaid employee. His job is to make everyone laugh. Taylor sits beside me and steals a fry just as I'm finishing up the story about Clara's mystery letter.

"She's going to do the things on Clara's list," Taylor says, nudging me with her shoulder and then dropping a fry to Ratface, who gobbles it up in one snap of his tiny jaws.

I give her a weak smile and feel Mrs. Grant's stare laser its way into my brain. "*Are* you going to do that?" Mrs. Grant wipes the countertop as she looks at me. I look up at her and then at Taylor. Taylor's smile is so wide I wonder how it's possible. Could my face even stretch like that anymore?

"I mean, if I'm going to take eighth grade by storm, maybe it would help with that?" I eat a fry and it suddenly has no taste.

"But, Amelia, honey, do you *want* to take eighth grade by storm?" Mrs. Grant sets her towel off to the side and puts her hand on my hand. For some reason, this makes me want to just cry and cry and cry. Because honestly? I don't know what I want. I just don't want to feel like this anymore.

I shrug. "At least it would be different."

"Different how?" Mrs. Grant is very good at asking questions, her voice so soft it's like the opposite of her eyes.

I shrug again. "Doing something would be a nice change. Does that make any sense? Like . . . I can't talk to Clara anymore. She can't roll her eyes at me. She can't be grouchy with me for borrowing a shirt. But crying all the time doesn't accomplish much, does it? It doesn't bring her back, and it doesn't make me miss her less." I choke back a knot in my throat. "So maybe I could get closer to her by trying to figure out why these things were so important to her? I don't know. It sounds stupid when I say it out loud."

Mrs. Grant and Taylor both stare at me. This is maybe the longest string of words I've strung together in about three years.

"Wow. You've been thinking a LOT about this."

Taylor's eyes are wide. Mrs. Grant's hand is still on mine.

"What does your heart tell you to do?" Mrs. Grant squeezes my hand.

"My heart tells me it doesn't want to hurt so much anymore." I look down at my half-eaten grilled cheese, the swirling tears in my eyes blurring it into a big blob.

"You're going to have to go to all the parties with me," I say, my voice thick with unshed tears. I clear my throat. "And help me figure out who the heck Billy is."

"Of course, of course! It's going to be fun, Amelia!"

I swipe at my eyes and notice the fountain through the front window. Some little kids are trying to climb the giant bird in the middle of the fountain. The bird stuck in stone forever. I don't want to be stuck in stone forever. Even if it's easier that way.

CHAPTER FOUR

"HEYA, KIDDO!" DAD GRABS ME up in a hug as soon as Mom and I walk in the door. Mom drops her keys on the kitchen counter and her bag on the floor. She looks like she's had a rough day. Is it possible for grown-ups to even *have* as rough a day as the first day of eighth grade? I thought the whole point of her doing this part-time consultant thing was to have *less* stress and *more* time at home. I think maybe she's doing it wrong.

"Did you ruin your appetite?" Dad smells like meat and barbecue smoke, his big hairy arms tickling my less hairy arms as he holds on tight. I don't say anything because I know he'll keep talking. Dad isn't big on silences. "You think you might want to try out some new sauces? I've been experimenting."

"Uh-oh." Mom cracks open a soda and tries to crack a smile, too. "More experimenting?"

Peabody's Pits 'n' Pieces is Dad's new adventure. He's always loved to cook on the grill. And he's always loved meat. So, after he went crazy a while back and quit his job as a computer programmer and spent like three months in bed, he finally decided he was going to start a barbecue restaurant.

I could tell Mom thought he was nuts. Those golden eyes of hers can't hide her feelings very well. But just like he didn't say anything when she spontaneously quit her job so she could "enjoy more family time" and then just as spontaneously asked for half her job back so she could "feel useful," *she* didn't say anything when he came back from the bank in his rumpled funeral suit with a grin on his face. She also didn't say anything when he went on and on about barbecue smokers and different kinds of wood and spice rubs. She didn't even say anything when he decided he'd rather have a food trailer than an actual restaurant, and parked a sleek silver bullet Airstream in our front yard until the neighborhood snobs made him move it. It's been a couple of years since Dad found his voice again (and Mom started working fake part-time), and since then, there has been a LOT of experimenting and tasting and talking about barbecue.

I don't really mind. The more he talks, the less I have to. And the more Mom is at work, the more Dad and I get to hang out. Plus, I like meat, too.

Now Dad takes my bag and herds me and Mom into the kitchen. There are little glass dishes all over the counter, filled with mystery sauces. There's also a slab of smoked, but sauceless, spare ribs. Dad drops my bag by the table, throws on his apron, and starts whacking at the ribs with a cleaver. He doesn't really need to whack them, though. The meat falls right off the bone.

His voice is soft as he says, "There's gonna be a cook-off at the lake later this month. Food TV people are going to be there. It could be huge for Pits 'n' Pieces. What do you both think about going? Cheer me on? Maybe get to make a silly face on national TV?"

Mom says nothing. I say nothing. I'm going to pretend I didn't hear him over the tsunami of saliva in my mouth. Not a lot of things make me legitimately happy these days, but a mouthful of rib meat dissolving on my tongue comes pretty darn close, even if my belly is full of fries and a grilled cheese.

I will not let a mention of the lake ruin that.

Dad clears his throat and starts pointing at the dishes of sauce. "I have spicy and mild. Sweet and tangy. And this one . . ." He gestures proudly. "I might have to make you sign a waiver before you try it. Ghost peppers." He waggles his eyebrows and makes a *whoosh* noise like a firework shooting into the sky.

Mom and I dig in while Dad watches with a look on his face that is both proud and terrified. He's like a kid at the science fair. Will the judges give him a blue ribbon? Or are his experiments too strange?

I point at the one that is suspiciously orange. "I like to eat this one, but I don't like to look at it." Dad nods and pulls a little notepad from his apron pocket. He jots something down and sticks the pad back in his pocket. "Noted," he says with a grin.

Mom points to the ghost pepper one, tears streaming down her face, sweat beading on her upper lip. "Wh-where's the waiver?" she stammers. I can't help but laugh.

"So, tell me about your first day of eighth grade, Amelia!" And just like that, Dad kills the mood. Suddenly, the sauce in his beard doesn't seem charming anymore. It is annoying.

Why can't he just let us have five seconds to live in a moment? All of a sudden, I feel like I might cry. I swallow around the growing lump in my throat and put down my rib bone. I lick my fingers as I blink back tears and shrug. "Fine?"

"A truer answer has never been spoken." Dad gives me the tiniest of sideways looks and then starts tossing the little dishes in the sink. "At least you have the big prank this year. That's something to look forward to, yeah?"

"Oh, Jim, don't start." Mom can't help but smile, though. He's still at the sink and she slides behind him, her arms around his big belly. They are so gross. I mean, come on. They were in eighth grade together. Heck, they were in kindergarten together. This town is like the La Brea Tar Pits, collecting souls, no escape.

For years my textbooks have had Mom's or Dad's name in them. (Small-town school funding, yikes.) Sometimes I've even had the same *teachers* they did. It's insane. So, yes, I know Mom's prank was yarn bombing a bunch of light poles on Main Street. Dad's prank was huge and had something to do with stop signs and getting in trouble for endangering the public. Or at least that's what I was always told. My hand clenches around Clara's letter folded in my pocket.

I have no idea what my prank will be. Like zero idea.

I leave the two of them in the kitchen and take my bag upstairs. Lying on the bed, I stare at the ceiling. There was never really a game plan for what Taylor and I would wear to school on the second day of eighth grade. I get up and open my closet.

There's a knock on my door and Mom sticks her head in. "You going to bed already?"

I don't know. I feel like I can never answer any of her questions. Even the simple ones. I shrug, which has become my signature move.

Mom sneak-attack hugs me before leaving the room. I close my closet door and look at the empty bed on the other side of the room. The quilt is the same. The pillows the same. Mr. Bear leans to the side, his left ear hanging by a thread. I walk over to the other closet, the big one, the one I was never allowed to open.

I open it.

There's a flowy top covered in a bunch of bright colors, and a jean skirt. That was the outfit Clara chose for her first day of eighth grade. The outfit she never got a chance to wear. And in the back, behind another flowery shirt and some white jeans, there's a black shirt with a streak of silver down the side. I take it out of her closet and put it in mine.

CHAPTER FIVE

"OKAY." MY HANDS ARE ON my thighs as I lean over, breathing harder than I have possibly ever breathed. "I—it's—can we stop now?"

Taylor jogs in place next to me. "Stop?!" She looks like I just told her Beyoncé is retiring. "We've only run half a mile. HALF a mile, Amelia! That's basically nothing."

"I might puke," I say to the ground, swallowing hard, my heart still pounding.

"You're not going to puke. After mile five, you can puke. Come on. Let's go!" She grabs my arm and gently pulls. I plant my feet and not so gently pull back. She stumbles toward me.

"Hey, hey, heeeeeeey!" A tall boy on a skateboard whooshes past, flips the board on its end, turns, and comes back toward us. He's wearing a helmet that looks like a shark is eating his head.

"Hi, Twitch," I breathe. "What's the story?"

"Same as always," he says, skating circles around us. "Though you freaked me out for a minute, out here in those sporty clothes doing sporty things. Thought for a second the ghost of Clara was haunting me." His lopsided grin doesn't match his sad eyes. Twitch and I used to see each other every day. He hung around Clara like a lost puppy, and she tolerated him because . . . well, I don't really know why. I guess because she could boss him around and he would do anything for her. It's hard for me now, to see him around. When he appears, it's like the world goes foggy and I zoom through some kind of time warp. I can only ever see him, soaking wet, running in from the lake, arms waving over his head, screaming her name in a voice I'd never heard before, or heard since. The kind of terror and panic he must have been feeling, it made his voice jagged, louder than possible, high-pitched. You could almost see the spiky words shooting from his mouth: *Help! Clara! Underwater! Boat flipped! Help! Help!*

I stand up straighter, taking my hands off my thighs, my posture suddenly reminding me of Twitch catching his breath as the grown-ups ran past him to a motorboat and then sped to the middle of the lake.

Can you be in love with someone when you're in the sixth grade? I don't know. But maybe Twitch was in love with Clara. I don't think she was in love with him, though. Maybe that's the saddest thing of all.

"Whatcha doing?" he asks, turning tighter and tighter circles. The silver bracelet he always wears glints in the sun and blinds me for a second. You'd think a sophomore in high school wouldn't care what little eighth graders were up to, but you'd be wrong. We have a weird connection, Twitch and I. When you've stood next to someone and breathlessly watched the world end, it gives you a bond whether you want one or not. That sounds dramatic, but it's true.

"Amelia is broadening her horizons," Taylor says, switching from jogging in place to jumping jacks. "She is endeavoring to break out of her shell."

"'*Endeavoring*'? You sound like my mom."

"I'm just saying you're attempting something big. Big things need big words."

I feel my eyes start to roll, but I try to stop them. I don't want to be grouchy with Taylor. She's trying to help. And I know I need help. I mean, I guess I do. Moping for three years? A huge cry for help, right?

"How is puking in the street broadening your horizons?" Twitch's eyes finally match his smile.

"I am not puking!" I put my hands on my hips. "At least not yet. Anyway, I'm doing it for Clara." I reach into the tiny zipper pocket in the back of my running shorts and pull out her letter, where I stashed it, folded as tightly as possible. It's a little damp from my sweat, but not enough to smear the ink, just enough to make it kind of limp in my hand. I hand it to Twitch.

"I'm going to make sure everything on her list gets taken care of."

He takes it, barely pinching it between two fingers.

"It's not covered in poison, dork, just my sweat."

"Why would I take your word on that? How do I know you aren't some kind of mutant? The risk seems high." Twitch is trying to hold the limp page in a readable position. He has to stop skating and arc his head toward the sun as his two fingers dangle the sweaty paper in front of his face.

I watch him read it, his face going from that smirking-joking-Twitch-expression to solid stone. The pink in his cheeks goes pale. When he's finished, he carefully folds the paper, following the creases that are already there. He hands it back to me. I don't think he cares about the sweatiness anymore.

"You're going to do all these things?" His voice is a little rough. He clears his throat and looks down at his board.

I feel my infuriating tears threatening once again and nod. "It's not like I'm trying to BE her, or anything. It just seems like I can help her do the things she didn't get to do, and she can help me . . ." I can't think of what to say. Be happy? Stop feeling terrible all the time? I don't want to say any of these things out loud.

Twitch's dark brown eyes gaze off into space. "Yeah" is all he says. After a minute where we're all kind of quiet and lost in our own thoughts, he smacks his foot on his skateboard and says, "Well, you lovely young women, have a wonderful day," and he's off down the hill, out of sight.

"Oh, Twitch," Taylor says softly. Then she looks at me, her eyes bright, her mouth doing a frown-smile thing. She looks so much like a grown-up sometimes.

"Come on, let's take a break."

"Milk shakes?"

"What else?" Taylor links her arm in mine and we head toward the General Store.

CHAPTER SIX

"I AM THE DRAGON BREATHING fire! Beautiful mane, I'm the lion!" I hold my spoon like a microphone and screech into it, eyes screwed shut, feeling the music snake its way into my body, making me move in a way I couldn't without the beat and the flow and . . . Man, I love music.

"Settle down, settle down. Your Beyoncé karaoke is going to scare away all my customers." Mrs. Grant jogs down the stairs and turns off the radio Taylor and I have cranked up loud. She looks at us with this expression of amusement and grouchiness, but also maybe fondness? Maybe?

"You knew that was Beyoncé?"

"Everyone within a twenty-mile radius knows that was Beyoncé, Amelia."

Taylor licks her spoon and points it at me. "She's right. Please don't make the whole town go deaf."

I roll my eyes, but in a joking way. Nothing like a milk shake and Beyoncé to cheer me up. Except . . . the ding-ding of the front door echoes through the store and, yep, it's Mom. Right on time. Ratface runs over to her to say hello. She leans over and pats him on the head, but even his cute lolling tongue can't stop my good mood from leaking into the air like helium escaping from a balloon.

"Everyone having fun?"

Why do moms have to say such dumb things? I can't even answer her. For some reason, though, Mrs. Grant and Taylor don't seem to think it's ridiculous and they babble on about how we're fine and how I'm going to be in great shape soon. Mom's face squinches in that way it does when she's confused. I do a zip-it motion with my hand, and Taylor's eyes go wide. Thank goodness for best friend mind-reading abilities.

Mom doesn't know about the letter.

"And here I thought it was strange that you woke up so early to meet Taylor. Now I find out you woke up early to go *running*? Who *are* you?" Mom's tone is light but those tiger eyes tell me she's weirded out.

"Just trying to get that mind-body thing going," Taylor says, her smile so big that it might blind us all. "Did you know that exercise can help depression?"

Mom turns to me and I watch her expression go

from weirded out to concerned. "You're depressed, Amelia?" Oh, good grief.

Taylor mouths "Sorry!" over Mom's shoulder. Only I can see her, and I try not to glare. This hole is getting deeper and deeper.

"Can we just go?" I pop my earbuds in, letting the music drown everyone out. I see their mouths moving, and I choose not to figure out what they're saying. I hope "Can we just go?" is not the last phrase I ever say to my mother, but right now, I want out of here and for her to stop talking and just . . . to find a hot shower. Is there any possibility I'll be in shape enough to try out for softball in four months? Do I even care?

I wave at Taylor and walk out of the General Store. I climb into Old Betsy, the cracked vinyl seat snagging at my running pants. I feel like everything is snagging at me these days. It's never enough to tear a hole, only enough to annoy me.

I wonder if Clara ever felt like Mom wouldn't give her enough space. She did put the thing on the list about being nicer to Mom. I think about how she used to mimic Mom when she was mad, using this ridiculous singsong voice. It always made me laugh, even when steam would shoot from Mom's ears.

To me, Clara always seemed like she had everything figured out. She knew what she wanted and went for it. But maybe she had doubts, too. Hmm. I pull the now-dry letter from my pocket and read over the list for the thousandth time. Maybe she didn't always go for it. Maybe Clara was an illusion like the rest of us.

"What do you have there?" Mom asks, her eyes meeting mine in the rearview mirror.

I carefully fold up the letter and shove it under my butt. "Nothing!"

Mom blinks at me and then her eyes are back on the road.

Sigh. Excellent work, there, Amelia. THAT wasn't suspicious at all.

"So, you know how I was late picking you up yesterday?" Mom navigates around the fountain, and I imagine what it must have looked like full of water sparkling from the sun. I bet it was loud, too, with all the rushing water. It must have been nice to sit on the edge and feel little splashes in the hot sun.

"Amelia?"

I snap back to attention. "Uh. Right. Yes. You were late yesterday."

"I was late because I finally had that meeting with Mr. Robertson. Remember the one I set up last year when school was almost out for the summer?"

My brain tendrils reach back into the recesses of my mind. I can feel the memory surfacing. Then it crashes through my body with an electric jolt. "Yes! About my possibly testing out of eighth-grade science and taking physics this year?" I had forgotten all about that! My body zings at the thought of escaping earth science and getting my hands dirty in the high-school physics lab.

"Well," Mom says as if she's a magician about to reveal a cornucopia of delights inside a previously empty box, "Mr. Robertson said you can come by the high school and take a physics benchmark test. You'll also have to take the eighth-grade earth science final exam to prove you know the material and will be fine skipping the class. Pass both of those and you're in."

I let her words fly around in my head as we drive by the lake. I listen to the monster under the water growl low and mean. Clara never got the chance to take earth science or physics. Well. I'll ace them both for her.

"Can I take *both* tests? Tomorrow?" I ask.

"Both? Tomorrow?" Mom's golden eyes dart back up to the rearview mirror. She catches my gaze and sees I'm serious. "That's not a lot of time to study," she says, but her voice fades halfway through her statement and she smiles. She knows I can do it. I'm not worried at all about taking two tests in one afternoon. I'm also not worried about having barely any time to study for either one. I'm only worried about Mr. Robertson, because I am about to come in and OWN that physics class.

I feel something weird happening to my face.

My cheeks are warming.

My lips stretch out a little bit.

Am I actually smiling? When was the last time *that* happened?

CHAPTER SEVEN

I PUT BOTH TESTS FACEDOWN on Mr. Robertson's desk.

"Done already?"

"Done already." I can feel another smile threatening.

"Well, okay, then." He stands up behind his desk and offers his hand for me to shake. It feels silly shaking it, because I've known Mr. Robertson since I was a baby. I've jumped in piles of leaves in his backyard. I've babysat his dog while he was on vacation. My parents bought our house from his mother before I was even born. It's a *very* small town. "I'll grade these and get back to you."

"How long do you think it will take?" I ask, eyeing the tests, and then his face. I like that he has these black freckles that mix in with his dark skin. I also like how his mustache sometimes hides his expression. I'm always trying to figure out his mood. He's good at being calm and collected, but more often than not, there's a little spark in his eye like a faraway star shining through a dark nebula.

"I think it will take me however long it takes me," he says, and I groan. That makes him laugh. "It won't be weeks, Amelia. I won't keep you in suspense any longer than I have to."

"Thanks, Mr. Robertson," I say. "I can't wait to start class."

"So bold," he says. "So confident." He winks and laughs. I can't help but smile as I walk out of the classroom—and directly into a person walking by.

Oof. The kid's books go everywhere. It's like a ream of paper exploded as we both go sprawling. I'm on the floor, dazed, when I hear a familiar laugh.

"You sure go out of your way to say hello, don't you?" It's Twitch.

"Oh my gosh, Twitch, I'm so sorry!" I quickly stand up and start gathering papers and handing them to him in big unorganized clumps. "What is all of this?" I'm not sure I've seen so much paper in my life. For a second I think I see Clara's name, but then it's lost in the pile.

"Just a project I'm working on," he says as he gathers up papers, too.

We pile all the pages together and he asks, "So what are you doing here, anyway? Not a lot of eighth-grade classes at the high school."

"Oh, I was just visiting Mr. Robertson," I say. I'm not sure why I don't want to tell him about the physics test. Maybe I don't want to jinx it. "He's my neighbor, you know? I, uh, watch his dog sometimes? So, I was . . ." I trail off on purpose, hoping Twitch will interrupt. He doesn't, so we both just stand there feeling weird. Or at least I feel weird enough for the both of us.

"Okay, well, I need to get going," I say.

Twitch smiles. "Nice *running* into you."

"Hey," I say over my shoulder. "I hardly recognized you without your helmet."

He smiles and tries to wave, even though he has about eleven million loose papers in his arms.

I wave and then run out of the building, making sure I don't mow down anyone else. Once outside, I look at my phone. Mom has a city council meeting tonight, and Dad is probably at the barbecue trailer getting ready for the dinner rush. I could either hang out here and wait for Mom to eventually pick me up, or walk over to Grant's General Store and call her from there. It's not *that* long of a walk. And I *am* still trying to get in shape for softball tryouts . . . I hike my backpack over my shoulder and set off.

Walking through town is kind of like walking through a good friend. That sounds weird and possibly gross or ghosty, but I don't mean it like that. I just mean no one is a stranger. Every storefront is familiar. People wave and yell hello from across the street. It's weird to me how I can know pretty much everyone in this place and yet still feel alone most of the time. With Clara I never felt alone. I felt irritated or annoyed. I felt like I couldn't breathe without being compared to her in some way, but when I compare that to how I feel now, I'd take it any day.

When I walk through the door at Grant's, the special is the *We're Gouda Together* grilled cheese. (Gouda and mild cheddar with a smidge of mustard.) Yum.

"How'd it go?" Taylor is behind the counter refilling ketchup bottles. Her apron looks like she's just murdered someone.

"Messy much?" I ask, and she looks down.

"Don't worry," she says, and laughs. "He didn't put up much of a fight."

"I think it went great," I say. "Knock on wood." We both rap our knuckles on the counter, even though it's Formica. "Mr. Robertson has to grade both the tests, and then he'll let me know. He promised not to torture me for too long."

"Ooh! Speaking of torture . . . I think we should add another half mile to our run tomorrow morning. What do you say?"

"I say, I'm going to put up more of a fight than the guy you killed earlier."

"Oh, come on," she says. "A half mile is nothing. You need to build your stamina. Maybe I'll let you speedwalk part of the way."

I look at her with some skepticism.

"I will!" She laughs.

Mrs. Grant walks behind the counter and says hello. I say hello back while I ponder this new half mile.

"Maybe," I say.

"Maybe counts as yes!" Taylor yells over her shoulder as she brings all the ketchup bottles to the storage closet.

"Can I get you a special, Amelia?" Mrs. Grant asks. She's already buttering the griddle, because she knows I could never say no to a *We're Gouda Together*.

"Yes, please," I say. And in a flash, I'm eating a hot, gooey grilled cheese like it might be my last meal. I think about last meals almost as much as I think of last words. I don't care if cheese replaces all vegetables in my life, I'm never eating anything that isn't worthy of a last meal, ever again.

"Have you figured out your prank yet?" Mrs. Grant asks, elbows on the counter, chin in her hands.

"I have not," I answer with my mouth full. "I want it to be something good, and I can't think of anything good."

"You will," she says with a smile. "I have no doubt."

"What about me?" Taylor asks, emerging from the storage closet. "Do you have your doubts about me?"

"Only when it comes to successfully filling ketchup bottles, my dear," Mrs. Grant says. She makes a "gimme" motion with her hand and Taylor strips off her apron. Mrs. Grant throws it in a basket of other dirty aprons and motions for Taylor to go sit beside me. She does, and I begrudgingly give her a bite of my sandwich.

"You know," Taylor says, swiping cheese off her chin, "we could do the best prank together. Come up with something doubly great, but only have to do half the work." She waggles her eyebrows. It's definitely a tempting solution. Plus, it would be fun to work on the prank with her. I don't even know why it's such a big deal. You'd think a town wouldn't want to encourage a bunch of eighth graders to run amok with practical jokes, but maybe by encouraging us to do them all at once, it kind of contains the trouble? Who knows. All I do know is that we have months to plan something before we blow everyone's socks off. That's plenty of time.

The bell on the door dings, and without even turning around, I know it's Mom.

"So?"

Yep. Mom. I turn and feel immediately annoyed at the cheerful inflection of her question. Why so annoyed so fast? How does that happen? What is the science behind this?

I feel myself go stone-faced. "It was fine," I say.

"That's it? Fine?" Mom is standing behind me now. She puts her hands on my shoulders. I shrug them off.

"Fine," I say, and I can hear an edge creeping into my voice. "Regular. Normal. Nothing spectacular." I can see her in the mirror behind the bar. She takes a step back from me and exchanges a look with Mrs. Grant. Mom's face seems to say, "Ouch, give me a break." Mrs. Grant's face seems to say, "Uncool, Amelia," and "I'm sorry, Jen," all at the same time. Now I feel like a jerk.

I turn to face Mom. "I just mean . . . it went fine. I think I did well. It wasn't hard, and Mr. Robertson was nice."

Mom licks her lips and says, "Great." Her voice is flat, the spark gone from her eyes. "Finish up so we can get home." She fishes around in her purse for some money to pay for my sandwich, but Mrs. Grant waves her off. The air in the store is suddenly thick with awkwardness. My fault.

I hop off the stool, wave bye to Taylor and Mrs. Grant, and walk out of the store.

CHAPTER EIGHT

"COME ON," TAYLOR SHOUTS, JOGGING backward. She's up at the top of the hill, and I'm at the bottom. I look up at her and imagine all the things I'd rather be doing right now. Going to the dentist, breaking my leg in a freak getting-out-of-bed accident, standing on a planet while its star goes supernova . . .

"AMELIA! Don't stop! What are you doing? Come on! Come on! I believe in you!" She's clapping now, creating a beat for me to run to. Ugh. I hate this so much. Halfway up the hill, I can't run anymore, so I listen to my screaming legs instead of my screaming Taylor, and I walk. When I get to the top, Taylor looks at me as if I've turned into a pile of dog poo. "I cannot believe you just did what I saw you do."

"What? Make it up Deadman's Hill without becoming a dead man myself? That seems impressive to me. I mean, if I were to ask myself—and I did ask myself—'What would Beyoncé do, if she were about to die on a hill?' my answer, and her answer, would be: Do not die on this hill. So, taking THAT into account, I think I did a great job."

Taylor just stares at me.

Her face is getting pinker by the minute and I can tell she's building up a head of steam. Now might be the time to run.

"You know I'm doing this to help you, right? You know I'm setting goals for you so that you can actually achieve something on Clara's list, right?" She crosses her arms over her chest. I look down at my sneakers. "Sometimes you are your own worst enemy, Amelia, I swear!"

I let her words sink in for a minute, even though I don't like them. Am I my own worst enemy? I don't know. I mean, I'm only doing the things on Clara's letter because Taylor seems so sure it will be good for me. I'm only doing this stupid running because Taylor thinks it will help me get on the softball team. Am I my own worst enemy? Or is SHE my enemy? Trying to make me do things that she knows I'll fail? But . . . that doesn't make any sense. She's my best friend. She obviously doesn't want me to fail.

"Hello. Earth to space cadet." Taylor knocks on my forehead like it's a front door. "What's going on in that head of yours?"

"You didn't tell me the extra half mile was going to be up Deadman's Hill." I can't help but sound sullen. I feel sullen.

Taylor throws her arms in the air. "I'm trying to push you, Amelia. I'm trying to get you out of your comfort zone. I'm trying to help you. Can't you see that?"

"I can. I do. I just . . . why can't we go for ice cream and talk about our feelings instead?" I offer a silly smile, but Taylor is having none of it.

"We can't talk about our feelings, Amelia, because YOU WON'T TALK ABOUT YOUR FEELINGS." She storms off.

"Taylor!" I shout after her. "Taylor, wait!" But she doesn't wait. She runs off, and I know there's no way I can catch up to her. Sigh.

I plod along the side of the street, trying to catch my breath, and not even close to catching my racing mind, when I hear the familiar gravel-scattering sound of skateboard wheels behind me. I turn.

"Heya, stranger. What's cookin'?" Twitch asks. The straps of his helmet dangle under his chin like tentacles. "You out running again? Is the world actually ending, or what?"

"Have I mentioned lately how much I hate running? I hate it with the fiery hot intensity of ten thousand suns."

Twitch laughs. It reminds me of the Before Days, when I'd hear him laughing in the game room when he and Clara would hang out with their friends, playing pool or video games. Twitch is like a human time machine. "I'm going to ask you a question," he says. "And I know it's going to sound crazy. You're gonna be like, 'OMG, Twitch, why would you ask such an insane question?!?!' but I'm going to ask it anyway, because I live on the edge." He pauses and takes a deep breath. "Are you ready?" he asks as he exhales and takes another dramatic, deep breath. "Why are you running if you hate it so much?"

I shove his arm and he laughs again. "You know why I'm running. I showed you the letter. I'm going to try out for softball, because Clara never got the chance to."

"But you hate sweating."

"So?"

"You hate sports."

"So?"

"Uh . . ." Twitch looks genuinely confused.

"I'm doing it because Clara wanted it. I'm trying to complete her letter for her. I don't know." I stop walking, turn, and peer up into his scratchy-looking face. "I'm hoping it will make me feel less sad all the time, okay?"

His face is serious now as he nods. "Yeah, okay. I get that."

We walk together in silence for a little bit longer, when he says, "Why don't you come home with me for a second?"

I can't think of how to answer him. Why would I go to his house? Even though we know each other in, like, the deepest, most horrible ways, we also don't know each other *that* well. He was Clara's friend, not mine. It would be strange to go to his house.

He holds up his hand. "I don't mean come over and sit on the couch and hang out. That would be weird."

I nod, feeling a wash of relief.

"I just mean, I'll grab my sisters' gloves and a softball and we can go play catch. Seems like that might be more helpful for tryouts than all this running."

I think about it for a second, and he has a point. "Okay," I say. "Let's play catch."

He smiles, and we pick up the pace. His house is just around the corner.

CHAPTER NINE

"GOOD!" TWITCH SHOUTS AS I actually catch the softball instead of trying to dive away from it. "Keep your eye on the ball. Nice work."

We've been out here for a long time, tossing the ball back and forth. Or really, he tosses it to me, I duck, it rolls away, I chase it, find it, throw it back, rinse, repeat. It's pretty fun, and I think I'm getting in more running than I did when I was actually running.

"When are you going to tell me what you were doing in Mr. Robertson's class?" Twitch asks as he catches my throw. He's still wearing his helmet as if afraid I might bean him on the head. He might be right.

I think about all the paper he was carrying and how maybe I saw Clara's name. If I answer his question, maybe I can ask him one in return. "I was taking a couple of tests to see if I can start taking high-school physics."

His eyebrows shoot up and are almost lost in the shark teeth encircling his helmet. "Cool. When do you find out if you can do it?"

"Not sure," I say, trying really hard to keep my eye on the ball as it hurtles toward me. "Soon, I hope." I catch the ball and continue, "What were all those papers that I made you drop?"

"If you pass the test, how will it work, do you know?" he asks. I can't tell if he didn't hear my question or if he's ignoring it. "Like, will you walk over from the middle school to the high school? Or do some kind of self-paced thing from home?" He catches my throw with ease and tosses it underhand back to me. I like underhand. I can catch those.

"I'm not really sure," I answer. "I think maybe I'll walk over. I've been trying not to jinx it by thinking too far ahead."

"Oh," he says. "Sorry."

"No, no," I say. "That's okay. *You're* not going to jinx it."

"Why wouldn't *I* jinx it?" he asks, pretending like I've hurt his feelings. "I have excellent jinxing powers."

I'm just about to ask him again about the papers when I hear: "Hey, Twitch." Some kid I don't know walks up to us and they do a kind of high five handshake thing. The kid looks at me and back to Twitch. "You babysitting or something?"

I feel my cheeks burn. Does he think I'm ten?

Twitch laughs. "Nah, man. Just hanging out with my friend Amelia. Amelia, this is Knute."

I hold up my hand in a way that I hope says, "It's not really nice to meet you, please go away," but, like, in a polite way.

Knute nods in my direction but is still looking at Twitch. "Some of us are going over to Grant's for a burger. Want to come?"

"Sure," Twitch says. "We're just about done . . . Aren't we, Amelia?"

I'm about to say something like "I guess" when Knute turns and actually looks at me for the first time.

"Amelia?" he says. "Clara's sister?"

I swallow hard and nod.

"I didn't recognize you," he says, walking over to me. I wish he wouldn't come closer. I feel like this is about to be a conversation I don't want to have. "I was at her party. The one where . . ." He stops and looks at the ground. "Anyway, you look different."

"It *has* been three years," I say, casting my eyes around, looking for anyone, anything, to save me from this.

"Man," Knute says. "That day . . . it was really—"

Twitch sees my face and our moment-of-trauma connection lights up. He grabs Knute by the arm and drags him away mid-sentence. "It was great catching up, Amelia," he says to me, interrupting Knute, and making a har-har sound at his bad pun.

"Uh," I stammer. "Yeah, it was nice to see you." And before I can say anything else, he's whisked Knute off in the direction of the General Store, leaving both gloves and the ball on the ground.

I stand there for a minute, not sure what to do or where to go, and then I realize I'm sweaty and hungry, so I take a deep breath, grab the ball and gloves, and head toward home.

"Heeeeeeey, kiddo!" Dad pulls something out of the oven. Something that smells really, really good. "What have you been up to?"

"Just some exercise," I say, going to the fridge and getting some water. "Nothing crazy."

Dad puts the tray on a towel on the counter. "Check it out," he says. "I'm testing out some desserts for the lake contest. I'm meeting the producers of the TV show up there in a little bit and I thought, why not bring them a little treat?"

I pretend he hasn't said anything about the lake (or about potentially bribing the producers of that stupid contest) and peer down at the tray. It smells super good. Like chocolate chip cookies, but with something . . . different added in.

"Can you smell my secret ingredient?" Dad asks,

pulling a cookie off the tray and tossing it from hand to hand so he doesn't burn his fingers.

I sniff the air. "Hmm," I say. "Is it something savory?"

"Ding ding ding!" Dad says with a smile. "But what?"

"Can I taste one?"

He hands over the cookie he's been tossing and I take a huge bite. It's warm and the chocolate is so gooey it gushes over my lip. "Mmmm," I say, my mouth full. "I taste vanilla and cinnamon and dark chocolate and something salty . . ." My eyes go wide. "Is that *bacon*? Dad! Did you put bacon in these cookies?"

He claps his hands. "Ten points to Ravenclaw!" he shouts. "You like?"

I swallow the bite in my mouth and think about it. I actually do like. I like it a lot. "This is weird and delicious, Dad. Nice work!"

"I really only have a few goals in life," Dad says, looking up to the ceiling with reverence. "To be weird, and to make delicious things."

"Well, if that's the case, then your goals are complete," I say, finishing off the cookie. "Yum."

"Think they'll help push me into the winner's circle at the contest?" he asks, eating a cookie of his own.

Man, man, man. I really don't want to talk about the stupid contest. That's going to mean talking about me coming to the contest, which will mean talking about me coming to the lake, and I am never going to the lake again. So.

"Amelia?" Dad's face is hopeful. He has chocolate in his beard.

"I don't think you need anything to push you over the edge, Dad. I mean, you're already in MY winner's circle." I bat my eyes at him and we both laugh.

"What are you two up to?" Mom is standing in the doorway. She's trying to sound playful, but her eyes have no sparkle. I wonder how long she's been listening. I know she hates it when Dad and I are buddy-buddy. She acts like we're leaving her out of some cool kids' club. It's not that at all. It's just that . . . Dad and I seem to get each other. Like, we're on the same wavelength or something. Mom has her own wavelength. Sometimes I think I can hop along for a ride, but other times, it just seems unreachable.

"Try one," Dad says, tossing a cookie to Mom. Dad seems pretty oblivious to the wavelengths.

Mom catches the cookie and takes a bite, nodding as she chews. "Pretty good," she says.

"Pretty good? Pretty good?! These are officially the best cookies ever made! I mean, come on!"

Okay. I take back the part about Dad being oblivious to the wavelengths. Now he's doing the thing where every word and gesture is about ten times too loud and too big because he's trying to make us laugh, and bring us all together in some kind of made-for-TV family bonding moment. Yeah, no thanks. I grab another cookie and shove the whole thing in my mouth at once so I don't have to say anything. Out the kitchen window I see Mr. Robertson and his dog hanging out on his front porch. Hmm. Would it be against some kind of secret rule if I went over there and said hello and asked how the test grading was going? I chew my cookie and ponder my choices. Go out there, ask about the test, have him refuse to tell me, feel embarrassed, learn nothing new. OR have to talk to Mom and Dad about the contest and the lake. Hmm again.

I head upstairs to shower. If he's still on his porch when I'm clean and have possibly eaten one more cookie for courage, I'll go out there.

CHAPTER TEN

"TINY!" I SAY, SQUATTING AND slapping my thighs. Tiny leaps off the porch, his tongue wagging almost as much as his tail. He leaps on me, knocking me backward, and covers my face with slobbery licks.

"Tiny! No!" Mr. Robertson's yell is half-hearted. I'm pretty sure he knows that Tiny is going to do what he wants to do. Humans only serve to get in his way.

I roll over onto my belly to avoid the licks, and push myself up to my knees and then my feet. This is the only way to escape a Tiny lick attack. I learned this years ago when he was a puppy, but still nearly twice my size.

Mr. Robertson is standing next to me now, in the little dip in the grass that separates his house from mine. He's holding Tiny by the collar, but only because Tiny is letting him. If that dog wanted to, he'd be free as a bird.

Dad smiles. "Deal."

I should've known something was up when Dad shoved a couple of bags into Old Betsy's trunk before we took off, but I was distracted by thoughts of chocolate scoops and sprinkles. So, once we were all in the car and rounding the bend past the lake, I shouldn't have been surprised when Dad turned down the little gravel road to the lake parking lot.

"Um," I say, feeling my heartbeat ratchet up to about 245. "This doesn't look like ice cream."

"Cookies," Dad says. "Producers. Remember?"

Mom stares straight out the windshield, arm stiff on the car door where the window is open. I get the feeling she didn't know about this pit stop either.

Ahead of us, over a grassy area and near the RV hookups, is Pits 'n' Pieces shining in the sunlight. There's a crew setting up a camera, and a woman in a floppy hat waves and walks to the car.

"James." Mom's voice is low.

Dad reaches over and squeezes Mom's shoulder. "It'll be quick," he says. "Just smile for the camera." He opens the car door and shouts a booming "Hellooooo!" at the woman in the hat.

The lake sparkles just like it did on that day. The color of the sky is the same, too. I can't believe he brought us here like this. I can't believe he's smiling

"I brought you some cookies, but . . ." I hold up the ziplock bag. Inside is a mound of crushed cookies. "Sorry about that."

Mr. Robertson smiles and takes the bag anyway. Tiny is immediately sniffing at it and trying to nip through the plastic to the bacon he knows is in there. Mr. Robertson taps Tiny's nose with one finger. "No. You've already ruined them. I get all the crumbs to myself." Then he turns his attention to me and tilts his head slightly. "You wouldn't be coming over here to pry certain information out of me, would you?"

"Who, me?" I say, feeling my cheeks get warm. "Of course not."

"Good," Mr. Robertson says. "Because it would be against district policy for me to tell you that you aced both tests. I could get in trouble for saying something like that, so I would never say it. I wouldn't tell you that you should prepare to start taking physics at the high school. And I definitely wouldn't give you an extra textbook to look at so that you're caught up with the class when you join us. Nope. Never would say anything like that. You're going to need to wait for the official call from the school counselor."

Wait. What?!

I jump up in the air and squeal, clapping my hands. This makes Tiny jump up and bark. He's not one to

miss a celebration of any kind, no matter how spontaneous or short-lived.

Mr. Robertson is pretending to look stern, but his
eyes sparkle. "Wait right here," he says. "And don't let
Tiny escape."

I nod. Tiny is on his two hind legs, his front paws
hanging over my shoulders. I hold him there and we
dance for a minute. Turns out Great Danes are very
good dance partners.

Mr. Robertson is back outside in a flash and he
offers me the textbook as he lures Tiny off my shoulders with a treat. "I'm not telling you to read up to
page twenty-five and be prepared for a pop quiz on
Friday. I'm not saying anything of the sort."

I try to look stern, too, but I feel my smile peeking
around the edges of my face. "Yes, sir," I say. "It's weird
how your mouth has been moving and yet I've heard
no sounds come out of it."

He nods back and I take the book. We both grin as
he pops a pinch of cookie crumbs in his mouth. "Tell
your dad these cookies are pretty good, but I think
maybe he mistook some bacon for chocolate chips."
He winks as I run back to the house.

"How's Mr. Rob—" Mom starts as I run in through
the kitchen door. She and Dad are sitting at the table
playing gin rummy, because they are apparently ninety-
five years old. I move as fast as I can to the stairs and

up to my room, hoping they didn't see the textb
my arms. I know I *should* want to tell them the
news, but for some reason I don't. I just want
with it for a little while, feel the goodness insid
all mine, before someone says something to ma
feel either less good or less mine. I shake my heac
I even make any sense? I have no idea.

In my room, I sit on my bed and open up the
book. I run my hand over the smooth pages. Th
are formulas and equations I could stare at all da
might stare at them all day. I look over to Cla
empty bed. "I did it," I whisper, and point to the bo
Then I remember that Clara had no idea I would
to get into high-school physics as an eighth grader. S
knew I was good at math, but hadn't seen me blo
through my science assignments. She never saw me wi
the science fair.

Already, the excitement I felt a few minutes ago ha
dimmed, just a little bit.

There's a quiet knock on my door, and then it squeaks
open. I scramble to hide the physics book as Dad
walks in.

"Want to go for a ride?" He jangles the keys to Old
Betsy. "Maybe grab some ice cream?"

I don't really want to go, but I also don't really want
to argue about not wanting to go. "Okay," I say. "But
let's do more ice cream and less riding around."

and talking to that woman and not feeling like his guts are going to burst into flames.

"Amelia, Jen . . . come meet Stacy, the producer of *Trailer Takeout*," Dad shouts at the car. "Amelia, grab the cookies from the trunk, please."

I feel shaky and blindsided. Mom squares her shoulders and swings the car door open so hard it bounces away from her and then slams shut again. Oh boy, Dad is in for it.

The rest of the next hour goes by in a fog. Along with every question Stacy the Producer asks me, I hear the lake growling in the distance. During every moment the cameraman zooms in on my face, I see Twitch screaming on the shore. Stacy the Producer explains the rules of the show, but I don't hear anything. I only hear Mom's sobs from that day. I only see horror reflected in the sparkles on the lake.

By the time we're all back in the car, I feel like I've run up Deadman's Hill six times. Mom is silent and seething.

"I'm sorry," Dad says as he puts on his seat belt. "But I knew if I asked you both to come with me for the interview, you'd find an excuse not to. Stacy really wanted the whole family for the background coverage. It's good for the show. Plus, I got to give her some of my cookies. This whole thing is for the success of all of us, remember? It could be a really big deal."

For once, Dad's enthusiasm is lost on me. This was not fun. This was not okay. It *wasn't* the whole family.

"Ready for ice cream?" Dad asks, his voice hopeful as he throws Old Betsy in reverse.

"Just take us home," Mom says, and right now her tone suits me just fine.

Dad sighs deeply while he backs out of the parking space. "I'm sorry," he says again. "But look at it this way . . . we all went to the lake, and now we're all going home. Together. Nothing bad happened. I know it wasn't cool of me to ambush you both like that. I do. But look!" He sweeps his arms wide, despite the fact that he's driving, and his right arm ends up in Mom's face. "It's a beautiful day! We're going to be on a TV show where we'll be made famous! And the lake was nothing but scenery. THAT is a successful afternoon, don't you think?"

Neither Mom nor I say anything. Though deep, deep down in the dark caves of my soul, I can kind of, sort of, maybe, possibly, see his point. Maybe.

CHAPTER ELEVEN

I'M EATING SAUSAGE—NOT BREAKFAST sausage, actual mesquite-smoked sausage, with jalapeños in it—when the phone rings.

"I can't believe you can eat that first thing in the morning," Mom says, walking to the phone. I shrug, dunk my sausage into Dad's special vinegar-based barbecue sauce, then wrap the dripping mess in a tortilla. I take a huge bite and feel my mouth water as the sausage and sauce bite back. Another man's football game snack is my delicious breakfast.

Mom's voice is ratcheting up in volume as she says, "Yes," then "Yes!" then "YES!" and I know this must be the school counselor calling about physics. Mom looks at me as I chew my spicy mouthful and she gives me a thumbs-up. I just stare at her while I chew. Sometimes, out of the blue, I get these flashes of her at the funeral. When she was crying so hard her whole body shook in waves, like human earthquakes. She made this animal noise . . . this wailing . . . that still makes the hairs on my arms stand up when I think about it. I look at her on the phone, giving me a thumbs-up, and for some reason, that's what I see. The sausage in my mouth has turned to dust. I look away.

I hear the beep of the phone hanging up, and in a nanosecond, Mom is by my side, breathless. "You did it!" she says. I can hear the smile in her voice, but my brain is still seeing her wailing at the funeral. "They've arranged for you to start this afternoon. Mrs. James will let you out of history ten minutes early so you can walk over to the high school. Go to the front office, check in, and then go to Mr. Robertson's class. You remember where it is, right?"

"The high school?" I ask, playing dumb.

Mom's face darkens. "You aren't happy about this? No excitement?"

Somehow, all of her excitement seems to be stealing mine away. I wonder if Mr. Robertson's physics lectures can explain that to me.

"I remember where the classroom is," I say, wiping my mouth and standing up. "And I am excited. I promise." I try so hard to smile for Mom, but I'm afraid it must look like I'm being electrocuted. She smiles back at me, looking dubious.

"I have to go," I say. "Don't want to be late."

"Don't you want me to drive you?" she asks as I open the kitchen door.

"Nah," I say. "Extra exercise."

She looks at me in this way I can't really describe. Like maybe I've turned into a very disappointing alien. I flee the kitchen. The cool air outside smacks me in the face and I take huge, deep breaths. Is Mom always going to remind me of the funeral? Is everything?

"Heeeeeeey!" Taylor jogs up next to me. She's back to her flowy dresses, just like I'm back to my T-shirts and jeans. So much for our Sandy-taking-over-the-school attire. Taylor links her arm in mine as we walk down the sidewalk. "You coming to the store after school?"

I nod. "I might be a little late, though."

"Okay, cool. I'm going to be late, too. Lacy and Katherine asked if I wanted to hang out after school." Her cheeks flush and she looks at the ground. I think of Lacy and Katherine, the inseparable duo who always seem to be giggling in a corner somewhere. Does Taylor want to be giggling in a corner somewhere instead of hanging out with me? "I mean, you could come, too, if you want . . ." she adds quickly. I can tell by her voice, though, that I wasn't part of the original invitation.

"It's all right," I say. And, truly, it is. As much as it

makes me feel a little itchy to think of Taylor not wanting to hang out with me, I would *much* rather be studying physics than trying to giggle in a corner. I lift my nose in a snooty way, to make Taylor laugh and lighten the awkward mood. "*I'll* be late because I'll be coming from the high school."

"From the—? Oh my gosh! You got into the physics class?" She stops walking and grabs my other arm. "Amelia! That's so awesome!"

I smile. "It is, isn't it?"

She grabs me up in a bone-crushing hug. "Good work, you!"

I can see her eyes drifting off as a million ideas come to her at once. "You'll be like our high-school spy! You can tell me everything that's happening over there. Who are the cool kids? Who are the ones to avoid? What clubs are the best for meeting people? Who are the cutest boys? Lacy and Katherine are going to pass out when I tell them we have a high-school infil-trator on our hands! Amelia! You're like a spy AND an explorer!"

I push her off of me and laugh a little. "No. I'm just a big nerd. But thanks for your confidence." I want to tell her that Lacy and Katherine totally won't care, but it makes me smile that she wants to brag about me. Even if it's because of my access to high-school secrets.

Taylor stares at me like a parent stares at a kid on graduation day. "First this, then you'll get on the softball team. Soon, you'll be asking out boys and hosting parties. My little Amelia is growing up." She pretends to wipe away a tear.

"Oh, good grief," I say. "Not everything is about that stupid letter, you know."

"It's so not stupid!" she retorts. "You're already coming out of your shell! High school, Amelia! OH EM GEE."

I hate it when she says *OMG*.

"This physics thing is totally separate from the letter," I remind her. "Clara didn't even know I was good at science." My voice catches at the end of the sentence. Great. Am I going to cry? It feels like I've avoided that travesty for the past few days. Ugh.

Taylor hears the waver in my voice and she stops talking. We walk through the front doors of school together and say nothing as we head to our lockers. Lacy waves at her from down the hall and she runs over, linking arms with Katherine along the way. I take a deep, wavering breath, push open my locker, and grab my stuff for first period.

CHAPTER TWELVE

"EVERYONE," MR. ROBERTSON SAYS, HIS deep voice booming through the lab. "This is Amelia Peabody. She'll be joining us for class this semester."

I hear a murmur go around the room, and several instances of people saying, "Peabody?" and "Clara's sister?" and "You remember that girl who . . ." and suddenly the shiny surfaces of the lab tables, the glimmer of the equipment on the shelves, the bright colors of the posters on the walls . . . it all dims. My mouth goes as dry and dusty as the firewood for Dad's barbecue smoker. How did I not predict this would happen? *Of course*, everyone in this class knew Clara. They were all in the same grade.

"Sorry I'm late," comes a voice from the doorway behind me. I turn and look. It's Twitch! He moves past me, drops his backpack on the floor beside a lab table, and pulls up a stool. "Got caught up in art." The glaring eyes painted on the sides of his helmet stare at Mr. Robertson, but Twitch smiles.

Mr. Robertson frowns. "Second tardy this week, Mr. Lewis. You know you only get so many each semester before—"

"I know," Twitch interrupts. "I'm sorry. It won't happen again."

"As I was saying," Mr. Robertson continues while all eyes swivel from Twitch to me, "Ms. Peabody will be joining us this semester. I expect everyone will treat her with just as much—or more—respect than you treat one another." His "or more" was directed at a girl and a boy across the room who were very clearly not paying attention.

"Amelia, you can take that seat there." He points to the stool next to Twitch and I feel a surge of relief. No questions about Clara with Twitch as my lab partner.

"How interesting to see you here," he whispers as we both take out our textbooks.

I smile. "Looks like you just got some hours added to your babysitting job."

He rolls his eyes and stifles a laugh. I'm ready to laugh with him when I see his notebook on the table. In the right-hand corner, scribbled in blue ballpoint pen, it says, "Billy Lewis."

Twitch is Billy?!

Oh em gee.

How did I not know Twitch is Billy? I mean, unless there are two Billys in town? But I'd know if there were two Billys in town. Except . . . there's one Billy in town and I didn't know THAT.

"Amelia? You okay over there?" Twitch looks at me, his forehead wrinkled in concern. I must be hyperventilating or something. The words from Clara's letter bang around in my brain like I'm an unstable atom. "Ask Billy to a dance. (OMG. Billy. Sigh.)"

Clara liked Twitch? How could that be? I remember her bossing him around, teasing him, always challenging him to silly competitions that she knew she'd win. *"Who can eat three Oreos fastest?" "Who can swim to the pier and back first?" "Who looks better in that dumb helmet?"* All of that meant she *liked* him? And now I have to ask Billy to a dance?! He's like seventy-nine years older than I am! Well, three years older than I am, but still.

"Earth to Amelia, psssshhhht, over." Twitch mimes like he's talking into a walkie-talkie, then waves his hand in front of my face. His shiny bracelet catches my eye and snaps me out of my spaciness.

"Huh? Oh, sorry . . ." I stammer. "I just . . . I was . . . what page are we on?"

"Twenty-five," he says, looking at me out of the

sides of his eyes as he bends his head over his textbook.

"Great. Excellent. Perfect," I say as I quickly flip to the right page and thank the Universe that he can't hear my heart beating at supersonic speed.

CHAPTER THIRTEEN

"AMELIA."

"Taylor."

"Amelia."

"Taylor."

I have just told Taylor that Twitch is Billy, and watching her reaction is like watching Ping-Pong balls labeled *O*, *M*, and *G* fly around behind her eyes. At one point, she lets out a squeal so sharp and loud I'm pretty sure a dolphin somewhere just looked up and said, "Huh. Did someone just call my name?"

"Taylor." I'm trying to keep my voice low and calm.

"Amelia!" Taylor grabs my shoulders and nearly shakes me off my stool. Thank goodness Mrs. Grant is in the storage closet right now, though surely she can hear us. "We are learning so much about Clara. Doesn't this excite you? It's like a new discovery every day!"

"Well, I wouldn't say every day—"

Taylor squeals again. "I love this! Mystery! Intrigue! Amelia, you're like a one-woman reality TV show!"

Mrs. Grant walks out of the closet holding an armful of folded paper napkins. "Who's on a TV show?"

"Amelia!" Taylor shouts with glee. "Well, I mean, she's not. Not yet, anyway. But her life is so exciting, it's like she's on one!"

"Taylor. Good grief. My life is not exciting. It's basically boring with a heaping helping of terrible."

Mrs. Grant gives me some side-eye that looks a lot like the side-eye Twitch gave me in physics. "What's going on?"

Taylor opens her mouth to blurt the whole thing, but I hold up my hand. It's my story. *I'm* going to tell it. "Remember how I'm trying to do all the things on the list my sister made before she . . . before she . . ."

"Yes," Mrs. Grant says, interrupting me so I don't have to say the part I don't want to say.

"Well, one of the things on the list is to ask this boy, Billy, to a dance. He's some guy she really liked, I guess." Then I tell her everything I've just discovered. She points to the chalkboard with the day's special on it. It's the *Romaine Calm*. (Gruyère with butter and crisp, cold romaine lettuce to finish.)

"I'm totally romaining calm!" I shout.

"Yes, I can see that," Mrs. Grant says with a laugh. "Would you like me to make you a sandwich?"

"Do you even have to ask?" I say, running my hands through my hair.

"You know Kite Night is only like a month away," Taylor says, sipping a milk shake.

"I'm not asking Twitch to Kite Night. The dancing is lame. Plus, that's like asking my dad to a dance. If my dad always wore a shark-attack skateboarding helmet and was fourteen feet tall."

"It is not like asking your dad, you goof!" Taylor says, shaking her head. "It's totally not. Look at Beyoncé."

"I love to look at Beyoncé," I say, trying to make it look like I have heart eyes.

"That's not what I'm talking about!" Taylor is getting frustrated with me now, and I like it for some reason. "Twelve years, Amelia. That's how many years separate her and JAY-Z."

"I have to say I'm on Amelia's side in this argument," Mrs. Grant says from the griddle. "Middle schoolers and high schoolers should not date."

"Gram," Taylor says, exasperated. "Amelia is going to be a high schooler next year. Plus, she's practically half a high schooler now."

I'm so tired of talking about this. Sometimes I think if I could just muster half the energy for things that

Taylor can, then I would be so much more . . . I don't know. Just so much *more*. Taylor is like the human equivalent of the word *jazzed*.

My eyes wander to the big window at the front of the store. People walk by quickly and I wonder where they're all going. Probably, they're going home to cook dinner. Or maybe they're going to take their kids to piano lessons. I see moms pushing strollers, and I wonder what the babies are thinking. Are they happy, hungry, sad? Which one of these people walking by will be the lake's next meal? What will be their last words? These babies who haven't even said their first word yet will have last words one day. Hopefully, they'll be old when that happens. But maybe they won't be. What will be the thing they say last? Will it be, "Oh good grief, no you can't come on the boat. You're such a baby." And then will the person answering yell, "I hate you! I hate you! I never want to see you again!" And then will that person always wonder whether she caused the accident to happen with just the will of her voice? Even though she knows that's impossible? Even though a million doctors and therapists and adults have told her it's definitely 150 percent not her fault?

"Amelia. Honey." Mrs. Grant's soft voice makes my eyes move from the window to her face. I didn't even realize I was crying. Taylor is behind the counter now, apron on, not looking at me, wiping down the work surface. Her mouth is open slightly and I can see her poking her tongue at the roof of her mouth, like she wants to say something angry, but is holding back.

Mrs. Grant takes off her apron and comes to my side of the counter. She puts an arm around my shoulder and helps me off the stool like I'm the old lady and she's the Good Samaritan. "Taylor, can you keep an eye on things?"

Taylor nods without even looking up. I wipe the tears off my face and catch some snot with them. Lovely. Mrs. Grant pushes aside the curtains hiding the stairs, and leads me up to their apartment. She throws her hip into the unlocked door and it opens with a bit of a crunch.

"This old building shifts every time it rains," she says. "One day we may not be able to get this door open. We'll have to live in the shop. Which we practically already do." She smiles at me. I can't quite find a smile to give back.

Mrs. Grant leads me into their small living room. I love it in here. It's so worn and comfortable. The Grant family has lived in this apartment since Mrs. Grant was a little girl. You can barely see what color the walls are because there are so many pictures everywhere. And every surface is covered in framed photos and little knickknacks. It's like visiting a very personal museum. I love that you can feel this history in every room. Even the pink bathroom, with the sink that only sometimes works and the tile that's cracked around the bathtub, has this heavy feeling of knowing so many secrets. I like to think that when Mrs. Grant was my age she looked in the mirror in that bathroom and wondered about her future.

"Take a seat, love," Mrs. Grant says. She hands me a tissue and I blow my nose. I feel like such a loser I can't even find the words to apologize. Three years, Amelia, my brain tells me. Three years means you need to stop crying like this. Taylor is right. You have to move on. You are stuck in the mud. I feel the tears well up again as Mrs. Grant brings me some boiling-hot tea and sits next to me on the couch. I can't even sip the tea because it's so hot, but the warmth of the mug feels really good as I hug it with my hands.

Mrs. Grant's hair is especially flyaway today, a tornado of white. She's tried to catch it with a purple scarf, to pull it back in a kind of ponytail, but without much success. She's holding a big old book on her lap. The leather cover is brown, and you can tell that years of being opened and closed, or even just touched, have made the edges a darker brown. She opens the book, and inside there are black-and-white photos stuck to black paper pages. Paper triangles on the corner of each photograph hold them in place. Mrs. Grant carefully slides one of the photos out of its triangles and hands it to me. I put my tea on the coffee table and take the photo.

There are two girls who look younger than me, though not by much. They have their arms around each other and are wearing swimsuits and laughing. The picture is wrinkled, but I recognize the lake behind them. The pattern of the trees on the far shore was the same then as it is now.

"That's me," Mrs. Grant says, pointing to the girl on the left. I hold the picture closer, and even though it's just a smidge blurry I can tell it's her. The crazy hair is a giveaway. "This is my sister, Rosalie." She points to the other girl. The shape of their mouths is the same, but otherwise she looks completely different. She's tall and super skinny, whereas Mrs. Grant was shorter and rounder. Her hair is long and straight, and even though the picture is black-and-white I can tell it was much darker.

"I didn't know you have a sister," I say, looking from the photograph to Mrs. Grant.

Mrs. Grant's face softens. Her eyes close for a second, and then she opens them, but it's like she's looking at something far away. "Rosalie died when she was fourteen," she says.

"What?" My voice comes out a strangled whisper.

"It was an accident." Mrs. Grant's voice is quiet,

but strong. "We were at the lake. I wanted to go out on our canoe, but she didn't want to. She said she was too tired. I was the youngest, though, and used to getting my way. I begged and begged, so she finally said yes. We took the canoe out to a little cove so we could swim, but it was a cove we hadn't been to before. It was closer in, so we wouldn't have as far to paddle back to the shore.

"I was still learning how to dive back then, but Rosalie was one of the best divers in town. She was so tall, and her body bent perfectly when she broke the surface of the water. Anyway, that afternoon, she stood on the tip of the canoe to show me how to dive properly, but what we didn't know was that the water was more shallow than we thought. We didn't know there was a huge boulder just under the surface that we had somehow missed paddling in. She dove in and hit her head."

Mrs. Grant is holding my hand as she tells this story, and I look up at her and see she has tears in her eyes. "I waited for her to surface. It felt like years, eons. Then, when I leaned over the edge of the canoe, I saw her long hair, floating." She stops talking abruptly and puts her hand to her mouth. Then she shakes her head, hard, as if to snap herself out of the memory.

"I'm sorry I never told you about Rosalie until now,

Amelia. I'm terribly, terribly sorry. Taylor doesn't even know about her. She's been my special, painful secret for many years."

My brain is whirling. I can't figure out what to feel or what to say. I vaguely remember, after Clara died, there were some headlines in the paper about the last lake tragedy being fifty years ago, but I didn't pay attention to any of the details. Everything was such a blur.

"I—" I start, but Mrs. Grant interrupts me.

"It's okay, Amelia. You don't have to say anything. I just want you to know that I really, really know how hard this is for you. I know it from the jagged depths of my heart, my dear."

I swallow hard, and my voice comes out a wobbly whisper. "Is it ever going to feel better?"

Mrs. Grant takes the photo from me and lays it on the coffee table next to my untouched tea. She holds both my hands in hers and looks me straight in the eye. "The pain will lessen over time. I promise. But it will always be with you. This grief is part of you now, Amelia. It's the thread that quilts together every other part of your life. I know that right now that must sound terrible to you. And it is terrible, Amelia. It's terrible what happened to Clara. It's terrible that you and your family have had to go through this tragedy. Never let anyone minimize that, okay?"

I nod.

"I can't promise it will get better, but I can promise it will be *different* over time."

I nod again and she wraps me up in a soft, strong hug. "Do you want to see the rest of the pictures?"

I nod for a third time and then we both blow our noses. She opens the photo album and lays it across both our laps as she turns the pages and shows me everything she can about her childhood with her sister.

I don't know how long we've been sitting there when I hear footsteps coming up the stairs. It's Taylor and Mom.

"What in the world are you two doing up here?" Taylor asks. "You're going to get in trouble for violating child labor laws, leaving me down there like that." She laughs and holds up her hand, mimicking the way Mrs. Grant does it. "But don't worry. Mom is down there now so I can get some homework done."

"Time to get home, Amelia," my mom says.

They've both just burst in talking, without even bothering to see what we're doing. Only now do they come over to us.

"What is that?" Taylor asks, looking over my shoulder.

Mrs. Grant closes the album quickly and stands up. "Just some old pictures."

"Ready?" Mom says. "Dad needs our help tonight. He's moving a bunch of equipment to the Airstream," she tells Mrs. Grant. "He's trying to get situated before all the hoopla with that TV show contest."

I give her a look. She was so mad when he tricked us into going to the lake, and now she's going back *voluntarily*?

Mrs. Grant just smiles politely. "See you tomorrow, Amelia?"

I keep looking at Mom, who nods and says, "Is that okay? I feel like I'm taking advantage of your generosity, Mrs. Grant."

"Never," Mrs. Grant says, walking to the door that leads to the staircase. She gives it a yank and it creaks open.

"Don't forget about Kite Night!" Taylor calls after me. I can't read the expression on her face. She doesn't look mad, but she doesn't look super happy either.

Mom shoos me down the stairs before I have a chance to respond. She says good-bye for us both and soon we're out of the apartment, out of the store, and driving away in Old Betsy. As we go past the lake, I hold my breath and stare at its black water in the twilight. It eats every fifty years, huh? Good to know.

CHAPTER FOURTEEN

DAD IS TOSSING SUPPLIES INTO his truck when Mom pulls in the driveway.

"Just in time!" he says with a grin, wiping sweat from his forehead. "I've almost got everything ready and then we can head to the trailer. I want to get it set up and ready for tomorrow."

I feel numb after my talk with Mrs. Grant. I can't catch any of the thoughts flying around in my head except for one: I am not going to the lake.

"Go find some grubby clothes, Amelia," Mom says. "We'll follow Dad over there."

Even if I *wanted* to help empty oil containers and fill sauce containers and stash wood for the smokers (which I don't), I still wouldn't go to the lake. No way.

"I have homework," I say. My voice is monotone

and I don't look back as I push the door open and walk into the kitchen.

"Since when does homework ever take you more than five minutes?" Mom asks, following me inside.

"Since today," I say, walking up the stairs now, still not looking back.

"Come on, Amelia. Get changed. We won't stay for long, just enough to help."

"HOW are you okay with this?" I ask her. "After that ambush?!"

She seems surprised at my bluntness, then she sighs. "Well . . . Dad *asked* this time. And he said he was sorry. This whole thing with the contest and the trailer . . . it's important for the family. Especially with me only working part-time now. We could use the money the show might generate. If he needs our help, we should help."

"Oh, Mom," I say, feeling disgust rise up from my toes. "Way to stand your ground." I shut my bedroom door and push the dresser up against it to prevent any unwanted bedroom breaches that might lead to heartfelt speeches or hugs. Nope. Not going.

It isn't long before I hear a knock. "Amelia. Come on. What's with the attitude?" Mom used to say that to Clara all the time. "*Clara Peabody! What's with the attitude?*" She turns the doorknob, but the door only opens a crack because of the dresser. "What the—" I hear her loud footsteps as she storms off. A minute later, Dad is knocking on the door.

"What gives, Amelia? I'm not loving this behavior. Let's go. Now."

I refuse to say anything. If they can't figure out why I'm so mad, then I'm not explaining it. I don't even know that I could find the words to say if I wanted to say them. Other than *No, Nope, No way, No how, Uh-uh.* Dad sighs deeply and I hear his heavy footsteps go down the stairs. A few minutes later his loud truck engine roars to life. Old Betsy is quiet. Either Mom rode with him in the truck, or she's still here. Doesn't matter. I'm probably not leaving my room ever again.

Lying on my bed, I stare at the ceiling. Mrs. Grant seems like a perfectly normal lady. She always has, ever since I've known her, which has been forever. She's funny and smart and always busy. Everyone in town loves her. It's blowing my mind right now that, even though a horrible thing happened to her sister (a horrible thing she blamed herself for), she's such a . . . regular nice person. She doesn't have a cloud of Dead Sister around her everywhere she goes, like I do. People don't whisper and point at her like they do to me. She goes about her everyday life in a way that seems happy . . . joyful, even. I mean, she whistles and sings to herself, and knows Beyoncé lyrics. HOW IN THE WORLD DOES SHE DO IT?

It's like, for Mrs. Grant, having a dead sister is a thing she keeps inside her, not because she's ashamed of it, or because it's a terrible purple bruise she has to poke, but because, I don't know. Because it's just part of her? Like, Rosalie is alive, but as part of her own soul.

I sit up with a start. How can I make Clara part of me like that?

I hear a commotion out my window that's louder than my racing thoughts. Tiny is barking like crazy, and there's someone shouting. Sliding my curtains to the side, I see Twitch on the sidewalk, holding his skateboard like a shield while Tiny jumps at him and barks. Twitch looks terrified, his helmet all askew, but I can tell by the way Tiny is shaking his booty he's trying to get something. I squint. Yep. There it is. Crumpled up next to the skateboard, gripped hard in Twitch's right hand, is a paper bag from Big Boy Burger, Tiny's favorite. I watch them dance for a second, but it doesn't look like Tiny is giving up anytime soon, and Twitch looks like he might wet his pants. Where is Mr. Robertson?

I push aside my dresser, throw open my door, and run downstairs. It only takes me a couple of seconds to run through the house and get outside.

"Tiny!" I shout, clapping my hands like Mrs. Robertson does. "Cut it out, nerd. You're scaring Twitch!"

Tiny turns to look at me for a split second. He assesses that I don't have a Big Boy burger and he goes back to barking at Twitch.

"TINY!" I shout again, marching up to him and grabbing his collar. "Stop!" He looks at me again and then lunges, licking my face all over. That makes me laugh and splutter. I'm trying to fend him off and signal to Twitch that he's safe.

"Get that burger out of here." I laugh. "You're torturing the dog."

"I'M torturing HIM?" Twitch asks, dropping his skateboard to the sidewalk and holding the burger bag behind his back. "I thought he was going to eat me."

"He just wants your burger. Those are his favorite."

"His fav—" Twitch looks at me, wrinkling his forehead. "You guys are tight, huh?"

Tiny is sitting by my feet now, though he's still nearly as tall as I am. He's happily panting and sniffing around for the burger, giving my face a lick here and there even as I try to shove his enormous head away from me. "We're BFFs for sure," I say. "You okay?"

Twitch gives a sheepish smile. "I'm fine. Maybe my ego is a little scraped up."

"Wait there," I say. "I'll be back in a second."

"Yes, ma'am," Twitch says with a salute. Such a dork.

I hook my finger under Tiny's collar and lead him to Mr. Robertson's backyard. I kick open the fence door and lead Tiny over to the covered porch where I know there will be a bowl of food and water for him. "Here you go, Tiny. It's no Big Boy burger, but it'll do." He gives me a look like, "NOPE," but he doesn't follow me when I go through the gate and shut it behind me.

Back on the sidewalk, I ask Twitch, "Did he jump over the fence?"

Twitch nods, his eyes huge. "It was like some kind of dog-shaped missile heading right at me."

I start to laugh. I can't help it. The image is too funny. Twitch's cheeks turn pink. They're almost the same color as the shark eyes on his helmet. "What are you doing over here, anyway? I never see you skate by."

"Oh," he says, his pink cheeks getting redder. "Actually, there are two burgers in this bag. One for you." He hands me a burger. "You looked a little freaked out in class today, so I thought I'd come by and see if you're okay." He follows me to my front porch, where we sit. "I've discovered that a Big Boy burger can momentarily erase all memories of people in physics classes acting like dummies."

He starts to eat like he hasn't eaten in weeks. I take a small bite out of my burger. It's warm and juicy and yummy, but I'm not that hungry.

"So how are you doing?" he asks, wiping ketchup drips off his chin with the back of his hand. "Is physics blowing your mind?"

I shake my head and roll my eyes. "Physics is the easiest thing of all the things in my life right now."

He pops the last bite of his burger in his mouth and says, "Well, I guess that's good, then."

I shrug and put my burger on the crumpled bag. I stare across the street at the setting sun. The sky is turning bloodred and orange. It's beautiful. "How come I never knew your name was Billy?" I ask.

Twitch squints and turns his head a little to the side. "Are you asking me why you don't know my name? Because I don't know how to answer that." He laughs quietly.

"I just mean . . . did Clara call you Billy or Twitch? I never heard her call you Billy."

"Are you talking about her letter? The part about asking me to a dance?"

Now it's my turn for my cheeks to turn pink.

Billy looks at his sneakers. They're old black Converses, and he's drawn a super-cool-looking, intricate pattern all over the white rubber that covers his toes and the sides of the shoes. "When we were together, just the two of us hanging out, she called me Billy. But when we were with other people she called me Twitch like everyone else." His finger traces the designs on his shoe. He pinches his lips together in a straight line and looks up at me.

"Pretty sure I came by to see how *you* were doing. And now we're talking about me. How do you do that, Amelia? You're some kind of magician."

"You don't want to talk about this, huh?" I say. I understand.

"Are you going to eat that?" Twitch points at my burger with only one sad bite taken out of it. "You can have it," I say. "I had a sandwich over at Grant's not too long ago."

Twitch nods and takes my burger. He eats it slower as we both watch the sky changing colors. "So you're doing fine in physics, then?" he asks finally, swallowing the last bite.

"The physics part is fine," I say, watching a cloud race by. "It's just . . . I guess I never thought about the fact that the class would be full of kids who used to have class with Clara."

"Yeah," Twitch says. "Welcome to my life."

"Do you want to go to Kite Night with me?" I blurt.

"Huh?" He turns and looks at me.

"The stupid town party thing—"

"By the fountain, with all nighttime kite flying and the terrible DJ and the corn dogs? Yes, I know what Kite Night is, I just mean . . . uh . . . no offense, but . . ."

"Uuugh, nooooooo." I shove his shoulder hard. "Not like a date, dummy. Just, will you go with me?" I reach into my pocket and pull out Clara's letter. I unfold it and point to number three.

3) Ask Billy to a dance. (OMG. Billy. Sigh.)

He flushes, and his mouth opens and closes without making any sound.

"It's. Not. A. Date. Dummy," I say very slowly. "Boys. Are. Gross. And. Girls. Run. The. World. But. Please. Help. Me. Cross. One. Stupid. Thing. Off. This. List. Please."

"Okay, okay, you don't have to turn into a robot. Fine. But it's not a date. Sophomores don't date middle-school kids."

"It's not a date!" I shout. That makes Tiny bark from all the way in Mr. Robertson's backyard.

Twitch laughs. "Fine, fine. Excellent. Don't sic your dog on me."

"Not my dog." I laugh. "But I will if I have to."

Twitch holds his hand out for a shake. "Yes, Amelia Peabody, I will go with you to Kite Night so that you can cross one stupid thing off your list."

"Excellent," I say, and we shake hands so hard his helmet wobbles.

Twitch's phone chirps and he looks down at the

screen. His eyes widen for just a second and then go back to normal. "I gotta jet. But you're okay, yeah?"

I nod. "You're okay?"

He nods and stands up.

"Wait!" I say. "I'll be right back." I run into the house, upstairs to my room, and back down in record time. I hand him the softball and two gloves. "You left these the other day."

He takes them from me. "Aha! I was looking all over for them. Thanks."

And then he's off, skating down the street, gloves on both hands like a dork, ball nestled in one glove, empty Big Boy Burger bag stuffed in his back pocket.

CHAPTER FIFTEEN

"YOU DID NOT."

"I did."

"You did not."

"I did! Also, I'm having déjà vu."

Taylor shoves a book into her locker and primps in the mirror that hangs next to a picture of Beyoncé.

"Well, was it weird? Did you get nervous? I can't believe you guys are dating." She makes a face in the mirror like she smelled a spoiled hot dog. Though her eyes are sharp and pointy as her reflection stares at me standing behind her.

"I told you. It's not a date."

"Well, then it doesn't count." She slams her locker shut and smacks her lip gloss.

"Of course, it counts," I say. "The letter didn't say 'Ask Billy on a date,' it just said 'dance.'"

Taylor makes a gimme motion with her hand and

I sigh. I pull the letter out of my pocket and hand it to her. "Exhibit A," she says, jabbing at the letter with her finger. " 'OMG.' " She looks at me pointedly. "And exhibit B." She jabs with her finger again. " 'Sigh.' " She folds up the letter and hands it back to me. "She was clearly . . . feeling *feelings* for him, Amelia. It has to be a date." She stops walking dead in the center of the hallway and I run into her. She whips her head around to stare at me. "You ARE sure Twitch is the right Billy, aren't you?" She wrinkles up her nose. "It's just very hard to believe."

"Yes, he's Billy. No, it's not a date. Yes, it still counts." I'm starting to get irritated with Taylor. Has she always been this bossy?

"I'll see you at gym." I wave as I walk away, my back to her.

"Are we running tonight?" she calls after me.

"Sure!" I yell over my shoulder. Though I'm not really sure I want to.

When I get to class, I see everyone through the skinny window in the door. They're chatting and goofing around, waiting for the late bell to ring. Some kids sit on the desks and laugh at things on their phones. Others stand in a cluster at the back of the room. Everyone is either paired off, like Lacy and Katherine (*how* do they get so many classes together?!), or in a group, and I know that in about two minutes they'll all have to be in their seats when the bell rings, but still. Two minutes of standing in there, not in a group or paired off, is basically two lifetimes. I don't think I can open the door and go in. Geography isn't calling to me today. I turn quickly and walk down the hall. There are still a bunch of kids milling around, so no one notices as I walk past. I don't turn around, I don't look to the side. I just keep walking, holding my breath, until I walk out the hallway door into the bright afternoon sun.

When I get past the open expanse of the soccer field, I see a cluster of trees and I take a deep breath. I move past the tree line, and then, dropping my backpack against the trunk of a tree, I slide down next to it, sitting in a pile of leaves.

I've never skipped class before. I have no idea what will happen if I get caught. Mom and Dad are already mad because I wouldn't go to the lake last night. I'm not sure they'll even know how to punish me if they find out about this. I'm the good girl. Clara was the handful.

I pull my knees up to my chest, hugging them. Am I really going to sit out here and stare at trees for forty-five minutes? Great plan, Amelia. This is definitely more constructive than actually learning something about geography. I sigh. It's not like I can just march back into class, though, can I? Why didn't I hide in the bathroom and go in after the late bell? I would have missed the two lifetimes of not talking to anyone, but I wouldn't be sitting out here like a dope. Maybe I can go back in and tell Mr. Holbrook I was in the bathroom. Or maybe I'll just stay out here and listen to the tree whispers instead of listening to the class whisper about me.

I'm rummaging around in my backpack, trying to find a granola bar and a book when I hear a crunch. My heart stair-steps into my throat. Wonderful. Now I'm going to be killed by an ax murderer. My palms start to sweat as I hold my breath and try not to make any noise. The crunching sounds are getting louder. And now I hear voices. One voice in particular sounds familiar.

Through the brush, I see three or four figures pushing their way into the woods. They aren't super close, so I don't think they've seen me. I hear laughing and a sound like someone is shaking a spray-paint can. I catch a flash of red and white from the edges of a skating helmet, and yep. That's Twitch. I can't really see who's with him because they're walking fast. Soon they're deep in the woods and I can't hear them or see them anymore. Wonder what they're up to. A small part of me wants to follow them, but a bigger part of me is feeling a wash of exhaustion after the rush of terror. I should get back to class.

I sigh and zip up my backpack. At the edge of the trees, I look around to see if anyone's outside, but the coast is clear. I run up to the door I came out of and bounce off it when I push on the handle. Of course, it's locked. Uh-oh. I didn't think about that. I run to another door and it's locked, too. How in the world am I supposed to get back inside?!

Like some kind of inept spy, I run along the side of the school trying every door, but they're all locked. The only choice is to go in through the front door, and I know from coming to school late after various dentist appointments and things, *that* door is locked, too. The front office people have to buzz you in. I look at my watch. Twenty minutes until gym.

I go hide under the bleachers and watch everyone run track for the next ten minutes. Coach blows her whistle and the girls line up to go through the double doors that lead directly into the locker room. Luckily, Coach goes in ahead of everyone. I jump in at the back of the line and sneak in.

"Amelia? What in the world are you doing?" Georgia, who has been holding the door for everyone, seems to have a voice louder than anyone else in humankind.

I hold my finger to my lips. "I'm working in the office this period, and I have a message for Coach." I pull Clara's letter from my pocket and wave it. "Very important. Top secret."

"Uh," Georgia says, but I just walk briskly past her. I find an empty toilet stall and hide in there until the bell rings.

Once everyone is mostly out and the next class starts trickling in, I flush the toilet and emerge, somewhat victorious.

"Amelia?" Taylor's voice is behind me, and it sounds aghast. "What in the *world*?"

"What?" I whip around, startled.

"Girl." Taylor shakes her head. "I just . . . *what* is going on with you?"

That's when I catch a glimpse of myself in the mirror. My hair is full of leaves. Leaves and twigs are snagged all over the back of my sweater. I look like I've just crawled in from the woods. Which I have.

Taylor picks leaves out of my hair as I walk to my gym locker and pull out my sweats. She opens her mouth to say something, but I hold up a hand. "I don't want to talk about it."

"Okay," she says with a small laugh, though her expression is concerned. "I'll see you outside."

Amelia Peabody: the only person in the history of time who can calculate gravitational potential energy but who can't calculate how to correctly skip one class.

CHAPTER SIXTEEN

"IS IT EVEN SWIMMING SEASON?" I ask. "Is anyone even *going* to the lake these days?" I can hear the whine in my voice.

"That's where they're filming the contest, Amelia. What can I do?" Dad throws his arms out in a helpless gesture.

"You could not be part of the contest," I mutter under my breath. Then I say it louder, because why not? "Why do you even *have* to do the contest?" I ask. "It's just some silly TV show."

Dad pulls his face back like I slapped him. His voice is quiet. "Because it's my dream to have a successful barbecue business? Because I want to provide for you and Mom? Because it will make me happy?"

"Doesn't anyone in this house care about what would make ME happy?" I shout. It's like I'm floating above myself and watching the scene. I can't even believe these words are coming out of my mouth. It's so stereotypical. So teenager-y. And yet . . . it's how I feel. *Don't* they care about me? Don't they see how *un*happy it makes me to even *talk* about the lake, God forbid go there. I make a loud harrumph noise. "Even my *thoughts* are italicized. *That's* how upset I feel."

Mom stares at me. She seems to be wavering between anger and sadness. Dad is clearly settling in for full-on anger.

"I have to go practice for softball tryouts." I storm out of the kitchen and onto the front porch.

"Who ARE you?!" Dad shouts after me. "Be home by seven!"

Be home by seven? He's not going to march out here after me and drag me kicking and screaming to the lake? Of course not. I know Dad would never do that. But still. Did I just win that argument? I feel very uneasy as I run down to the alley behind the General Store where Taylor's "front door" is.

I knock on the door but no one answers. Weird. I know we had plans to run this evening. I jog in place for a minute and try to figure out what to do. I'm definitely not going home. And by myself, I don't know if I have the oomph to force myself to keep running when I want to give up. Hmm.

An idea lights up my brain. Perfect.

"Amelia? What are you doing here?" Twitch is standing in the doorway holding a bowl of ice cream. He looks different and I can't quite figure out why. Aha. It's his jaggedly crazy hair. He looks like a completely different person without that shark-bite helmet.

"Are you eating ice cream for dinner?" I ask, jogging in place.

"Are you jogging on my front porch?"

A voice from inside the house yells, "Who is it, William?"

"Amelia, Mom!" Twitch shouts back.

"Amelia Peabody?" Twitch's mom comes up behind him, wiping her hands on a dish towel. She sees me and smiles. It's that sad smile I know soooooooo well. "How *are* you? How are your parents?"

"She's fine, everyone's fine," Twitch says. He hands her his bowl and shuts the door behind him before she can say anything else.

"Twitch!" I laugh. "I mean *William*! That was so rude! Also, how many names do you *have*?"

"Well, she was asking personal questions," he says, shaking his head. "And Billy is a nickname for William. Twitch is a nickname for, uh, everything." A tiny smile plays at the corners of his mouth.

"She was just asking how I am," I start, but he holds up his hand and I laugh. "Okay, yes, I saw the look in her eyes. The 'here's the girl with a dead sister' look. I am very familiar with it."

"Well, you're welcome for saving you from it," he says. I give him a little bow and say thanks.

"Do you want to play catch?" I ask. "I have been stood up for my jogging date with Taylor."

"Sure," Twitch says. "Don't move." He runs into the house and in a minute he's back out with the gloves and a ball. "You know you're going to have to get your own glove if you make the team."

"Details," I say, with a dismissive wave. We both laugh.

We go out into the street to throw the ball. I want to ask him what he was doing in the woods during school hours, but if I ask him then he'll know *I* was in the woods during school. Conundrum.

Mostly, we just play catch in silence. It's really, really nice. He seems to be kind of lost in his own thoughts, but I don't mind. No one is pestering me with questions, no one is giving me looks of pity or confusion. It's just catch. Plain and simple. My mind thinks: THROW and then it thinks CATCH and that's it. I wish I could do this forever.

"THERE YOU ARE, YOU DWEEB!"

My head swivels around. Taylor is jogging up the street. "Where have you been?" She's out of breath and sweaty.

"I went to your apartment and you weren't there," I say, confused.

"I was waiting at Deadman's Hill. Where we said we would meet." Her hands are on her hips. Twitch wanders over to us.

"What's up, Taylor?"

"My blood pressure, *Twitch*," Taylor says with an edge to her voice. "Amelia asked me to help her train for softball tryouts, but when we do train together, all she does is complain. And now today, she left me high and dry." She taps her foot angrily. "Looks like she found a more appealing trainer."

"What?" I say. "No! Taylor, come on." Why is she acting so mad?

"No, it's cool. Play catch with your boyfriend, Amelia. I get it." She runs off before I can say anything else.

I whip around just as Twitch is about to say something. "I've told her a million times you're not my boyfriend."

Twitch looks relieved, then says, "Do you need to go? Talk to her?"

I shake my head. "I do not. Now get back to where you were."

"Yes, ma'am," he says, and jogs back to his spot. I throw the ball way off to the side and he has to chase after it. Ugh. Stupid Taylor, ruining my Zen. But I do feel bad. Did I say I was going to meet her at the hill? I can't remember.

For the next few minutes, Twitch and I make a feeble attempt at throw and catch, catch and throw, but both of our minds are somewhere else now. Finally, I toss the ball back to Twitch, then I toss the glove.

"I gotta go," I say. "Thanks for practicing with me."

"No problem," Twitch says. "See you tomorrow."

"Bye." I watch him lope up the porch stairs and through the front door. It's dusk out now and the lights inside the house seem extra bright. I see Twitch go into the kitchen and say something to his dad. His two older sisters are sitting on the couch still in their soccer gear. His mom walks by the front window, sees me staring, and waves. Her wave startles me. She makes a gesture for me to come in, but I shake my head and run off like some kind of feral cat.

CHAPTER SEVENTEEN

SOMETIMES, DURING CLASS, I FIND myself mesmerized by Mr. Robertson's mustache. It is very, very shiny and very, very black. I wonder if it ever tickles him. I wonder if he has some kind of special mustache oil or shampoo to make it that shiny. I wonder if he goes out with friends and tries to pick up ladies and the ladies are all, "Oh, Mr. Robertson, you seemed like a regular man until you turned around and, *wham*, your mustache rays pierced my heart."

"Amelia?"

I blink. Everyone is staring at me. "Uh . . ."

Mr. Robertson taps at a formula on the whiteboard. "Can you . . ."

"The frequency of sound is . . ." I look over the numbers and do some calculations in my head, "292.66 hertz," I say quickly, solving the formula.

"I just wanted to know if you could name the

formula, Amelia." Mr. Robertson crosses his arms. "But good work solving it." He's eyeing me like he can't tell whether he should be mad at me for not paying attention, or impressed I could do the math in my head.

"Oh," I say. "Sorry. That's the Doppler shift formula." The class is all staring at me like my hair is on fire. I want to say, "What? *I'm good at physics.*" But I don't. Mr. Robertson's mustache quivers just a little bit as it does a bad job of hiding a smile.

I wonder where Twitch is today. It's weird sitting here at our table without him. I feel exposed or something, which is an irritating feeling. It's not like he's my protector, except that sometimes he is. I like it that he steers conversations away from uncomfortable things, and that he includes me in other things. I'm not some freakazoid middle-school physics genius to him, I'm just another kid in class. The way he treats me like a normal human seems to make other people treat me like a normal human, too. Without him here, I feel like my normal human mask is hanging off just enough to show the weirdo underneath.

As if my brain conjured him out of thin air, he bursts through the door, out of breath and sweating, drops his bag on the ground next to our table, and straddles his stool. He stares directly at my textbook, and my notebook, then grabs his own notebook and starts working on the problems on the page without saying a word.

"Ahem." Mr. Robertson looms over our table. I can smell Twitch's spicy boy smell mixed with something else . . . what is it? Nail polish? I look at his hands. His fingertips are red and blue. It's not nail polish, though. It's spray paint. Twitch stands up and follows Mr. Robertson to his desk, where they have a very quiet, but very heated, conversation. Twitch comes back to the table, grabs up his stuff, and storms out of the classroom.

Later, when the bell rings and I'm zipping up my backpack, Mr. Robertson strolls over, hands in his pockets. "How are you?" he asks. He jangles change in his pocket. That is maybe the only thing I don't like about Mr. Robertson. He's a change jangler.

"Fine," I say.

"Class treating you well?" *Jangle, jangle.* "You seem to be thriving." *Jangle, jangle.* His shiny mustache bends light toward his mouth, making his bottom lip shine, too.

"I love it," I say. "Really."

"Good," he says. "I'm glad to hear it." *Jangle, jangle.* I want to reach over and grab his hand out of his pocket to make him stop.

I throw my backpack over my shoulder and head to the door.

"Amelia," he calls after me. *Jangle, jangle.* "You make such good calculations in class, be sure to think carefully about the calculations you make outside of class, too. Think of the butterfly effect and how decisions you make now might affect your whole future." *Jangle.*

"Uh, okay," I say as I walk into the hallway. "Bye, Mr. Robertson. See you tomorrow." What in the world is he talking about? What calculations am I making outside of physics? Other than the fact that I'm calculating right now how to steal all of his change to keep it quiet.

The halls are full of kids flooding out of school, and I join the flood. My mind is wandering to what grilled cheese special is on the board at the General Store today, when I see Twitch duck out a side door with a couple of other kids. Hmm. I calculate that I want to follow him.

I wait a few seconds and then peek my head out the door. Twitch and the kids are walking toward the woods. I slip out of the door and try to quietly run close enough to them to see where they're going, but not be seen by them. Not an easy task when you're crossing a soccer field. They walk fast and I have to kind of run/skip to not lose them. I'm not even sure why I'm following them.

Out of nowhere I realize that, even though I am

constantly reminding Taylor that Twitch and I are just friends, I've always thought of him as *Clara's* friend. And while I want to know why Clara treated him the way she did, but still seemed to crush on him, I also just . . . well . . . I just want to know more about him. He's becoming more of *my* friend and less of Clara's former friend. And even though we aren't *best* friends or anything, it feels weird to realize he does things that I don't know about. That sounds very stalker-ish, but it's true. I just . . . I want to know what Twitch is up to.

We're in the woods now, and I'm trying to keep up without making a huge racket. It's pretty useless, though. Twigs break under my feet, and I trip at least nineteen times and go "OOF" each of those nineteen times. So it isn't a surprise when I hear a girl's voice, "Come on over, whoever you are. You are a terrible spy." Some people laugh.

I feel my face burn as I catch up to them. Twitch is standing in a small clearing with two girls, a guy, and someone whose back is to me. That person is bent over something and is shaking a spray-paint can.

"Amelia?" Twitch's face crinkles up in confusion as he sees me emerge from the trees. He's flanked by the girls, who both have their arms crossed. One has fiery dyed-red hair in a Mohawk. The other has a completely shaved head and huge silver hoop earrings.

"I . . ." I start. But I only now see everything surrounding us. There are tiny rocks creating a mosaic
on the ground. It isn't finished, but it's huge and it
takes my breath away. It's painted a deep, dark blue;
the kind of blue that looks like it goes on forever and
ever. Scattered everywhere in the blue are tiny golden
stars. I can't tell if they're painted or if they're actual
little stars glued onto the rocks. I squat down. They're
painted. Whoa. So many of them. And around the
edge of the whole thing is a red rim and white jagged
triangles. I stand up so I can get a better view. Is it . . .
teeth? It's like the shark teeth around Twitch's helmet.
Am I standing in a giant deep-blue mouth filled with
stars?

"I was actually going to bring you here," Twitch
says after clearing his throat. "But I wanted it to be
finished first."

That's when I realize the girl with the Mohawk is
Maureen. And the bald girl is Desiree. They were
on the boat with Twitch at Clara's party. The boy is
Henry. The other boy stands up and wipes his hands
on his pants. Jake. Everyone stares at me through the
shadows of the trees. They were all on the boat when
Clara drowned. I haven't seen them together since the
funeral.

"We're getting really close to being finished," Twitch
says. "Remember all those papers I dropped when we

ran into each other at school ages ago? That was a bunch of research into figuring out how we can get city funding for an art project . . . maybe move this somewhere where other people can see it. Or maybe leave it here, but protect it. Anyway, we've been getting together more often lately so we can finish it." Twitch sighs and looks off into the distance. After a second he turns back to me. "We needed to do something. For Clara. Together. And we didn't know what. This just kind of . . . happened."

I can't quite figure out what I'm feeling. I want to cry. Not because I'm sad. I mean, I'm *always* sad, but I'm not extra sad or anything. I just . . . I think maybe I feel left out. No one thought to ask if I wanted to help? Just like Clara, this art that they've created for or about or because of her is so beautiful . . . and a little bit scary, and . . . familiar to me. But no one wanted to tell me about it until it was finished? They didn't even think to include me. Would Twitch have planned to tell me about it if we hadn't become quasi-friends?

I look at them all looking at me. Then I turn and run.

CHAPTER EIGHTEEN

I'VE SLOWED TO A WALK now that I've made it to the town square. I'm making my way to Grant's, brain still whirling, when I see Mrs. Grant pop out of the Enchanted Florist. She's holding two bunches of yellow flowers that look like daisies.

"Swamp sunflowers," Mrs. Grant says to me when we meet on the sidewalk. "Terrible name, beautiful flowers. Thought I'd spruce up the place a bit." She puts her hand on my arm. "Amelia, dear, are you all right? You look like you've seen a ghost."

I shake my head. I can feel hot tears swirling into my eyes. Stupid. It's stupid to cry. What am I even crying *about*?

"Here," Mrs. Grant says, handing me one of the bunches of flowers. She links her empty arm in mine. "Let's walk and talk."

"But the store . . ." I start. She shushes me.

"The store doesn't need a walk and talk right now. You do."

All I can do is nod and feel the tears spill down my cheeks, hot with anger over crying again, and also hot with, what . . . sadness? Left out–ness? Aloneness? Maybe that's it.

"I feel like there's no place for me," I whisper, my chin trembling. "I feel like everyone has a spot in the world. But I don't. It's like Clara and I shared a spot and when she died I lost my place, too. But that's not like Taylor, who has so many friends and always knows what she wants and how to get it. It's not like Twitch, who has these friends who are all creating art together. It's not like Dad and his barbecue, or you and your store, or Mom and her work. I don't have anything. I just float around and feel sad and invisible."

Mrs. Grant tightens her arm around mine. "Does it help if I tell you everyone is sad in their own way, and you are definitely not invisible?"

I shrug. As we're walking, a bunch of workers are setting everything up for Kite Night. It's really coming up so soon?

Our walk and talk mostly ends up just a walk as we make a loop around the town center in companionable silence. When we get to Grant's General Store, I feel better, even though there wasn't a lot of soul-searching or talking. Sometimes just walking with someone is nice. Kind of like just playing catch.

"Amelia!" Taylor screeches as soon as we walk through the door. My peacefulness shatters. "Now you're out exercising with *Gram* instead of me?! Do you even *want* my help anymore?!" She glowers at me for a split second and then storms upstairs before I even have a chance to respond.

"I don't think she's used to seeing you on your own so much," Mrs. Grant says, pulling on an apron over her sweater and jeans. "Give her time. She'll figure it out."

I'm not sure I want to give her time to figure it out, though. It's annoying to always be yelled at, especially when I don't feel like I've done anything to deserve the yelling. I've seen her at school with Lacy and Katherine. It's not like she's pining away for me, or something. She has plenty of friends and projects and things. Can't we be friends without her having to know about every tiny thing I do?

Taylor comes back downstairs holding Ratface. She bites her lip and takes a deep breath. "Sorry I just yelled at you. That wasn't very cool. I just . . . I'm here to help you, Amelia, you know that, right?"

"Of course, I know that," I say, feeling like maybe I have whiplash from her mad–not mad switcheroo.

"And you know that sometimes I have to figure things out on my own, right?"

She nods, but she doesn't look convinced. Ratface leaps out of her arms and runs to the front door to greet a customer.

"Why don't you two get behind the counter, wash your hands, and help me cut some cheese?" Mrs. Grant asks.

Taylor and I both burst out laughing, and for just a second it feels like old times.

CHAPTER NINETEEN

"COME ON," I SAY. "TAYLOR. This is stupid." We're standing in her kitchen. She's draped red fabric over the window so that the small area glows like the inside of an eyelid. There's a long tablecloth hanging off the kitchen table and a candle in the middle. On one end of the table is a Ouija board.

"No, Amelia. You need closure. We're going to fix you for good." She smiles brightly and gestures to a chair nearest the board.

I sit and cross my arms. "Um, (*a*), I don't need to be fixed. And (*b*), this is a game, Taylor. There's no such thing as ghosts."

Taylor sits across from me and shakes her head like I just told her the earth is flat. "Girl, all you ever DO is talk about how you wish you could stop feeling sad, how you wish you could be normal, how you wish you could be as beautiful as me." I stick my tongue out at her, but I smile a little bit. She's such a booger, but I do love her. "This is your brief opportunity to break through the bonds of this world," she continues with a twinkle in her eye, "and peek through the veil of the next world. This is your chance to have some new last words with Clara." Her voice has softened and she puts a hand over mine. "Okay? I know it's silly, but maybe it will help?"

I nod, and swallow back tears. It's stupid. But fine. Taylor deserves a normal friend, and I would love to launch into the world of Taylorville where everything is fun and no one is sad and the only thing that makes me angry is when my best friend doesn't exercise enough.

"So, what do we do?" I ask.

The Ouija board has the alphabet in the middle of it, split into two lines and bent in a kind of rainbow shape. Under the alphabet is a line of numbers going from one to nine, with a zero at the end, and under that it says GOOD BYE. It says YES and NO in the top corners. There's a plastic thing in the middle of the board that's sort of in a heart shape, and in the middle of it is a magnifying glass so you can see what's under it.

"Put two of your fingers here," Taylor says, showing me how to hold the plastic thing. "And I put two of my fingers *here*," she says, putting her hand on the other side of it. We look up at each other and burst out laughing.

"Dumb . . ." I say with a smile.

"Zip it, you," Taylor says. But she's smiling, too. "Make sure you don't push it or anything. Just let your fingers barely rest there."

We sit like that for a second. "Now what?" I say. The red light filtering in probably isn't any warmer than usual, but I'm starting to feel hot and claustrophobic in the small kitchen. I'm ready to get this thing done. I need closure for my closure.

Taylor makes a face. "The instructions weren't in the box. So . . . I guess we just ask questions?" She clears her voice, and in a very dramatic voice says, "Hello, spirit world. I hope you are doing well today. We would like to talk to Clara Peabody. Is she available?"

"It's not a voice mail—" I start to say, but the plastic thing under our fingers jerks over to the YES by a drawing of a smiley sun. What the—?

Taylor and I lock eyes. "Oh em gee," she whispers. "Spirit world," she continues in her silly deep voice. "Just to confirm we have the right Clara, can she tell us her sister's name?" The plastic thing glides under our fingers to the *A*. Then it jerks to the *M* and my heart starts to bang in my chest like I've just sprinted half a mile. When it moves toward the *E*, I yank my hand off of it, my eyes meeting Taylor's in a kind of panic.

"This isn't real," I say. "This can't be . . ."

"Put your hand back on it, Amelia," Taylor says. Her voice is firm, but not mean. "This is your chance to talk to Clara. Make things right."

I swallow hard. How can this be real? There's no such thing as the spirit world or ghosts or any of that. When you die, you die. I have seen death. There is no filmy fog of a soul floating up to the sky. And yet . . .

My voice comes out as a croak. "Clara? Do you hate me?"

The plastic thing pulls our fingers to the NO, and I feel something inside me break open. A rush of tears pours down my face. I stare at the board and sob, "I had no idea you were going to die. I was mad you wouldn't let me on the boat. I didn't actually mean I never wanted to see you again. I didn't actually mean I hated you."

The plastic thing moves to *I*, then *K*, then *N*, then *O*, and finally *W*. It stops for a second, and Taylor and I just look at each other, stunned. I feel movement under my fingers and now it moves to *L*, and *O*, and *V*, then *E*. Then it slowly moves to *U*.

I bury my face in my hands and cry and cry. Can this be real? Is it actually Clara speaking to us from . . . wherever? Does she really not hate me? I'm sniffling and wiping my face as Taylor stands up and comes over to me. She kneels next to me and puts her arm around my shoulders. She's about to say something, when a streak of white light crashes into the kitchen. Our red eyelid opens to reveal Mrs. Grant standing in the doorway at the top of the stairs from the store.

"What in the world?" she says. Ratface runs past her and over to us, wagging his tail and hopping around.

"Ratface, no!" Taylor hisses, making a grab for him. She misses, though, and he runs under the hanging tablecloth, barking. The tablecloth ripples as he runs around under the table. Now he's growling and barking and I hear . . . what was that? A "*shhh*"? From *under* the table? Wait. What?

I hear it again: "Shhh!" and that's when Taylor puts her hands over her face. Ratface is going absolutely berserk now and the shushes become "*ow!*" and "*stop it!*" Then the tablecloth lifts up and Twitch rolls out from under the table, Ratface attached to his back pocket, trying to free a stick of beef jerky. Twitch's helmet is all cockeyed on his head, and he's holding a big U-shaped magnet that I recognize from physics class.

Taylor peeks at me through her hands. My mouth hangs open. Twitch sits on the floor and says nothing. Mrs. Grant has her hands on her hips. Ratface eats the jerky.

Finally, I find my voice. "This was a JOKE? You were . . . You thought . . ." My face feels like it's going to catch on fire.

"Amelia," Taylor pleads. "It wasn't a joke, I swear. We just wanted to—"

But I don't hear what she has to say. I don't WANT to hear it. I fling myself from my seat, and fly down the stairs. Taylor and Twitch call after me, but I don't turn around. I'm never speaking to either one of them again.

Ever.

CHAPTER TWENTY

HOW COULD THEY? HOW COULD they? I'm pacing circles in my bedroom, raging mad. I feel like every bond of friendship or trust or *anything* has been shattered into a billion tiny pieces.

When I came home, I flew past Mom, who was at the kitchen table reading and having a snack. She called upstairs after me, but I didn't answer. Now she's knocking quietly on my door.

"Amelia? Taylor's here."

"NO!" I yell, spluttering. I'm so mad I can't even find complete sentences. I have turned into a cavewoman. A very, very angry cavewoman. "GO!" I shout, pointing at the dresser shoved in front of the closed door. "GET OUT! AAAARGH!"

"Amelia?" Taylor's voice is small outside my door. I want to destroy something. I breathe fire and smoke as I cast my gaze around the room. It lands on a picture of me and Taylor making goofy faces. I tear it up into tiny shreds and then shove the tiny shreds under the corner of the bottom of the door that isn't covered by the dresser.

"I was just trying to help," Taylor says through the door. "I thought this would fix everything. I thought it would make you . . . you . . . again."

The rage inside me, which I thought had already hit "exceeds maximum," boils up even faster and angrier. "THIS IS ME!" I scream. "I AM ME! I CAN'T BE FIXED! THIS IS WHAT YOU GET! THIS BIG MESS OF A PERSON IS ME NOW! THE ME I WAS ISN'T THE ME I AM ANYMORE!" The words I'm screaming make perfect sense to me, but I can hear how they might sound like Dr. Seuss having a very bad day. I don't care. Taylor can figure it out.

"Amelia, please," Taylor says. "I wasn't trying to hurt you. I was trying to help." I can hear that she's crying, but I don't care. Good. Let *her* cry for once.

"Amelia." It's Mom now. "Take a deep breath, baby. Deep breaths."

There's some quiet talking that I can't understand, and I hear footsteps going down the stairs. After a minute, it's Mom again. "Taylor went home. Can you open the door now, please? Can you tell me what happened?"

I don't really want to tell Mom what happened,

but it crashes over me that I have zero friends now. And I really, really need to talk about what happened, if only to get the whole yucky story out of me. Like barfing when you've eaten bad fish. I push the dresser out of the way and open the door. Mom rushes in and grabs me in a bear hug. Neither of us says anything while I cry and cry until I can't anymore. Then we sit on my bed and I tell her the whole story.

Mom is quiet for a bit when I'm all talked out. Then she says, "Well, that was a very poor choice on their part."

I start to laugh through all my tears and snot. I wipe my face with the back of my hand and my voice comes out blurry, "You think?!"

Mom laughs, too, as she nods. "A terrible plan."

I lie back on my bed, my nose completely stuffed up from all the crying. "Why would they be so mean? Why would they do something like that?" My voice has gone from sounding blurry and wet to sounding like I have a very bad cold.

Mom lies back next to me and we both stare at the ceiling. "I think people are good at heart," she says quietly. "I think Taylor and William really were trying to help you, even though their execution was terrible. I think people who have not experienced hard things have a difficult time understanding what it's like, and so they might do or say things that feel insensitive. They might do or say things that ARE insensitive."

"But then is it my job to tell them that?" I ask. "I don't want that job. I want them to be able to figure it out on their own."

"I know, honey," Mom says, taking hold of my hand. "It shouldn't be your job or my job to comfort the people who are supposed to be comforting us. Grief is hard for everyone. It takes a toll."

I don't say anything. All the anger is slowly dissipating, like the steam on a road after a particularly violent thunderstorm.

"How could they do that, though?" I whisper.

"They just wanted to help," Mom whispers back.

"That's not good enough of an answer," I whisper.

"I know," Mom whispers back. And we lie there together, on my bed, until the sun sinks and the moon rises and Dad comes home, walks up the stairs, and stands in my doorway. Wood smoke drifts off of him.

"Everything okay in here?" he asks.

"Not really," I say.

He comes over and lies on top of us both, squishing us until we can't help but laugh and squeal for him to get off.

"I brought dinner," he growls into our hair, making us squeal and squirm more. His huge arms dig under us both until he's lying on us *and* hugging us, and all three of us are giggling. "Guess I better bring this giant, heavy cord of wood down to the smoker," he says, trying to lift us from the bed. "Guess it's time to see how this new flavor will rock everyone's taste buds." We're too heavy for him, or he pretends we are, or he loses his balance, I'm not sure which, but Dad makes a startled grunt and rolls off us onto the floor.

"Man down," he groans. "Man down."

Mom stands up and offers him a hand. I stand up and offer him my hand, too, and together we heave him to his feet.

He and Mom share a quick look that seems to say, "What in the world?" and "I'll tell you later, but it's okay now."

"Time to eat?" he asks.

"Let's eat," Mom says. She puts her hands on my shoulders, I put my hands on Dad's shoulders (which I can barely reach), and we conga-line down the stairs to the kitchen.

CHAPTER
TWENTY-ONE

"OKAY," MR. ROBERTSON SAYS, CLAPPING his hands loudly, one time. "Ready to shake things up a bit? How about we have a little fun for once?"

Someone interrupts, "But we always have fun in *your* class, Mr. Robertson!" and everyone laughs.

Mr. Robertson clears his throat and says in a deep, grave, booming voice. "Of course, you do." A few people whistle and hoot in excitement, but I have no idea why. Mr. Robertson continues in his grave voice, "For the next couple of classes, we are going to explore the physics behind ghost hunting." Someone who's sitting next to the light switch flashes the lights a couple of times and everyone laughs. I feel my heart start beating a little faster. "We're going to learn what exactly ghost hunters look for when they're searching for life after death, and we're going to use our scientific minds to ask ourselves: Can physics *really* explain the unexplainable?"

The class is full of murmurs and excitement. My mouth has gone dry. I can't believe this. It's like a *school-sanctioned* Ouija board unit. Now, more than ever, I don't want to think about ghosts. And even though I don't believe Clara is lurking somewhere in the clouds, I hate to even imagine the possibility she might be trapped somewhere trying to communicate with me but is unable to get through. Stupid Twitch and stupid Taylor made me think, for just a second, that she was out there somewhere, and it was both the most wonderful and most terrifying feeling ever. It makes my stomach flop just to remember.

"If the next few classes are going to make any of you uncomfortable," Mr. Robertson says, staring directly at me, "feel free to let me know after class. I can give you an alternative assignment and you can work independently in the library."

Yeah, great, like the girl who's already known as the One with the Dead Sister is really going to be the *only* one who excuses herself from ghost class. Can you *imagine* the pitying looks I'd get from everyone? Thanks to Twitch and Taylor, I know with absolute surety that ghosts don't exist. I can handle this.

* * *

The next day speeds by like a freight train headed for a cliff. It's the first time I've ever dreaded physics, and my feet drag as I walk over to the high school. The woods whisper in the wind off to the side, and I think about ducking in there to hide. But no. I trust Mr. Robertson. I think. I mean, physics is math. And math is solvable. No mysteries. Right? I take a deep breath. Everyone else might try to use these lessons to prove that ghosts exist, but I'm going to work to prove they don't. I square my shoulders and march into school.

Twitch is already at our table for once, and he looks at me like Ratface does after I yell at him for eating my shoelaces. Fine. Let him look that way. I'm never talking to him again, so he's just going to have to get used to it. I sit on my stool and turn my back to him so I don't have to see his dumb face or his stupid helmet or any of him at all.

Mr. Robertson launches into a lecture on Einstein's theory of relativity. He writes $E=MC^2$ on the board. He talks about how energy can neither be created nor destroyed, so does that mean once a person has been alive their energy is floating in a little ball somewhere, a ghost of their former selves?

I raise my hand. "Mr. Robertson, that's the dumbest thing I've ever heard." Everyone turns quickly to stare at me.

"Excuse me?" he says. His mustache is very, very sparkly today.

"Well, what I mean is . . ." I say, "if energy is neither created nor destroyed, then when we're created as humans we're using energy that's already been around, right? So when we die, that energy goes back to where it came from, don't you think? We all came from stardust, and we're all going back to stardust."

The class is completely silent.

"Stardust, huh?" Mr. Robertson says as my words hover over everyone.

Stardust.

Did I really just say that?

My mind immediately goes to the woods, to the tiny golden stars painted all over the mural. Is Clara stardust? I feel my eyes start to swim.

I gather up my stuff in a rush and dash out of the classroom.

"Amelia?" Mr. Robertson shouts after me, but I don't stop. I run all the way to the woods, pushing through the branches and leaves until I get to the right spot. I throw down my backpack and heave myself onto the rock next to the art project Twitch and everyone have been working on for so long.

I stare at the tiny stars, the deep blue, the jagged teeth.

Can Clara be nowhere and everywhere all at once?

Bits of dust float in the air, riding on sunbeams that cascade through the tree branches. They are golden, too, like tiny daytime stars taking flight. I hold my hand out, and the little bits of dust and dirt dance around my fingers in the brightness and heat of a slant of sun.

"Amelia."

It's Twitch, and he just about gives me a legitimate heart attack.

"TWITCH!" I shout, jumping up. "You scared me!" A wave of dizziness makes me wobble as my breath tries to catch up with my heart rate.

"Sorry," he says. "I'm sorry for everything."

I hold up my hand. I don't want to hear it.

"I—" he starts, but I point at him.

"No," I interrupt. "I don't want you here. I'm . . . I'm thinking about the theory of relativity, okay?"

He holds up his hands. "Fine. I'll leave you to think. But, Amelia, I really am very sorry." He pushes his way through the trees and is gone. I hate that my first instinct is actually to call him back over. I know I said I didn't want him here, but if I'm being honest with myself, I don't really want to be alone either. I don't call for him, though. I let him go.

"Oh, Clara," I whisper. "If you're everywhere, why do I feel so alone all the time?"

CHAPTER TWENTY-TWO

"READY?" MOM PEEKS HER HEAD into my room.

I look up from the homework spread out all over my desk. "Not going," I say. "Why are *you* going? I thought you hated Kite Night."

Mom is awkwardly holding a box kite with reflective tape all over it. Her eyes are bright. "Dad was right about the lake. Maybe he's right about this, too. Why don't you come with us?"

"I was going to go," I say. "But ever since the thing with Taylor and Twitch, eh, I'm just not feeling it." Kite Night has never been a huge thing for me. Not like with Mom and Dad. I've seen pictures from when they were kids and went, and then the pictures from when they took Clara and me when we were super tiny. I guess it used to be a big deal for them. Mom hasn't been since . . . well . . . she hasn't been in a long time.

"Fair enough," Mom says, and I think I might fall out of my chair. She isn't going to argue with me? Tell me I need fresh air for a fresh soul or something silly like that? "If you change your mind, you know where to find us."

"Eating delicious corn dogs and flying ridiculous kites and winning at dancing!" Dad yells upstairs.

"If I change my mind, I know where to find you," I say. "Have fun. Don't get into any trouble."

Mom laughs. "We'll try not to. Though Dad is going to be handing out free samples of his bacon chocolate chip cookies, and I'm pretty sure he needs a permit for that."

"Then I'll be here to bail you out of jail if I have to," I say. Mom gives me a thumbs-up and pulls my door shut. Wow. That conversation was just . . . almost fun, and not full of arguing? Huh.

I look back down at my homework, but my concentration is broken. I take Clara's letter, which is getting pretty beat-up, and I flatten it out on my desk. It doesn't actually say "go to a dance with Billy," it just says ask him to a dance. So, technically, I can still cross this off the list, right? I'm mulling over the semantics when I hear a tap-tap-tapping at my window. I slide the curtains to the side just as a handful of pebbles scatter over the surface, sending me back on my heels, startled. I go closer to the window and look down.

Twitch.

He's pretending like he's going to throw the softball next. Down at his feet are two gloves. I shake my head. He makes an exaggerated pout. I shake my head harder. He falls to his knees and holds his hands up like he's begging or praying or both. I sigh and unlock the window. I push it open and stand there, hands on my hips, shivering in the breeze.

"Catch?" he shouts up at me.

I don't say anything.

"Come on, Amelia. Please? Just for a minute? It's about to get dark anyway."

In that moment I feel really, really tired. I don't want to hate Twitch. I don't want to hate Taylor. But what *do* I want? "Don't move," I say down to Twitch. I close the window, grab a sweater, and go downstairs. Once I'm on the front porch I wave at him to come over and sit beside me.

"Here's the thing," I say, after a few seconds of us sitting quietly next to each other. "I know you said you were sorry. I just . . . I don't know why it doesn't feel like enough. I don't know what to do about that."

Twitch tosses the softball from one hand to the other. "I could stand on Mr. Robertson's desk and shout to our whole physics class about how I did a stupid thing and now I'm sorry. I could take out an ad in the newspaper. I could invent a time machine, go back in time, not do the Ouija board thing, come back and tell you I didn't do it, and you'd be super confused because it had never happened. Though I guess if I invented a time machine, I'd go back and stop Clara from getting in that boat. But then you and I wouldn't be friends."

I snatch the ball from his hands. "Time travel is complicated."

"Everything is complicated," he says, standing up and putting on a glove. He jogs down the front walk and punches the glove. "Right here. Hit me as hard as you can."

I throw the ball with a ferocity I've never tried before, and it slams into the mitt with a satisfying *pow*. Twitch looks at me and smiles. "Again," he says.

Over and over I throw the ball as hard as I can, until I get lost in the rhythm. Wind up, release, step back, catch. My shoulder starts to ache, my fingers are going numb, but it feels incredible to fling this angry energy out of my body.

"Did I ever tell you why people call me Twitch?" Twitch asks, throwing the ball to me a little harder than before.

"No," I say.

"Clara never said anything about it?" *Wham.* The ball lands hard in my mitt.

"She didn't," I say, throwing it back.

"When we were in third grade, Clara and I were at school walking together to bring the attendance sheet to the front office when I collapsed. I don't remember it at all. I only remember waking up in the hospital after. It was my first epileptic seizure."

"You have *epilepsy*?" I had no idea. And now I feel this awful dripping, sinking feeling down to my toes because I know Clara, and I think I know where his story is going. The ball lands even harder in my glove, and my palm stings through the leather.

Twitch pushes up his sleeve and shows me the bracelet I've always seen but never paid close attention to. "That's why I wear this." Then he knocks on his ubiquitous shark-mouth helmet. "And this. Though, technically, my medicine works great now and I don't have to wear the helmet like when I was little. I still like it anyway. It makes me feel, I don't know, safe or something."

I toss the ball back. His Adam's apple bobs for a second, then he continues.

"Apparently, after the ambulance took me away, Clara told everyone I'd had a 'Twitchy attack.' She showed them how I'd seized up and shaken and wet my pants. When I came back to school a few days later, everyone welcomed me with imitations of my shaking and whispers about my pants wetting." The ball pounds into my glove. I throw it back and give my hand a shake, to try to disperse the painful tingles. "It took a while to get my epilepsy under control, so I had a few more seizures at school and I had to start wearing a helmet. A real freak show. And lots of Twitchy attacks to entertain my classmates."

"That's so awful," I say. "Why were you friends with her after that? Why do you let people call you Twitch?"

Twitch laughs, but it's sharp and not the ha-ha kind of laugh I usually hear from him. "There's not a lot of 'let' to it, Amelia. People are going to say what they're going to say. It took me a long time, but I learned that instead of getting mad, I had to take over the nickname on my own terms. Does that make sense?" The ball slams into my mitt and I wince.

"So, you asked them to stop and they didn't," I say.

"Yes, but it became more than that. I wanted to control this mean thing and turn it into something boring, something that would melt all the meanness out of it. So, they called me Twitchy, and I started calling myself Twitch. I turned it into something that belonged to me. I introduced myself that way to teachers and new kids and everyone. YOU didn't even know my name was Billy."

"That's because I didn't know Billy was a nickname for William!"

He smiles and shakes his head. "I took control of the name and, by doing that, I took away its power to hurt me. I was mad at Clara for a long time, but we were eventually friends again—because eventually I believed her when she said she was sorry, and because I took the thing she did to me and turned it into my own thing."

I toss the ball back to him even though it's getting super dark now and hard to see. I thought I'd known how his story was going to end, but I'd actually only figured out part of it. "Are you telling me that I should start calling myself Ouija and keep being mad at you for a while?" I try for a smile.

"No," he says, with a real laugh this time. "I'm saying that people can be mad at each other and they can forgive each other and they can be mad at each other again and they can do stupid things and they can do smart things. The best part of being a human, Amelia, is *being a human*. We are all whiteboards that can be covered in terrible words, erased, and re-covered in better words." I lower my glove a tiny bit, feeling that sink in, just as he throws the ball really fast. It clips the edge of my mitt, takes out the wind chimes hanging from the top of the porch, and smashes through the plate glass window right into the kitchen.

My mouth flies open as my head swings from Twitch to the smashed window and back to Twitch again. He drops his glove, runs up to me, and puts his hands on his head.

"I hope my parents are as good at forgiving as you are," I say as I start to laugh. Then he starts to laugh, too, and soon we're both buckled over laughing so hard we can barely breathe.

"Are you going to say, 'You should see the other guy'? Because I don't want to see the other guy," Dad says, coming up behind us. He's holding a couple of bags, and his arms hang limply at his sides. He gives Mom a helpless look. Her mouth hangs open much like mine and Twitch's just did.

"Are you at least friends again?" Mom says, rubbing her forehead.

Twitch looks to me and shrugs. I take a deep breath and say in a quiet voice, "Yes?"

"Well, good," Mom says. "Then it will be more fun when you rapidly, rapidly, RAPIDLY work together to raise the money to fix this."

"William," Dad says, shaking his head. "Go around back and find the big blue tarp in the shed. Amelia, go get the broom and dustpan." Dad goes inside, and Mom follows him. They drop the bags they're carrying and stare at us through the former window. "Go!" Dad says. It looks like he's trying to be mad, but really he wants to laugh. Kind of.

Twitch and I both disappear to the shed as fast as we can.

CHAPTER TWENTY-THREE

"GOOD MORNING, NOLAN RYAN," DAD says as he wanders downstairs and into the kitchen, still in his pajama pants. His hair stands up all over his head, making him look like a cartoon character that's just been struck by lightning.

"Who's Nolan Ryan?" I ask, pouring myself a glass of orange juice. The tarp covering the window makes an ominous *whap whap whap* noise as the wind outside tries to rip it loose from all the duct tape holding it to the window frame.

"Amazing pitcher for the Texas Rangers," Dad says. "Probably broke dozens of windows in his day." Dad is trying to start the coffee, but is not quite awake yet. Coffee beans go everywhere as he tries to pour them into the grinder, and he curses under his breath. Dad has never been much of a morning guy. For a while after Clara died, he wasn't an anything guy. He just never got out of bed. He got some medicine, though, to help with that, and now he's back to not being much of a morning guy.

"Technically, Twitch is Nolan Ryan, then," I say, helping him clean up the spilled coffee beans.

"Technically, I am going to flip my lid if we don't get this window fixed as soon as possible. Did you sleep at all last night?" He rubs his eyes, and I wonder if that same move is something he did when he was little. He kind of looks like a pouty kid right now.

I shrug. "I slept okay. Why?" Right on cue the tarp makes the *whap whap whap* noise again, and Dad gestures to it with a frustrated arm fling.

"That! That noise! All night, *whap whap whap*. I can't take it, Amelia."

"It's going to take a little while to figure out how to pay for a new window, though, Dad," I say, popping some bread into the toaster. "It's not like Twitch and I can just whip out a credit card and get it fixed."

Dad points at me and frowns. "I feel like your voice has more of an edge than it needs to, ma'am. You guys broke it, and you're going to have to pay for it. However"—his pointing hand is now stroking his beard thoughtfully—"I *do* have a credit card, so here's what's going to happen."

Mom comes downstairs now, all dressed for work. She steps on some coffee beans we missed and they crunch under her heels. She kisses me on the top of my head as she goes over to the coffeepot that is busy grunting and whirring as it works to create its addicting elixir.

Dad kisses Mom quickly and then turns his attention back to me. "I am going to pay for a new window. Think of it as a loan. You and Twitch will owe me the full amount of the bill. Possibly I will charge you interest."

I'm about to protest, but Dad holds up his hand. "In order to pay me back—and, Amelia, this is nonnegotiable—you and Twitch will work at Pits 'n' Pieces after school and on the weekends until your debt is paid."

"Ooh, good plan," Mom says, stealing a bite of my toast.

"What?!" I say, feeling my heart start to pound. "No! Not a good plan. Terrible plan. The worst plan. I can think of something better, just—"

Dad sits at the table across from me and puts both his hands on it, palms down. He stares at me. "Nonnegotiable," he says slowly and leans forward so that his nose is close to mine. "I am the boss of you still, and this is what I am currently bossing you to do." He sits back and crosses his arms over his chest, a look of satisfaction spreading across his face. Mom stares at him like she has no idea who he is, but she likes what she sees.

"After school. Today," Dad says, stabbing the table with his finger. "I'll call Twitch's parents to let them know."

"And I'll call Mrs. Grant to let her know you won't be at the store," Mom says.

I stand up in a huff, my chair squealing across the floor. "Not fair," I say, trying not to panic at the prospect of having to go to the lake TODAY. "Not fair!"

Dad lifts his hands in a "what are you going to do?" shrug. "We are all familiar with the unfairness of life, Amelia," he says. "I'll see you this afternoon."

I angrily gather up my school stuff and stomp out of the house. I turn back to see if Mom and Dad are gloating in the kitchen, but I only see the huge blue tarp mocking me. Aaaargh.

My pace is fast as I grouchily walk to school. I see Taylor walking ahead of me and think about running to catch up with her. Maybe she could help me figure out how to get out of going to the lake. But then I remember I'm mad at her. We have not yet broken a window together to make up. I sigh. I could run and catch up to her and tell her that I'm not mad anymore. I could ask her if we can go back to how everything was before. She glances back and sees me. I lift up my hand to wave, but she whips her head around and quickly jaywalks across the street to where Lacy and Katherine are motioning to her. Okay. Well, I guess we'll have to talk later. For just a second I allow myself to imagine chasing after her and blocking her path to Lacy and Katherine and making her talk to me, but then . . . ugh. Who can blame Taylor, really? For three years I've been a sad mess of a friend. No wonder they seem so shiny and fun. A rock would seem shiny and fun compared to me.

I slow down a little now, because I don't want to get to school too early. If I get there now, I'll just have to wander around and stare at everyone hanging out together and be reminded of my tragic lack of friends. So much for being the queen of eighth grade. I feel more like the court jester, except court jesters are funny. Maybe I'm the guy who sings all the sad songs at the big castle dinners. The one with the cautionary tales of woe.

The woods are to my left, with school looming up ahead. Maybe I could go back in the trees for a few minutes and take a closer look at the art Twitch has been working on with the other boat kids. Right at that moment the wind blows through the tops of the trees and it sounds like a quiet "Yesssssssss" being carried on the wind. My mind jumps to the Ouija board and I feel my pulse quicken. Then I remind myself all of that was fake and stupid. Clara is not trying to talk to me. It was just the wind. Even so, I feel compelled to tromp through the leaves and undergrowth. I mean, I could hide out in the middle of a forest, or be early to homeroom. The choice is not difficult, by my calculations.

It's a cloudy morning, and the cover of the trees makes it even darker. When I get to the clearing it looks different than last time. The blue is almost black and the stars don't glimmer. The red surrounding the edges is deep and bleeds into the white of the teeth. It feels sinister today instead of sparkly and amazing. It makes me think of the lake, actually, and how on a hot summer day it shines and shimmers like a giant has thrown a handful of glitter over the surface. But then, on cloudy days, or at night, the water looks fathomless and black, with an eerie stillness. It's so interesting how the same place can look so different.

I sit on a tree stump and run the sole of my shoe over the deep blue mosaic. They must have poured and smoothed concrete and then laid out all of these pebbles. Except, it looks like they painted the pebbles first, because when I lean closer I can see that the grout holding everything together is an ever darker blue. It is a magnificent piece of art, both beautiful and a little bit scary. Clara would have loved this. It's just like her.

"They're making me go to the lake today," I whisper. The trees rustle around me. I pull Clara's letter from my pocket. "I've been trying to do some things for you," I say, still whispering. "I figured out who Billy is, and by the way, you were super mean to him when you guys were small. I can't believe he forgave you." The painted stars sprinkled throughout the blue are different sizes. I didn't really notice that before. I stand up and walk around the edge of the giant mouth. "I've been training for softball tryouts, too. How crazy is that?" I look up at the trees blowing in the wind. "Probably not as crazy as talking to myself in the woods."

I fold up the letter and put it back in my pocket. "I don't know about throwing a party, though. I don't actually have any friends, expect for Twitch. And I don't know if I can be nicer to Mom, because she's colluding with Dad to make me go to the lake." I'm quiet for a minute, just listening to the trees. "I miss you," I say, my voice the smallest of whispers. Then, out of nowhere, there's a huge crack of thunder so loud I can feel it slam into my chest. I duck instinctively, grabbing on to the stump I was sitting on a minute ago. As soon as the reverberations from the thunder stop, buckets of rain start to fall. It's a deluge, what my grandmother would have called a frog strangler. And even sheltered by the trees, I'm getting sopping wet. I grab my backpack and run from the woods, knowing that when lightning strikes, you do not want to be standing under tall things that can transfer that electricity to your body. Of course, you also don't want to be the tallest thing running back to school.

I burst from the edge of the trees just as it starts to rain even harder. I'm soaked to the bone now and laughing hysterically. Twitch and I won't be working at Pits 'n' Pieces today, because Dad doesn't open the trailer in weather like this. No lake for me! Unless you count the lakes growing in my shoes.

I'm laughing and running and I'm sure I look like a crazy person, but I don't care. I stumble up the stairs to the front entrance of school, but the doors are locked. What! I look at my watch. Oh my gosh, I'm fifteen minutes late. Is there some kind of time warp in the woods?! I pound the buzzer and wave to a woman in the front office who sees me standing there, drenched. She buzzes me in and I bolt through the door, running to class. I slip and slide the whole way, my shoes having turned into skates.

I barrel into homeroom and squelch into my seat, also trying to squelch my hiccupping laughter. Taylor stares at me with her mouth open, as does pretty much everyone except for Mrs. Henderson, who apparently didn't see or hear me come in. How is that possible?

She's writing something on the board about parent-teacher conferences.

I lean back in my seat, water pooling on the floor around me, and I smile at the ceiling. I totally don't believe in ghosts or the afterlife or anything like that. But I have to say, a spontaneous frog strangler occurring just after I whisper to Clara that I don't want to go to the lake? Coincidence? Ha!

CHAPTER
TWENTY-FOUR

I TAKE A LONG, SLOW bite out of *Quiche Your Face*, today's special. It's two thin pieces of bacon and spinach quiche acting like pieces of bread, with sharp cheddar cheese melted between them. Very messy. Very tasty. Very perfect for a rainy day.

"How do you like my experiment?" Mrs. Grant asks, rubbing her hands together like Doctor Frankenstein.

"I like it very much," I say. And I do. Its yumminess is distracting me from Taylor, who's standing just behind the curtains leading to the stairs. She's staring at me and I'm pretending I don't notice. I think of everything Twitch and I talked about, and how humans are lucky to be imperfect so we can keep trying new things. If he could forgive Clara for being such a terrible jerk, surely I can forgive Taylor, who wasn't *trying* to be jerk but was one accidentally.

I look over at her and our eyes lock. Her eyes squint as we look at each other, and her lips pucker into a frown. She flips her long hair as she whips around and stomps up the stairs. Well, maybe *now* she's trying to be a jerk? How did I go from being pretty sure I knew every thought in Taylor's head to now knowing zero things banging around in that mind of hers?

Mrs. Grant has seen all of this, of course, and sighs. "This might be partly my doing."

I look at her, startled. "How?"

"I told her about Rosalie the other day. And then I told her how, when I was young, I tried the Ouija board to contact her."

My mouth falls open. Mrs. Grant holds up a hand. "I didn't tell her to try that with you, I promise. But I'm afraid I gave her the idea. Also, she was upset that I told you about Rosalie but hadn't told her." She sighs again. "I guess I can't blame her for that."

The rain and my reprieve from having to go to the lake have put me in a good mood. I want Taylor to be in a good mood, too. I want to tell her that Clara made it rain. I want this stupid fight to be over.

"Don't let anyone eat this," I say, taking one more bite and jumping off my stool. "I'll be right back." Mrs. Grant nods as if, of course, someone would wander by and attempt to eat a partially eaten sandwich.

Before I'm even halfway up the stairs to the

apartment, Ratface is barking like I'm leading a herd of armed robbers to storm the building.

"I don't want to talk to anyone!" Taylor yells through the closed door at the top of the stairs. It sounds like Ratface is throwing his barks at the door.

"I'm not coming to talk to *you!*" I yell back. "I'm coming to talk to Ratface. He seems upset." I can hear him throwing *himself* now, bodily, up against the closed door. Tiny *thwumps* are like little commas between his barks. "I think he feels bad about the other day. Don't you, Ratface?" The more he hears his name, the more frenzied he gets. I know Taylor hates this, and even though I feel sort of guilty, I love that I'm riling him up. "Ratface wants to say he's sorry, doesn't he? Doesn't he?" I'm using my goofy talking-to-a-dog voice now, and Ratface's barks are turning from ANGRY STRANGER barks to *hellohelloyou'remyfriend* barks. "Don't you want to say you're sorry for ruining a top-notch plan to fool me into thinking my dead sister was communicating with me from beyond the grave? Don't you, Ratface?"

Ratface goes nuts, slamming into the door and barking. He's throwing in a couple of whines here and there, and I'm starting to feel bad for teasing him.

"Amelia—" Taylor's voice is calmer now. I hear her mutter, "Ratface, no!" She sounds closer to the door.

"Ratface, your voice sounds weirdly like Taylor's.

How do you do that?" He barks at me. "Did you want to say you're sorry, Ratface? Do you want to use Taylor's voice to say you're sorry?"

"Amelia, I—" Taylor starts to talk but there's a huge crash downstairs in the store.

What the heck?

I run down the stairs and see a bunch of people huddled by a collapsed display of homemade jams. Glass jars are shattered, and ones that aren't are rolling around. Someone is on the ground, but I can't see who because of all the other people. Someone yells, "Call nine-one-one!" just as I push through the people.

It's Mrs. Grant. She's on the ground, one arm splayed to the side, one leg bent in an impossible angle under her. There's a big goose egg growing on her head. Her eyes are closed. Her face is the same color as the old gray ashes in our fireplace. It is not a color a human should be.

"TAYLOR!" I scream, but she must have heard the crash, too. She's right behind me, phone already out. "She needs glucose," she says to herself and runs behind the counter. Ratface is at my feet, no longer barking. He runs to Mrs. Grant and licks her face over and over and over again like he's a prince and she's Sleeping Beauty and maybe enough of his kisses will wake her up.

A siren wails in the distance.

"Amelia." Mom's voice is quiet, and she's shaking my shoulder. "Honey, wake up." I struggle to surface from a dream. Her voice is like the light you can see when you're deep underwater, and I make my brain reach for it until my eyes slowly open. It takes a second for me to remember where we are.

The hospital.

I sit up straight, with a start. The waiting room is entirely empty except for me and Mom. Where are Taylor and her mom and dad?

"Did—" I start, feeling panic crash up through my chest like a tsunami.

Mom puts her hand softly but firmly on my arm. "Everything is okay. Taylor and her parents are in the room with Mrs. Grant. The doctors were able to stabilize her. Something happened with her blood sugar and she got dizzy and then hit her head when she fell. She's going to stay for a few days, but should be fine."

I wipe drool off my cheek from where my face had been smushed up against the armrest of my chair. How in the world did I manage to fall asleep while all of this was going on? "She's . . . Mrs. Grant . . . she's going to be okay?"

Mom nods and the tsunami of panic crashes over me as a wave of relief instead. She takes her hand off my arm and picks up her purse from where it's been leaning against her chair. "We should get home and get some rest. You have a big day tomorrow."

I stand up and rack my brain. Big day tomorrow? It's not my birthday. It's not Taylor's birthday. No exams at school.

"Softball tryouts," Mom says with a soft smile. "It's been written on the calendar for months."

Well, *now* I'm awake. With everything that's been going on, I guess I hadn't realized they were coming up so fast. Oh my gosh. Am I ready? Should I not do it because Mrs. Grant is sick and Taylor might need me here at the hospital? Is that just an excuse to not do it? I should do it. I mean, Clara made it rain for me, I should definitely get on the softball team for her. But . . . there's no way she made it rain. She doesn't exist anymore. So then, if I miss tryouts, it won't bother her. Because she wouldn't know. But I would know. I'm doing this for me, right? I look around for Taylor. I need her to talk me into this. I need her to remind me why I'm doing it. I'm breathing fast. Panicking.

"All that running. All that playing catch," Mom says, taking my hand as we walk out of the waiting room. "The brave sacrifice our kitchen window made on your behalf." Mom is quiet for a second. Then she says, "You've really put a lot into preparing for this, Amelia. I'm proud of you."

My panic disappears and I want so badly, all of a sudden, to tell Mom that I'm doing this for Clara; it's not really for me, I'm doing it because it's a goal Clara never got to achieve. But Mom is looking at me with such hope, her eyes are practically screaming, "HAL-LELUJAH, AMELIA IS DOING A THING NOR-MAL KIDS DO," that I can't bring myself to tell her.

The lights in the hallway are so bright they make me squint. Rooms on either side of us have closed doors but big windows so the nurses can see in. I try to look ahead and not into the rooms, even though I wonder about the people in each of the beds, and I also wonder about the people sitting in the chairs next to the beds, or about the empty chairs next to so many of them.

At the end of the hallway are double doors. Mom and I stand dumbly in front of them, waiting for them to open, but they don't. I push on them but they seem to be locked. Then I see there's a big square button on the wall you have to push to open them. I smash my hand into it right when I hear slapping feet running behind us. I turn around and it's Taylor, bare-foot, hair flying around her shoulders. She runs right into me and we both let out a little "*oof*" as we stumble into the button I just pushed, which pushes it again, closing the doors this time.

Taylor is squeezing me tightly, a hug to rival all hugs

before it. "I'm sorry," she whispers into my neck. I can feel her hot breath and damp cheeks. "I was stupid, and I'm sorry. I won't try to make you stop feeling sad and I won't ever stop being your friend."

I'm not sure what to say. Earlier today, *she* was the one who was mad at *me*. Am I also supposed to say I'm sorry?

"It's okay," I manage to say. "It's all okay. I'm not mad anymore. Are you mad at me?" Taylor releases me from her hug but doesn't let go of my arms. She pushes me away from her so she can look at me. Her blue eyes x-ray through me for a few seconds, and then she pulls me into another hug.

"I was mad at you for being mad at me. And I was jealous of Twitch. And then I found out Gram was pouring her heart out to you, and it felt like everyone was just pushing me away and leaving me out of everything. Like, no one even noticed I was alive anymore. But now none of that matters. It's all so stupid." She's crying into my neck again, and I don't think I've ever seen Taylor like this before. She's always the one who knows exactly what to do and say. She's always the one in control. She's never *ever* the invisible one. I hold on to her while she cries. We're still leaning on the button and the big doors keep opening and closing until a nurse gives us a look and Mom gently pushes us away from it.

"Ratface says he's sorry, too," Taylor says with a sniff.

"Well, I'm never forgiving him, so that's too bad," I say. Taylor laughs.

"Poor Ratface," she says. "He was only trying to help."

"All anyone is ever trying to do is help," I say. "Don't you think?"

Taylor nods. She pushes herself away from me and wipes her nose with the back of her hand. We look at each other for a minute and I start to feel a little embarrassed at so much emotion spilling out everywhere.

"Good luck at tryouts," Taylor says.

"Thanks," I say, deciding not to tell her I had actually forgotten about them until about five minutes ago.

"You're going to do great," she says. "Clara would be so proud."

Mom perks up at the mention of Clara and gives me a quizzical look.

"Tell Gram that we love her and hope she feels better so soon, it's really yesterday that she's feeling better."

Taylor laughs. "I will definitely tell her that. Good night, Amelia."

"Good night, Taylor," I say. We smile and it feels so good to not be mad anymore.

Mom punches the button and the doors open. We walk through and, as they start to close, Taylor yells after us, "Who run the world?"

"Girls!" I yell back.

She gives me a thumbs-up. "Kick butt tomorrow, Amelia."

The doors close, and I follow Mom through the lobby and out to the car.

CHAPTER
TWENTY-FIVE

A CLOUD OF RED DIRT blows over my face as I lie on the ground, motionless, a slug drying in the sun.

"Peabody? Is that your name? You okay?" A girl leans over me, offering her hand. I grab it and she heaves me to my feet. "That was an epic miss, my friend," she says with a laugh. "But at least you committed." Several other girls are standing near us, trying not to laugh. A few more are actually laughing. The coach is off to the side, face squinched up like she's just smelled Ratface's breath.

"Sliding into first base is unnecessary," the coach says, walking over, "when the first baseman has already caught the ball and is standing on the bag."

My cheeks burn as I begin to realize that, maybe in addition to all the running and catching and throwing, I should have been learning the actual rules of how softball is played.

"Now," the coach says, walking away, "let's see who can throw."

After about fifteen minutes of watching incredibly athletic girls whip softballs into one another's gloves, I know the answer to this mystery: It Is Everyone But Peabody. I mean, it's not like I'm not trying, but good grief. I feel like a child among Olympians.

Coach finally tells us we can take a water break. I am covered in dirt and sweat and my arms might not ever work again. My hand shakes as I lift a paper cup of water to my lips.

"Amelia?" One of Coach's assistants, a girl who looks just like Twitch, but taller and prettier, comes up to me. She holds out her hand. "I'm Danielle, Billy's older sister."

I shake her hand. "I've been borrowing your glove a lot," I say because I don't know what else to say.

She nods as she looks me up and down, taking in my exhausted appearance. "And how's that been working out for you?"

I start to laugh. "Well, I'd heard it was a magical glove that made anyone who used it the best on the team. But maybe I've been using it wrong?"

Danielle laughs. "It's always made *me* the best on the team, so I'm not sure what to tell you." She winks as she walks away.

I look up at the blue sky and out at all the girls

running the bases. I imagine Clara out there shouting for the ball, throwing pitches, knocking home runs between the trees. She would have been good, I bet. Really good.

I crush up my paper cup, toss it into the metal trash can by the dugout, and walk over to the coach. "I think I'm going to leave now, if that's okay," I say, squinting up at her enormous frame.

She gives me a measured look. "If you give me time, I can turn you into a player." She pauses and taps her chin as she looks me up and down. "Probably."

I hold up my hand. "That's okay." I give her my glove. "Can you get this back to Danielle? I'm going to go home and take a shower."

Coach takes the glove and nods. "Nice effort, Peabody. Keep practicing. And, hey, maybe think about trying out for the high-school team next year."

"I probably won't do that," I say with a small laugh as I rub the growing bruise on my hip. "But thanks for your optimism."

Coach tips her hat and I walk away, limping, but only slightly.

CHAPTER
TWENTY-SIX

MRS. GRANT IS PROPPED UP in her hospital bed with a little wheeled table perched over her lap. Her glasses are on the end of her nose as she reads. I wave at Taylor through the window and her face visibly brightens when she sees me. She taps Mrs. Grant on the shoulder, and she looks up and waves me in.

I've come straight from tryouts, so I'm still super sweaty and covered in red dirt. I don't want to stay long, I just wanted to tell Taylor what happened.

"Well, you definitely smell really sporty," Taylor says, wrinkling her nose as I sit on the armrest of her chair. "How did it go?"

"Great!" I say. "I was so good the coach not only added me to the starting lineup, she made me captain."

Taylor's mouth hangs open in surprise. Mrs. Grant sets down her book and stares at me. I start to laugh.

"You should see your faces! Of course, she didn't make me captain. I left tryouts before they were even over." I stand up and slide my pants over my hip to show them the top of the bruise blooming from my misguided slide into first. "I'm not really cut out for sports."

Now they're both flinching. "Do you need some ice?" Mrs. Grant asks. "Taylor, get this girl some ice!" I wave them off.

"I'm fine," I say. "How are YOU?"

Mrs. Grant taps her chest and raises her eyebrows in a "who, me?" kind of way. I laugh. "You look pretty good. I mean, compared with yesterday when . . ." I make a "yikes" face.

"Oh, please tell me I didn't look like *that*," Mrs. Grant says. "I was imagining a more dignified concussion. At least with my mouth closed."

"You scared us," I say, remembering her on the floor. "A lot." She opens her arms and snaps her hands at me in a "come here" way. I stand and walk closer and she grabs me up in a hug. She feels solid and warm. I hold on for a very long time.

She lets go of me first and I acquiesce. I have to get home and shower and change so I can meet Twitch at Pits 'n' Pieces. Stupid lake. Maybe Clara will make it rain again. I look hopefully out the window facing the parking lot, but the sky continues to be bright blue and completely cloudless. Dang.

"I have to go," I say. "But I wanted to stop by and see how you were doing. And to tell you to feel better."

"I'll be out of here faster than Ratface can eat a dropped hot dog." Mrs. Grant smiles.

Taylor stands. "I'll walk you out. Be back in a second, Gram." Mrs. Grant nods. She's already back to whatever it was she was reading on the little table. Taylor and I walk out into the hall, through the doors, and to the lobby.

"We haven't really talked a lot about the prank," Taylor says.

"I know," I say, looking at my feet. "And we're running out of time."

Taylor swallows hard and looks over my shoulder, avoiding eye contact. "Lacy and Katherine and I . . . well . . ."

"It's okay," I say. "Do the prank with them. I'll figure something out."

"But—" Taylor looks at me now. Her face is a mixture of relief and something else. Sadness? Oh, it better not be pity. I feel my eyes go squinty as Taylor says, "I don't want to abandon you, Amelia. You'll have to do one all alone. Why don't you just join us?"

"It's fine," I say. And it really is. I'd rather do it by myself than join a group that only wants me because they'd feel bad about themselves if they didn't offer an invitation. "I have a million ideas."

Taylor looks at me with only relief now. "Good! I mean, I'm sorry that I kind of went rogue on this, but . . ."

"Don't worry about it," I say. "Things got weird and Prank Day is coming up. I get it." I do get it. I still feel a smidge of a sting that she joined a group without telling me, but having a conversation like this in the lobby of a hospital where people are waiting for surgery and crying about terrible things and all of that . . . it puts stuff like school pranks into perspective, you know?

"See you at school tomorrow?" Taylor asks as I make my way to the sliding glass doors.

"Yep," I say. I walk outside and the blue sky is welcoming at first, such a contrast to the inside of the hospital. But then I remember what the rest of the day holds, and suddenly I can't even really think about the stupid prank anymore. The lake is looming in my future. I wonder how slowly I can walk home. I wonder how slowly I can shower and change. Maybe by the time I'm done it'll be dark and Pits 'n' Pieces will be closed. I sigh. That won't work, because then I'll just have to go tomorrow.

I look down the sidewalk like it's the longest pirate plank in the world.

CHAPTER
TWENTY-SEVEN

THE LAKE RIPPLES IN THE breeze. The trees along its edges are the kind of green that seems to pulse with life. It's a beautiful Saturday. The sun is warm on my face, and I close my eyes for a second so I can soak it up. The redness of the inside of my eyelids makes me remember Taylor's kitchen and the Ouija board, which makes my eyes snap open. The sun glinting off the shiny silver of the Pits 'n' Pieces Airstream is so bright I think it might burn through my corneas. The line in front of the window is about ten people deep. Dad must be loving this.

I walk past Thai Me Up, Thai Me Down—the Thai food trailer that won the Best Almost Fast Food award last year. Their line is pretty long, too. Next, I pass Leafy Queens, a salad trailer. I actually like the black bean salad they serve, but I'd never tell Dad. He thinks salads are only good for rabbits and feeding compost bins.

Behind Pits 'n' Pieces, Twitch is adding wood to one of the smokers.

"Hey," I say. He's sweaty and wearing big gloves to protect his hands from the mesquite splinters.

"Hey," he says. "You're late."

"Well, technically, *I* didn't break the window."

He gives me a frowny look, but then smiles. "Nice try, Peabody. Last I remember, you're the one who couldn't catch." He stands up straight and his eyes get big. "Oh! How were tryouts?"

I start to laugh. I can tell from his ridiculous face he already knows. "Did Danielle tell you?"

He reaches under his crooked helmet and scratches his head—he's trying so hard to pretend he doesn't know anything. "Uh," he says. "No. I just . . . how did . . ." He looks more and more uncomfortable the more I laugh.

"It was awful!" I shout at him. "Twitch. You should have seen it. I flopped around like a Muppet."

Now he's laughing, too. "Danielle said you had a lot of heart."

I punch him in the shoulder. "That's what they say about people who are TERRIBLE," I snort.

"It is indeed," he says, punching me back, but much softer than I punched him.

"What!" Dad yells out the little back door of the trailer, "is going ON out there?! Amelia! Come help me! I'm drowning in here!"

Time slows to a pinpoint as we all hear what he just said.

I swear I can hear the lake laughing.

Dad blinks once. Twice. And time goes back to normal again. "Can you just get up here and help me?" he asks, voice softer now. "If we're this busy now," he mutters under his breath, "I can't even imagine how it might be if we win that contest." His brow is wrinkled. It's the first time I've seen Dad look really stressed out in a long time.

I nod and run up the stairs after him. Only then does it strike me that for the few minutes Twitch and I were talking I completely forgot that we were even at the lake, and what the lake means.

But now, as I stand beside Dad, filling cups with barbecue sauce and looking out the windows onto the lake, it's like I've been taken back in time. Of course, Dad didn't have the trailer then. We were just normal people having a normal birthday party at the lake, like the people I can see today, down by the water's edge tying balloons onto a picnic table and setting up coolers.

I wore my yellow swimsuit, the one I thought made me swim faster. Clara was wearing a two-piece with big red flowers on it. Her hair was jet black and scraggly at the ends because neither one of us had had haircuts in ages. Her skin was so brown from all the days we'd spent in the sun, it made the colors of her swim-suit pop.

"I hate you!" I screamed at her. "I never want to see you again!"

Those were my last words to my sister, as she stuck her tongue out at me and zoomed away on the boat full of her friends. Those were the last words she ever heard out of my mouth.

"Pulled pork sandwich and potato salad." I hear a familiar voice, and it snaps me back to the moment. It's Desiree, Twitch's friend from the woods. She's wearing those giant hoop earrings again and they shine in the sun. Gathered around her are Maureen and Henry and Jake. Everyone from the boat that day. Everyone from the woods.

"Hey, Amelia," Jake says, running his hands through his curly hair. "Twitch said you guys were going to be up here today. We thought we'd come up for lunch. And, you know . . ."

"For support," Maureen finishes for him. "The lake can be, I don't know . . ."

"Kind of hard to deal with," Henry finishes for her. Desiree nods.

Twitch comes around from the back of the trailer and sees them. "Heeeeeeeey!" he shouts. "You came!" They all awkwardly group-hug. Dad looks at me and at them. The line behind them is really long.

"Go out there for a second," Dad says. "But then get back in here." He swipes really quickly at his bright eyes. I guess Dad must remember them from that day, too. How could he not? It's a day emblazoned on all of our brains. Every detail. Every second. Seared in there forever.

I run out the back of the trailer and around front and join in the awkward hug. "I can't believe you all came out here," I say into the pile of armpits surrounding my face.

"We're all in this together, kiddo," Desiree says. "At least, now we are." She tightens her arm around my shoulder and it feels really, really good to feel really, really sad with other people. Isn't that weird? How can a person feel good and sad at the same time? It's like these guys have created some kind of new way to feel inside of me. Happysad. An accidental gift.

"Pulled pork and potato salad!" Dad yells from the window, holding a paper plate full of food. "One for everyone." He hands plates down to me, and I hand them to Clara's friends. My friends, now. Henry pulls out some cash, but Dad waves him off. "Just tell everyone you know it's the best barbecue you've had in your entire life."

"Deal, Mr. Peabody," Jake says, mouth full of sandwich. They all make their way to a picnic table nearby as Twitch and I walk back around the trailer.

Twitch smiles at me as I go up the little stairs. "I thought they might help the day go by a bit easier."

"Well, you thought right," I say, smiling back.

And it works. Every time I look out the window and see the lake looming, I also see Maureen and Desiree, Jake and Henry, camped at the picnic table playing cards, goofing around, or waving back at me and Twitch. I still don't love being at the lake, but I've stopped feeling the horrible dread and gloom that I did on my way over here.

Finally, Dad puts out the CLOSED sign, and Twitch and I help clean up everything for the night. "If the day of the TV show goes anything like today, we have first place in the bag," Dad says. He pulls at his beard, and his eyes look out over the water. After a minute, he snaps back to reality and says, "Winning that contest could really change things." For just a blink of a second his eyes seem kind of sad, then he brightens and smiles at us. "Who's ready for bed?"

"It's eight thirty, Mr. Peabody," Twitch says.

"Exactly," Dad answers, and we all laugh as we head to the car.

CHAPTER TWENTY-EIGHT

"HEY," I SAY, KNOCKING ON Mom and Dad's bed-room door. Mom is in bed with her glasses on and a bunch of paperwork spread around her. She looks up. Her laptop is on her lap, and its glowing screen reflects in her glasses. Dad must be downstairs watching TV.

"Hey, Amelia. What's up?" She slides a bunch of papers out of the way and pats the bed next to her. I sit down, awkwardly at first, but then I lean back on her inclined pillows next to her and I have a flash of memory from when I was little and used to climb into bed with Mom and Dad after a bad dream. Without even thinking about it, I tilt my head until it rests on her shoulder. She tucks my hair behind my ear, like she used to, and pushes her glasses up onto her head like they're a headband.

"Seriously," she says, "what's going on?"

For a second, I want to tell her about the letter. I want to tell her about softball. I want to tell her about the art project in the woods. I want to tell her everything. But there's so much to tell I can't find the words. I don't know where to start. I don't even really know why I suddenly want to tell her all this stuff right now. That's not why I came in here. But with my head on her shoulder, and her Mom smell reminding me of when I was little and when things were simpler, I don't know. I guess . . . I'm just really, really aware all of a sudden of how tired I am. Not like in a sleepy way, but in an everything way. I feel like I'm always swimming upstream. I'm always trying to push my way through things instead of just being carried along. I want things to be easy again, like they were when Clara was alive. Back when I didn't even know things were easy.

"I'm thinking about my prank," I say, which is about one-ninety-ninth of all the things I'm thinking about. "Do you know who's in charge of deciding how public art gets money?" Mom turns to face me, making me have to lift my head from her shoulder. She blinks. I don't think she thought this is what I was going to ask.

"Well," she starts. "Grace McNeil oversees the distribution of public funds, but she's not the one who makes the final decisions. Often there's a town vote if the funds are going toward something that isn't already a budget line item."

I hear her words, but they don't make a lot of sense, so I start over. "I have some friends who made this really cool art project. They're trying to figure out how to, like, protect it and turn it into something the whole public can enjoy. I was thinking maybe I could use their art as part of my prank. Or something." The truth is, I haven't really thought out much of anything. But I would like to help them get the money they need to preserve their art. "How can they turn their art into something for everyone?"

Mom scrunches up her face. "Unsanctioned public art? Is that what you're getting at? This sounds a little bit like you're talking about vandalism. You know vandalism is against the rules for Prank Day."

"It's not vandalism," I say, and my usual irritated-with-Mom feelings start rising to the surface. She gives me a look like she's not sure she believes me, but then goes into minute detail about grants and permissions and land ownership and all sorts of things that sound super boring. While she's talking, it hits me. I know *exactly* what to do with the art project. I know *exactly* how to turn it into something public without having to jump through all those hoops.

"You look excited," Mom says, interrupting herself

in mid-sentence. "I had no idea you have such a passion for small-town bureaucracy."

I jump up and kiss her on the forehead. "Thanks, Mom!" and I run back to my room to start planning.

All I need is a saw that can carefully slice concrete, the ability to lift super-heavy slabs, some kind of flatbed truck . . . aaargh. I drop my head on my desk. This isn't going to work at all. But there has to be *some* way . . . if I can figure out how to move the artwork from the woods and get it to the fountain, this will be the best prank ever in the history of pranks.

I slip on my jacket and tiptoe downstairs. I ease the kitchen door open as slowly as possible so it doesn't squeak, and walk as lightly as I can across the porch, down the little stairs, and onto the driveway. I look over my shoulder. No one is chasing after me, so I think my escape worked. I jog down the street until I see the lights of the town square, and I slow to a walk. It's pretty late, so not many people are out.

I sit on the edge of the broken fountain and give it a long, hard look. It's tiered, kind of like a cake, with a small circle on top in the shape of a very shallow bowl, a larger circle-bowl in the center, and then the big basin at the bottom. Shooting out of the top bowl is a giant bird with its mouth wide open. I guess years and years ago water shot out of the bird's mouth and cascaded down into the lower circle, where it over-flowed into the basin. The basin is about knee-deep and maybe twelve feet in diameter.

I briefly imagine having some kind of magical skills to break up and transport the art project to the fountain, and then reassemble it in the basin of the fountain. I sigh. Yeah, there's no way I'm going to be able to do that. For one thing, the art wouldn't fit. For another, I don't think there's any way to move it. For another, even if there was a way to move it, it would weigh like 5,735,385,753 pounds.

BUT. What if I re-create the art, and add a little something extra?

I look around to see if anyone can see me, but the town square is deserted. I climb into the empty basin, rub my hands together, and reach up onto the middle circle, pulling myself up and hanging on by my elbows for a second. Then I heave myself up until I'm standing on it. I can just barely peer into the bird's mouth, but it's really dark in there. I think I can see some kind of piping going way down, which would make sense. The pipe would have to recirculate water from the basin up into the bird's mouth so that it would shoot out and keep the fountain going. What if . . . My mind is really spinning now. As long as the piping from the basin to the bird's mouth isn't broken, or there's room for a hose, I might be able to . . . My heart leaps and I laugh out loud. If I can manage this prank, it might be the best prank ever AND it might be the perfect public art to complement the project in the woods. I leap down into the basin, hop over the edge, and run to Twitch's house.

It's late, so I don't bother going to the front door. I throw a handful of pebbles at his bedroom window like he did to mine. A few seconds later, the window rises and he looks down at me. He's wearing a T-shirt that's ripped along the neck.

"Amelia? What are you doing down there?"

"I just had the best idea!" I whispershout up at him.

"It's eleven o'clock at night!" he whispershouts back. "Have you not heard of phones?" But he's smiling, so I know he isn't mad.

"Come down here for a second!" I say.

He gives me an exasperated look but closes the window. In a minute, he's standing in the grass next to me and I'm asking him if he has any paint left over. His smile grows wider and wider as I explain how we can turn the fountain into a mirror of the art in the woods. "I love it," he whispers. "I'm sure we can do it. We have to tell the rest of the crew."

I nod and smile, so excited.

Twitch holds up a finger. "I think we can text them, though. Let's not get busted the first night out, okay?"

I nod again and pull my phone from my pocket.

Twitch tells me everyone's numbers and I send out a group text. We both watch as my phone blows up with responses. Everyone is in.

This is going to be the best prank in the history of eighth-grade pranks.

CHAPTER
TWENTY-NINE

THE NEXT FEW DAYS ARE a blur. Twitch's crew and I have spent hours in the town library, and our hands are cramped from so much work with scissors. We've gathered all the paint we need, and now we're all lying on the floor in my bedroom trying to take a quick nap before the sun goes down. Tomorrow is Prank Day and we're going to need the whole night to finish. Tomorrow is also the day they film *Trailer Takeout*, because of course. I've barely seen Mom or Dad in days. I have no idea how they're going to be able to see my prank and how I'm going to get down to the trailer for the contest. We'll just have to wing it, I guess.

I'm not sure if anyone has actually slept at all, but we've been quiet as the light has moved from the top of my window to the bottom of it, casting the room in a light orange, evening glow. Mom knocks on the doorframe (the door is open because GIRLS AND BOYS

IN ONE ROOM AHH NIGHTMARE SCENARIO), and she's holding a big brown bag covered in grease stains.

"Sausages and fries?" she asks. "Before the big night out?"

We all sit up, looking kind of groggy. Mom sets the bag on the floor in the middle of us and puts down a roll of paper towels. She disappears and comes back with a twelve-pack of soda and a smile.

"I hope Amelia has told you all thank you for helping her this week," Mom says, and I can't help but roll my eyes.

"Oh, Mrs. Peabody," Desiree says with a genuine smile. "Amelia is the one who has been helping us."

Mom doesn't seem to know what to say to that, so she gives me a quizzical look as she backs out of the room. Then she disappears down the stairs.

"Music?" Twitch asks, hooking his phone up to my speakers. Something bouncy and thwumpy plays, and we all get up and dance while we eat our sausages and fries. It's all so silly and spontaneous . . . and fun.

"Hey!" I shout. "Am I having a party right now?"

"I don't know!" Jake shouts back. "It kind of feels like a party." He offers up his soda and we all yell, "Cheers!" as we crash our cans together.

I set down my food and drink and pull Clara's letter from my pocket.

4) *Throw an awesome birthday party on the lake. (Invite everyone, make sure the boat is working, have enough ice cream for the whole town, make sure everyone knows it's YOU, Most Beautiful Queen of the Universe, in charge.)*

I look up at everyone laughing and dancing in my room. It's no one's birthday, and we're definitely not at the lake, and sausages are not ice cream, and yet . . . this totally counts as a party. I cross number four off the list.

"What's that?" Mom stares over my shoulder. I hadn't heard her come back in my room. She's holding a box of cookies, but she sets it down on my dresser as she leans closer.

"Is that . . . ?" she says, her voice quiet.

"Clara's," I finish for her. "Mrs. Henderson accidentally gave me Clara's letter at the beginning of the school year instead of mine. I've been trying to do all the things she never got to do." The music is still thumping, but no one is dancing anymore.

"Oh, Amelia," Mom says. "Oh, honey." She grabs me up in a hug. And suddenly everyone is hugging us. It's an enormous group hug with lots of sniffles. After a few minutes, we break apart and I hand the letter to Mom so she can see it better. She reads over it, then takes my pen and scratches off number one, the part that says "be nicer to Mom and Amelia."

"Looks like you've completed the list," she says, kissing me on the top of my head.

"Hey, guys," Twitch says. "I hate to interrupt, but it's eight o'clock. We need to get going!" We all scramble around to grab our supplies. I'm the last out of my room, with Mom beside me. She hugs me again and says, "You're a wonder, Amelia."

Those are really nice words to hear.

CHAPTER THIRTY

THE SUN IS JUST STARTING to rise, painting the sky in beautiful orange and pink streaks, when we finish. The fast-drying paint is a little bit sticky still, but not enough to smear. We've checked and rechecked the tubing, and set up the table next to us with golden paper, pens, and scissors. The Clara Peabody Memorial Stardust Fountain is ready for business.

We've painted the inside of the fountain a deep, dark blue, just like the project in the woods. The edges of the basin are painted red and jaggedy white, just like the project, too. And as for the stars . . . my fingers are crossed that it's going to work.

People are starting to gather around the fountain now, because everyone in town gets up early on Prank Day to see what's new and crazy. It's a town tradition, and I think some people look forward to it more than Christmas. You never know what's going to come from the minds of eighth graders given free rein, and as long as it isn't destructive or dangerous, everyone cheers us on. I hope they don't count painting the fountain as destructive, but I guess we can always paint it white again if they make us.

I look at Twitch, who nods. Desiree and Henry give me a thumbs-up, and Maureen and Jake smile encouragingly. I lean down to the hole next to the fountain where we've rigged our tubing and a small but superstrong fan. At the end of the tube I attach a huge plastic bag filled with golden stars cut from fancy paper. I put the fan (still turned off) in the other end of the bag and secure the edges so none of the stars can fall out. The crowd is bigger now, murmuring and looking at the painted fountain.

I flip the fan's switch and it turns on with a forceful whir, blowing the stars from the bag up through the tubing. I'm afraid they've all jammed up in there and gotten caught, but then stars begin to shoot out of the bird's mouth, gold catching the early morning sun and glimmering bright.

Everyone in the crowd sucks in their breath at the same time as the beauty of the gold stars flutters overhead. Maureen is by the bag now, filling it with more and more stars. They're flying out of the bird's mouth and into the air, some landing in the fountain, but others landing in people's hair or on their shoulders or their shoes. It's like snow, but with stars. I can't help but laugh out loud with the joy of the moment. It worked! My idea worked!

I hear someone say, "What's this?" A woman is looking at a star and trying to make out the words we carefully wrote on each of them.

"Every star has a name on it," I say. "Each star is for a person who lived here in town at some point in history but has now passed on. If there's a person you'd like to add, we have a table here with pens and papers and scissors. You can make your own stardust for the people you love. They don't have to have lived here, they can be from anywhere."

Mrs. Grant hands me a paper cup of hot tea and puts her arm around my shoulder. She squeezes tight. "This is beautiful, Amelia. Just beautiful."

I reach into my pocket and hand her a star. On it, I've written *Rosalie* in my best handwriting. Mrs. Grant takes the star and kisses me on the forehead. She goes to Maureen and puts it in the bag so that it can fly out of the bird's mouth, making Rosalie part of our stardust morning.

I see my parents in the crowd, and I feel this huge relief that they made it! I was so afraid they might miss the fountain because of the contest. Their faces are pointed at the sky, small stars falling all around them, smiling. I go over to them and hug them both. "I fixed what you broke, Dad."

Dad's eyes fly open. "How did you—"

"You told Clara, and she told me," I say.

"That stinker! She wasn't supposed to tell anyone."

"Well, technically, I guess, she didn't," I say, digging in my pocket for her letter. I show it to Dad. His face goes from happy to happysad as he reads it. He carefully folds it up and hands it back to me.

"Mom told me you had this, but I didn't know she mentioned the fountain." His eyes are shiny bright.

"So, how did you break it?" I ask.

"We filled it with concrete," he says. "It was a dumb idea. We thought watery concrete would come out of the bird's mouth and harden so there would always be a stream of 'water' coming from its mouth. Instead, we mucked up all the piping. But it looks like you fixed it?" His bright eyes are now big with wonder.

"No," I say. "We couldn't get anything to work with those pipes, but there was enough room next to them to snake in some tubing of our own."

"Quite ingenious," Mom says.

I smile. The stars continue to fly around us.

Mom and Dad both grab me up in a big hug. "We hate to do this, Amelia, but Mom and I need to run," Dad says, looking at his watch. "Filming starts in half an hour and I'm sure everyone down there is freaking out that we aren't already there."

"We'll see you later?" Mom asks.

Before I can answer, Taylor runs up to us, out of breath. "You did all of this? Whoa, Amelia, it's gorgeous!"

"I had a lot of help," I say, gesturing to the crew. "These guys made it all possible, for sure."

Mom and Dad wave as they run to Old Betsy. I wave back.

"It's stunning," Taylor says, lifting her face to the falling stars. "Amazing."

"Where's your prank?" I ask. "What did you do?"

Taylor waves her hand dismissively. "Lacy wanted to find a bunch of chickens and let them loose in Town Square and have a 'Running of the Chickens' day, like the running of the bulls in Spain. But the chickens all just stood around pecking the ground, and none of them would go anywhere."

"Points for effort?" I say with a laugh.

Taylor laughs, too. "No points for anything. Except, all the chickens are still alive—and well fed. So, I guess maybe points for that?"

Hours go by as people wander over and marvel at the stardust fountain. Some people smile big, some cry a little. It's kind of like a giant bonding moment for the whole town.

Mrs. Grant brings over drinks and snacks, and I remember—*bam*—I need to get down to Pits 'n' Pieces!

"Do you guys think you can keep helping out for a little bit?" I ask everyone. "I have to go help with the TV show stuff." And even though I know they all have to be just as tired as I am, everyone shouts out, "You bet!" and "No problem!" and "Good luck!"

Mrs. Grant jangles her car keys. "William, can you take Amelia to the lake? And not wreck my car?"

"Yes, ma'am," Twitch says, his face very serious. Mrs. Grant points at her car parked in the alley by the General Store. It's about a thousand years old and looks like it's held together with duct tape.

"I'll try not to wreck it any more than it's already wrecked." Twitch winks at her and she slaps his arm before she hands over her keys.

"I mean it!" she says. "Not a scratch."

"Do you think they'll let us keep the fountain like this? Forever?" I ask Mrs. Grant, even though I know she doesn't know. "Like a monument to everyone's loved ones?"

"I don't know," Mrs. Grant says. "But you should definitely ask."

She kisses my cheek, and then Twitch and I run to the car.

CHAPTER
THIRTY-ONE

"HOW'S THAT POTATO SALAD COMING along?" Dad asks. The TV show crew are outside the trailer taking video of the line. I finish stirring the big pot, cover it with plastic wrap, and push it into the fridge. "It's going to be great. Best potato salad ever." I've never made potato salad before, but Dad was insistent that today was the big day . . . today was going to be the first day of my potato salad reign.

Mom is in the cramped corner mixing cookie dough at Dad's request, which is hilarious because I'm not sure she's ever actually worked *in* the trailer before. Sure, she helps Dad stock stuff and set things up and whatever, but she always said she'd never set foot inside the trailer as an employee. "This is your thing," she'd say, pointing at Dad. "Yours." But today he weirdly asked for help cooking, and the two of us said okay. I guess we both know how important this is to him.

Dad strokes his beard nervously. "I know I keep saying this, but if we win this thing, it could really change our lives. I would probably have to start a real restaurant, or buy a few more trailers and put them in other towns. Our popularity would skyrocket. And so would my workload."

I look at him and tilt my head to the side, like he does to me when he isn't sure he understands what I'm saying. "Do you want that, though?" I ask. "I thought you liked having the small trailer and experimenting with flavors and stuff. I didn't think you wanted to go corporate, or whatever."

Dad tugs his beard some more, wrinkles getting deeper at the sides of his eyes as he smiles at me. "How did you get to be so smart?"

"Must be in the genes," Twitch says, coming up the small stairs into the trailer. He goes to the sink in the back and washes his hands. "The crowd out there is huge. I thought you might need a hand."

"The crowd in *here* is huge," Mom says. And she's right. Four people inside this trailer is super-close quarters.

"Tell you what," Dad says. "Let's all agree right now that it doesn't matter if we win. The only things that matter are flavor and fun. Deal?"

Twitch and I both smile big. So does Mom. "Deal," we all say together.

"Jen, why don't you give me the cookie dough and go outside to take orders." Dad takes the bowl from Mom, who's face goes slack with relief.

"Excellent," she says. "I'm outta here." She grabs an order pad from the counter and thumps down the stairs.

With more room in the trailer, Dad, Twitch, and I become a well-oiled machine. The afternoon is a blur of crowds and cameras. People interview us over and over and take all kinds of video of us cooking and handing out plates of food and tossing wood into the smokers and a million other things. By sunset, Dad, Mom, Twitch, and I are all sweaty and smoky and exhausted.

Producer Stacy comes over, headphones dangling around her neck. "Ready to come outside? We're going to announce the winners."

We all climb out of the trailer and follow her to the beachy part of the lake. She makes us stand in the sandy dirt with our backs facing the water while she sets up the cameras. The Thai Me Up, Thai Me Down guys are here, too, and the Leafy Queens folks. We all wave to one another. No one really seems to care who wins, we're all so exhausted.

After what feels like forever, the host of the show

bounds over to us, all smiles and full of energy. He announces that—drumroll, please—Pits 'n' Pieces has been disqualified.

What!

Everyone stares at him.

Apparently, because I helped make the potato salad, and Mom helped with the cookies, and neither of our names was on the chef roster, our team has been disqualified from the competition. Thai Me Up, Thai Me Down is the winner.

What!

What!

Dad laughs really hard and pats me on the back. Mom's eyes are huge, but then they narrow and she smiles. She turns to Dad, and they share a glance before she pushes him hard in the shoulder and they both laugh. Did Dad *know* we were going to get disqualified? Twitch looks at me and I shrug.

Stacy jogs over to us once the cameras are off and being packed away. "You knew the rules. I remember going over them with you. So, why did you throw it?" she asks Dad. "You would have won, hands down, you know."

He shrugs.

"Having my family cook with me makes me feel like the big winner," he says. "Everyone together, having fun . . . at the lake." He throws his arm over my shoulder and gives me a squeeze. "That's the prize I wanted, and that's the prize I got."

"You!" I wiggle away and point at Dad. "You *knew* you were disqualifying us?! Dad! You sacrificed the contest just to get us to the lake?"

"It was a game-time decision," he said. "I don't need a restaurant. I don't need more trailers. I don't need to work myself to a nub. I have everything I need right here." He grabs me up in a big hug, and then drags Mom into it, too. After a second, he even grabs Twitch. "Now let's go swimming," he says. And before I can say or do anything, he runs from the sand, onto the wooden pier, and cannonballs into the lake. Twitch lets out a hoot and runs after him, doing the same thing. Then *Mom* gives a yell and flings herself off the pier. What! Ha! Before I can even believe what I'm doing, I run after them, too, leaping from the scratchy end of the dock, feeling the wind whip at my hair and then the freezing water engulf my body. I open my eyes underwater and see Dad still down there, his eyes open, too. He smiles and waves and then grabs Mom and hugs her from behind. She opens her eyes and makes a goofy underwater face. I smile and wave. Twitch does a handstand, before floating to the surface. It's all so silly, this wild underwater tableau. We all swim up to the surface and shake the water from our hair and ears.

Dad is in the lake.

Mom is in the lake.

Twitch is in the lake.

I'm in the lake.

And it isn't eating any of us.

There are a bunch of splashes and suddenly Maureen and Desiree and Jake and Henry are in the lake, too. Where did they come from? Then Mrs. Grant and Taylor come flying into the water and we're all laughing and spluttering and splashing.

"We ran out of paper, so we shut down the fountain . . . for now . . ." Mrs. Grant says, her white hair shimmering like a mermaid's. "I hope that's okay."

I can only smile and look around me. We're all in the lake, laughing and splashing and smiling. The sky is a deep, deep blue and the sun is setting behind the trees. The first stars of the night begin to twinkle overhead, leaving just a hint of stardust in our hair.

ACKNOWLEDGMENTS

Writing a book is such an interesting phenomenon. You're alone for much of the process, but you're also surrounded by the characters you've created. You technically spend your days by yourself—but having conversations and arguments, solving problems and going on adventures, making discoveries and amends. And then . . . your story is done. You turn it in to your editor and your brain is quiet and alone again. Except, you're *not* alone. There's a whole team who springs to life to bring your book to readers. Agents, editors, designers, copy editors, marketing whizzes, public relations teams, and more. But while they're all working you're . . . by yourself. Your characters have been whisked away and you no longer visit their towns and adventures every day, because everything is off being polished and perfected.

All this to say, being a writer is not an easy job. It's arguably one of the best jobs in the world, but it's hard. And when you have a hard, sometimes lonely, job you have to learn to trust other people to help you out. Some of the people who help me every day are Samuel and Georgia and Isaac. They know that I sometimes have to live in my head and in my heart, and that means dinner might be late or burned. The school field trip might be missed. They know I will have to leave them sometimes so I can visit other children and talk about my books. They know this, but they don't complain. (Well, sometimes they complain, but mostly about my terrible cooking.) My kids are my confidants, my beta readers, my support staff, my champions, and my heart. I love them dearly, and I'm not sure they always realize they are the top notch number one most important team members in getting *all* of my books written and published.

It's also imperative, when you're a writer, to have a whip-smart publishing team who seems to miraculously know how to get things just right. From editing to design to marketing to everything in between, I could not be luckier to be working with the team at Scholastic. Erin Black seems to live in my brain. Sometimes I think she sees my words before I do. (I hope she does, because when we're on the phone talking about a project, I get so excited I talk right over her and I have to depend on magic for her to understand me.) Melissa Schirmer is a brilliant production editor, keeping everything in line and in tip-top shape, and Baily Crawford has reached into my heart and created a design that can't be surpassed.

My agent, Ammi-Joan Paquette, deserves confetti cannons and jubilant trombone salutes for all of her hard work. She never asks "why" and always asks "why not," which keeps me constantly on my toes. Joan gives me confidence, which gives me freedom to write. Joan also gives me brutal truth, which gives me freedom to write *better*.

And to Shannon, my love. You are my stars and sunshine, my first thought every morning and my last thought every night. You believe in me, and that makes *me* believe in me. Every day I wonder where you came from. Maybe science can't prove fate, but maybe it doesn't need to.

ABOUT THE AUTHOR

Kari Anne Holt is the author of several books for young readers, including *House Arrest* and *Rhyme Schemer*, each of which was a Bank Street Best Book of the Year, and *Gnome-a-Geddon*. Dreaming up sandwiches with punny names and barbeque sauces she'd like to try are just a couple of her hobbies. Kari Anne lives in Austin, Texas, with her family, and you can find her online at www.KAHolt.com.

ABOUT THE AUTHOR

Kari Anne Holt is the author of several books for young readers, including *House Arrest* and *Rhyme Schemer*, each of which was a Bank Street Best Book of the Year, and *Gnome-a-Geddon*. Dreaming up sandwiches with punny names and barbeque sauces she'd like to try are just a couple of her hobbies. Kari Anne lives in Austin, Texas, with her family, and you can find her online at www.KAHolt.com.

WRANGO

Also by Brian Burks

Runs With Horses

Soldier Boy

Walks Alone

Brian Burks

WRANGO

HARCOURT BRACE & COMPANY

San Diego   New York   London

wm
J.
Fic
Burk
16.00

Requests for permission to make copies of any part of
the work should be mailed to: Permissions Department,
Harcourt Brace & Company, 6277 Sea Harbor Drive,
Orlando, Florida 32887-6777.

Library of Congress Cataloging-in-Publication Data
Burks, Brian.
Wrango/Brian Burks.—1st ed.
p. cm.
Summary: When young George McJunkin leaves his
home in Texas and joins a cattle drive along the Chisholm
Trail, he experiences the hardships of being a Black cowboy
after the Civil War.
1. McJunkin, George—Juvenile fiction. [1. McJunkin,
George—Fiction. 2. Chisholm Trail—Fiction. 3. Cattle
drives—West (U.S.)—Fiction. 4. Cowboys—West (U.S.)—
Fiction. 5. Afro-Americans—Fiction. 6. West (U.S.)—
Fiction.] I. Title.
PZ7.B9235W1 1999
[Fic]—dc21   99-12381
ISBN 0-15-201815-8

Text set in Meridien
Designed by Linda Lockowitz

First edition
F E D C B A
Printed in the United States of America

To the memory of
George McJunkin

George McJunkin, circa 1911

FOREWORD

A T THE CLOSE of the Civil War, in 1865, the Texas economy was in a severe state of depression: Jobs were difficult to find and money was scarce. But Texas had cattle, millions of cattle. In order to sell them, the cattle had to be taken to railroad towns and loaded onto trains to be delivered to large meat-packing centers, such as Chicago. Thus the era of the great trail drives began.

It is estimated that between 1867 and 1895, more than five thousand African American cowboys helped drive nearly ten million cattle up the trails from Texas. The life of a cowboy on the open range held more financial opportunities and less discrimination than any other profession open to blacks at the time.

One such cowboy was George McJunkin. This is a story based on his early years, what little is known of them.

WRANGO

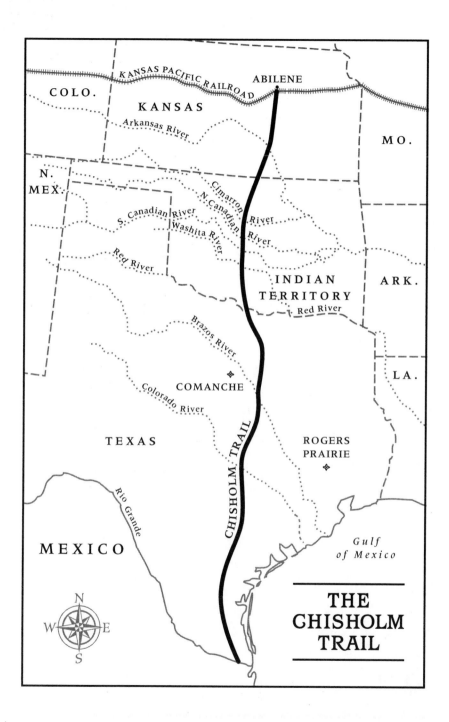

KANSAS PACIFIC RAILROAD

ABILENE

COLO.

KANSAS

Arkansas River

MO.

N.
MEX.

Cimarron River

N. Canadian River

S. Canadian River

Washita River

Red River

INDIAN
TERRITORY

ARK.

Red River

Brazos River

COMANCHE

Colorado River

TEXAS

ROGERS
PRAIRIE

LA.

Rio Grande

MEXICO

CHISHOLM TRAIL

Gulf
of Mexico

N
W   E
S

THE
CHISHOLM
TRAIL

ONE

GEORGE MCJUNKIN lay on the ground, desperately trying to regain his breath. He rolled to his side, wheezing, his eyes fixed on the blue roan that had just bucked him off.

The last thing he wanted was to get on the horse again. But if he was ever to be considered by the hands on the ranch as one of them, there was no choice.

Finally his lungs caught a little air, then a little more. He heard laughter and men speaking to one another in Spanish.

Two vaqueros sat on top of the corral fence snickering. One spoke. "You are a good farmer, George. Soon your nose will have plowed up all the ground here, and we will buy seeds and plant a big garden."

Behind George, a pair of strong hands hoisted him to his feet. His legs shook as he turned to face Senor Valarde. The man's beard and long hair were

completely white. Yet his straight stature was that of a much younger man, and his large brown eyes were clear and bright.

He held George by the shoulders and smiled. "Today, the *caballo*, he laughs. Maybe tomorrow you will laugh." He gestured at the setting sun. "It is late. Your papa is waiting for you."

George, still breathing hard, dusted off his worn bib overalls and inspected a long tear along the elbow of his red flannel shirt. He only had one other shirt, and his mother was sure to be angry about what had happened to this one.

A horse snorted, and George turned to see the roan standing at the far side of the corral. The small, Spanish-bred horse was shaking his head and pawing the ground with his left front foot.

George set his jaw and walked to the roan; the men on the fence laughed again. He paid no attention and reached for the rope reins trailing on the ground.

"Senor," George said to the old man, "there's enough daylight left for me to try to ride him one more time."

He held the ends of the reins as the horse backed away. Carefully he positioned them on either side of the horse's neck. His heart pounded. Every time he had been thrown, it had hurt. He put a bare foot into the stirrup, knowing that the longer he waited to get on, the worse the shaking in his arms and legs would become.

When he swung into the saddle, the roan reared, tottering back and forth on his hind legs, then came down hard on his front feet. The jolt threw George

forward, and the large Mexican saddle horn sank into his stomach.

Before he could settle back in the saddle, the horse windmilled, making a half circle in the air, and returned to the ground with all four feet as stiff as fence posts. The grinding shock of the landing shot up George's spine to his head.

He lost his balance, sliding to one side. He started to reach for the saddle horn to pull himself up but in a flash decided not to. The vaqueros rode bucking horses without grabbing leather. He wouldn't grab it either, even if it meant being thrown again.

The roan jumped forward, and George slid farther to the side. Only the calf of his left leg was still in the saddle seat.

He could see the ground rushing past him. The ride was all but over. The only thing left to do was to let go of the reins and feel the bone-jarring slap of the earth.

But suddenly the horse spun, so swiftly and powerfully that the motion forced George back up into the saddle. His feet found the stirrups and he braced himself.

The roan began to pump-handle buck in a straight line. The seesaw effect of the horse landing alternately on his front and hind feet was much easier to ride. For the first time, George felt as if he might succeed.

Then all at once the horse stopped, standing completely still. Senor Valarde and the other two vaqueros waved their hats in **approval,** shouting, *"Patéalo. Patéalo."*

The men were telling him to kick the horse, something he wasn't sure he wanted to do.

Ever so gently, he thought. He pressed his heels into the horse while taking up the excess slack in the reins. If there was anything his years of helping around the ranch and watching and learning about horses had taught him, it was that they were unpredictable. The roan, judging by his past behavior, shouldn't buck anymore. But that didn't mean he wouldn't. Today the rules of the game could change.

The horse took a hesitant step forward, then another. George held his breath and kicked harder. The roan moved into a trot, circling the corral as if he were the gentlest horse on earth.

George let out his breath in relief. He pulled the horse to a stop near Senor Valarde, who was standing with his back against the inside of the corral fence. George slid to the ground.

"Bueno," Valarde said, smiling. *"Muy bueno."* He held the horse's reins while George unfastened the latigo that held the cinch, and removed the saddle and blanket, putting them into a wooden box located just outside the corral.

The two vaqueros who had been watching were walking toward a low, mud-roofed structure made of poles that served as the ranch bunkhouse. They talked in Spanish and nodded. Neither of them looked back.

It didn't matter. George knew word would get around to the other hands that he had finally ridden the roan. His tired face broke into a smile.

Senor Valarde led the roan out of the corral, and George walked beside him. "I'll be back tomorrow . . ."

He caught himself, remembering that tomorrow was Sunday. As always, he would be going to church. After that he'd have to help his mother shake out their beds, wash clothes, and clean the house. The chicken coop and pigpens would have to be raked out, too, and then he'd have to help his father clean the blacksmith shop and the horse stalls in preparation for another week's work. It would be dark before he was finished with all his chores.

"I'll try to come back Monday," he said. "Maybe you could help me with my roping. I've been working on braiding a reata, like you showed me, but it's not coming out right. I'll remember to bring it with me."

Senor Valarde answered slowly, his voice soft. "I will not be here."

"Are you going to be out with the cattle? 'Cause I don't mind helping you. I could bring my reata."

"No." Senor Valarde half turned and patted the roan's neck. "The Sanchez Rancho, it has been sold. The new *ganadero* has his own vaqueros. There is no longer a place for me here. I will be leaving mañana."

"But you can't go! You've been here as long as I can remember. You belong here. No one is a better cowboy than you. And . . . and no one knows this ranch better than you do."

Senor Valarde pulled his sombrero down farther on his forehead. "I must leave."

George stared at the ground. This man had taught him to ride and rope. Almost everything George knew about horses he'd learned from the old

vaquero. And Senor Valarde knew things about him, too, about the shame he felt that he and his family had once been slaves. About how some of the townspeople hated them only because they were now free.

George raised his head. "Where will you go?"

"Perhaps there is work on the Kansas Trail, moving the *ganado* north. A man in a wagon came by here. He told me a large drive was being formed near Comanche. Maybe the *ganadero* there will have need of me."

George had heard about the Kansas Trail. Sometimes people called it the Abilene Trail or the McCoy Trail, and recently he'd heard a man at the store in Rogers Prairie call it the Chisholm Trail. He wished he could see it. He wished he could be a cowboy and ride up the trail until he was far, far from Rogers Prairie.

George had seen a herd of longhorn cattle passing through town a few months back. He'd watched carefully, especially the dozen trail riders who were with the herd. There were four black men and three Mexican vaqueros; and the other five cowboys were white. Each one was mounted on a good horse and wore sturdy boots and good felt hats, even the black men.

At noon, when the cowhands gathered at the chuck wagon to eat, the black men and the Mexicans lined up to get their plates filled just like the white men did. George had never seen such a thing. In Rogers Prairie, whites were always served ahead of blacks. Just yesterday, his father was asked to wait

outside on the steps until old Mrs. McMurdy finally decided which color of ribbon she wanted before the store clerk would fill his order.

George looked to his friend. "Do you think the boss of the herd at Comanche might hire me?"

Senor Valarde smiled, putting a hand on George's arm. "You have learned much, and you learn quickly. Someday you will ride with the best vaqueros. Now you should go. It will be dark before you reach your casa. Your mama and your papa are waiting."

The vaquero led the roan a few steps, then turned. "On my way early mañana, I will stop by to look at your reata."

Senor Valarde hadn't said he wouldn't be hired. Did that mean he might have a chance?

He broke into a run. He had a lot of work to do to convince his father to let him go. There wasn't a lot of time left before morning.

TWO

THE POUNDING of a hammer on steel rang through the air. George stopped running when he could make out the lantern-lit doorway of the blacksmith shop. He hesitated for a moment, feeling a tinge of guilt, and then hurried on in the dim moonlight. If he had stayed home and helped his father instead of going to ride the roan, the day's horseshoeing work would probably already be done.

Beyond the blacksmith shop he could see the candle burning in the only window of their two-room cabin. This had been his home as long as he could remember, but his parents didn't own it. His father didn't own the shop, either. Everything belonged to the ranch owner, old Master McJunkin.

Until the end of the war, when all slaves were granted freedom, he and his mother and father had worked for Master McJunkin. They had labored many hard years in the cotton and cornfields but

hadn't gotten themselves even so much as a foot of ground to call their own. And now it took nearly all the money his father could make shoeing horses and mules just to pay the rent and keep food on their table. Master McJunkin was richer than ever.

The hammering stopped as George stepped into the shop. His father pushed past a mule, grabbed a hot shoe with a pair of pincers, and dropped it into a bucket of water. As usual, his overalls were dark with smoke. His mother—a woman so slender she seemed almost frail—stepped out of one of the stalls with a rake in her hand.

"About time you showed up, George," she said angrily. "I see your face is dirty and your shirt's tore. You been out trying to ride them mean bronco horses again, haven't you?"

"Yes, ma'am. I know I should have stayed and helped you and Pa. But I rode today. Well . . . not every time. But I rode a bucking horse until he stood still."

His father reached into the water and pulled out the now-cold horseshoe. He spoke to his son as he continued to work. "The only thing them bucking horses is going to do is get you crippled or killed. Even old Master McJunkin wouldn't let his slaves get on them wild, crazy horses. Slaves was worth too much money. He didn't want to lose them. You ought to at least think as much of yourself as a slave owner would."

George chewed on his lip for a moment, but he couldn't keep quiet. "But we're free, and that's what freedom is about, isn't it? Being able to be a cowboy

and ride a bucking horse if that's what a body wants to do. Or being able to go wherever you want, whenever you want. What good is freedom, anyway, if we won't use it?"

"We are using it." His mother stepped closer, her eyes flashing. "Your father's shoeing that mule because he wants to. Nobody's making him do it. And he is getting paid. I never knew a slave to get any money."

He watched his father nail the shoe in place. The man's hands were thick and gnarled, and his back was bent from years of this hard work. George had learned farrier and blacksmith skills, and he could shoe a horse almost as well as his father. But he didn't like the work, and he didn't like the name that went with it.

Shoeboy. That's what his father was called.

George decided there was no use in waiting any longer. "Senor Valarde lost his job at the ranch. He says he heard about a cattle drive forming near Comanche. In the morning he's starting out on the trip over there to ask for a job." George fingered the straps on his overalls. "I want to go with him. Maybe the boss there won't hire me, but I want to see if he will."

His father twisted the end off a nail with the claw of his hammer and set down the mule's foot. He stood as straight as he could, placing a hand in the small of his back, and stared George in the eye.

"Cowboy work won't help you to get ahead in this world. Right now there's so many cows in Texas that they aren't hardly worth anything. The more of

them you own, the poorer you are. That's why there's a big push on to drive them all up north, where the prices are better."

The man stepped closer to George. "Sure, those cowmen need help from most anybody they can get now. But it won't last. In a few years, when most of the cattle are gone, they won't be hiring you anymore. White cowboys will be getting all the regular ranch jobs."

George was silent.

His father pointed the end of his hammer at him. "Son, what you need to do is go to school. A man that can read and write can do most anything he wants. The Freedmen's Bureau has already promised us a school, and someday we'll have it."

Someday. It was always *someday.*

There was nothing he wanted more than to go to school. But he had a feeling it was never going to happen. In fact, he was certain it wouldn't, not in Rogers Prairie. Even if the Freedmen's Bureau did build a school for blacks, plenty of whites in town had already threatened to burn it down.

He tried to keep from raising his voice, tried to will his heart to slow down. He had to convince them. "Some of the cowboys probably know how to read. Maybe one of them will teach me."

His mother shook her head. "You are barely sixteen years old, George. You don't need to be going off alone. We'll be getting that school just like your father said. Meantime, Master McJunkin just bought fifty head a' Mexican broom-tail horses, and he wants them all shod by the end of next week."

"That's right. I need you here to help me." His father's tone was steady. "I've told you this before. Someday I aim to save up enough money to buy this shop, and the cabin, too. It'll be yours when your mama and me are gone. You can live good just staying here and working. It's a whole lot more than lots of folks have."

George nodded and turned away. He walked to a bed of coals that lay waist-high on a rock hearth and began to pump air on them with the bellows. He hoped that someday his parents would own the shop, the house, too. But like the school, he doubted it would ever happen. And even if it did, he really didn't want any part of it. He wanted a different kind of life.

THREE

"Pass those biscuits, George, unless you mean to keep them all to yourself." George's father watched him finger the new reata Senor Valarde had dropped by on his way out of town earlier that morning.

George shoved the plate across the table.

"Now, don't carry on so. You act like the world has come to an end."

George continued to stare at the rope. His father didn't understand. Senor Valarde was his best friend, his only friend. And now he would never see him again.

Suddenly the riffle of hooves from a dozen or more horses sounded outside. George's father pushed his chair back and went to the window.

His mother moved the curtain. Her voice faltered. "Looks . . . looks like trouble. It's the men—the men that wear the sacks."

George followed his parents outside. A group of men had stopped their horses in front of the cabin and now stood in a choking cloud of dust. One held a torch, even though the sun had been up for almost an hour. They all wore white sheets, and their heads were covered with flour sacks that had holes cut out for their eyes.

"You and your mother get in the house," George's father ordered.

George didn't move. He knew who they were. Many black people around Rogers Prairie had been beaten and a couple of them killed by men dressed like these.

One of them spoke, his voice muffled by the sack. "You have yourself a problem, Shoeboy. We heard about what you did at the store the other day. Seems you forgot your place and stepped through the door ahead of a white lady. Now, you know we can't be having that kind of thing happening around here. You get yourself on over there to one of those trees and take your shirt off for your whipping."

"But I—I never stepped in front of any white woman. I—"

"Get, I told you!"

The riders stepped off their horses and George's mother grabbed his father's arm. "My man hasn't done anything to anyone. You leave him be. He—"

The hooded man who had spoken went to her and yanked her by the hair and threw her to the side, where she fell in the dirt.

George knew what to do. He reached inside the open door, stepped out on the porch, and brought

the butt of a rusted shotgun to his shoulder. He pointed it at the man who was talking.

"Mister," George said loudly. "You better ride out now or I'll have to pull this trigger and put an extra hole in that flour sack of yours."

No one moved.

George held the gun steady. The leader of the riders took a step back and spit tobacco juice on the porch.

"You're not very bright, boy. I wonder how your mama's gonna like seeing her baby boy hanging from a tree? 'Cause we'll come back for you."

George glanced at his father, who was helping his mother to her feet. "I told you to leave," he said, closing one eye and leveling the sights of the gun.

The man held up his hands. "All right. All right. We're leaving. But I promise, we'll be back."

He swung up onto his horse, and the others did the same. George held the shotgun on them until they were down the road and out of sight.

"George." His mother's shoulders drooped. "You know that old gun don't have no shells in it. Just what did you aim to do if those men wouldn't go?"

"Leave him alone, Mama." His father took the gun from George's trembling hands. "He only did what he thought he had to."

FOUR

THE AIR HELD the faint scent of wood smoke. George scanned the grassy plain around him, trying to determine the source.

Nothing. He couldn't see so much as a wisp. He shifted the burlap sack his mother had packed from his left shoulder to his right and forced his weary legs to walk on.

When the smoke scent grew stronger, he stopped again. In the distance was something he hadn't seen earlier. A patch of green that looked like the tops of trees, or perhaps it was bushes, big bushes. The vegetation could mean that water was there. Though he still couldn't see any smoke, the spot was the only one around that might offer wood for a campfire.

George moved on, heading toward the site. Five days had passed since he'd left Rogers Prairie, and leaving his parents had been harder than he had imagined.

He could still see his mother standing motionless by his father in the dim moonlight, watching him go. At least a dozen times he'd turned around and started back home. But then he'd realize that going back wouldn't solve anything. The men in the hoods would be waiting for him, and his return might put his parents in more danger than they were already in. If it hadn't been for his mother and father's insistence, he would have never left home in the first place.

But maybe, George thought, his going was for the best. It was the only way he would ever have a chance to become a cowboy. He only wished it could have happened differently. And the fact that he was at least a full day behind Senor Valarde didn't help things, either. Most of the time he wasn't really sure if he was even headed in the right direction.

Every so often he found himself looking back, wondering if someone might be following him.

There was no law in Rogers Prairie. He remembered a story his father had told him about a black man who was sitting on the top of a fence when a sheriff from a nearby town rode by. The black man was happy about his newfound freedom from slavery and, wanting to rub it in a little, started whistling "Yankee Doodle."

The sheriff stopped his horse, pulled a pistol, and with slow, deliberate aim, shot the man between the eyes. The sheriff rode on, and the black man lay where he fell until his corpse rotted and there was nothing left but bones.

In some ways black people were worse off now

than they ever had been, the way George saw it. At least when they'd been slaves, the white people around didn't seem so hateful. If his family had still been owned by Master McJunkin, they would have been safe from attacks like the one yesterday. Slaves were worth money, and anyone who whipped or killed them had to answer for it.

Now that blacks were free, it seemed, there was no protection, no help, and little hope.

THE PATCH OF GREEN was getting closer, and George could now see a faint trail of smoke, which quickly disappeared in the soft breeze. Whoever was camped there should be able to tell him where the town of Comanche was. And they probably had food.

Two days before, George had eaten the last of the corn bread and fruit his mother had packed for him. And though he'd been able to fill his milk-bottle canteen with water at creeks he'd crossed, it was almost empty.

And now he was lost. He had found out that Comanche was more than a hundred miles to the west, and that to get there, he would have to cross the Brazos River. But that was all he knew. He could only hope that the shallow, muddy river he had waded across yesterday was the Brazos. Whether he was anywhere near Comanche, he had no idea.

A horse neighed and George felt a touch of fear, a tightening in his stomach. He slowed his pace. What if whoever was ahead were dangerous people? What if they were like the men who wore the hoods and sheets in Rogers Prairie? Or it could be Indians. He'd

only seen wild Indians once in his life, and that was at a distance, when he and his father were taking a wagon load of feed out to a line shack on the McJunkin ranch; but he'd heard stories.

There were small bands of Kiowa and Wichita scattered about, but it was the Comanche who claimed most of the land in north-central Texas and were the most feared. They were known for their fighting abilities, excellent horsemanship, and the cruelty they sometimes showed their victims.

Senor Valarde's whole family had been killed by Comanche. He never would talk about it; he only said that as a young man he had left home for a week to tend a herd of goats, and when he returned, his home was burned to the ground. His mother and father and all his brothers and sisters were dead.

George wiped the sweat off his brow with his shirtsleeve. For mid-April, the day was unusually warm. He removed the burlap sack from his shoulder and, holding it in one hand, bent down to keep as low as he could. If there were Indians ahead, he wanted to see them first. Then he could change direction and skirt around them, or perhaps find a place to hide until they'd left.

The green he had seen was the tops of cottonwood trees. He could make them out clearly now. They grew out of a large oval-shaped depression in the earth. He reached the edge of the basin and was astonished at its size. A hundred men and horses could easily hide below, in the thick foliage.

Again a horse whinnied. George dropped, flattening himself on the ground. He could see nothing,

no movement. If he wanted to know who was down there, he would have to get closer. He was going to have to sneak through the trees and bushes.

He felt an urge to turn around and leave as quickly as he could. Then reason took over. It was probably just a family who was camped below him. A good family with children, who would share their food and water, and would tell him where he was and where he needed to go to reach Comanche.

The gnawing in his empty stomach helped him make up his mind. He would move closer.

He worked his way through the greenery and peered out through a small opening in a plum bush. He saw two horses tethered to a rope line, and the white, speckled rump of a third.

Voices reached him. Men were speaking in Spanish. Their speech was too low for him to understand, but he was glad to hear the familiar tones. Indians didn't speak Spanish—at least, he didn't think so.

It would look better, he decided, if he called out and walked into the camp rather than be seen trying to sneak around it.

He was about to stand, when something hit him from behind. He was pulled backward by the straps of his overalls and then shoved to the ground. An Indian stood over him, straddling his stomach. The man wore very little clothing and his face was painted red. In his hand he held a knife.

George saw the long blade coming fast. He kicked out with his legs and flung his burlap sack at the attacker.

The point of the knife stuck into the flesh of George's throat, and he lay still. The Indian raised his chin and let out a shrill call.

Other warriors emerged from the trees. They grabbed George by the arms and legs and carried him through the brush.

He could barely think or breathe.

They tossed him into the air, and he landed hard on open, grassy land. Another man stepped toward him. His boots were all George could see—black boots with tall tops, and shiny spurs strapped to them. On the side of one of the spurs were small crosses etched in what looked like gold.

Someone shouted. "Riders are coming! Many riders!"

The man kicked George in the side with one of his black boots. Pain rushed through him, and he jerked his head to see the man's face. It was a white face—whiter than any face he'd ever seen. Almost ghostly.

Then something slammed into George's head and everything turned to black.

FIVE

WHEN GEORGE WOKE, he was staring at a ceiling. There were cracks in the plaster, and bare spots where pieces of it were missing.

Finally he began to remember the red-painted Indian and the knife, and the boots, and being kicked. He raised himself up on his elbow. His head began to pound, and a sharp pain flashed in his side.

He lay back down, touching his forehead. A bandage was wrapped around it. He felt his side and found another bandage tightly circling his waist.

Taking a deep breath that brought more pain, he forced himself to sit up. The room started to spin.

Bars. A jail. It made no sense.

With great effort George managed to swing his feet off the cot, stand, and stagger to the cell door. It was locked. To his left, in a corner of the building, a man with a bushy black beard sat reading a newspaper, with his chair rocked back and his feet propped

on the edge of a desk. A lawman's badge was pinned to his leather vest.

The officer glanced at George and laid the paper down. "Looks like maybe you'll live after all. The doc said he wasn't sure whether you'd ever wake up or not. You took a pretty good whack on the back of your head."

George grasped the bars with both hands to steady himself. His throat was dry, and his voice hoarse. "Where am I? What am I doing here?"

"You're in Comanche. Been here since last night. You're in my jail, and you'll stay in it until I find out who you are and what you were doing traveling with them Indians."

Dizziness washed over George, and he waited a moment for it to pass, still holding tightly to the bars of the cell. He told his name and how he came to be in the Indian camp.

Slowly he told about the warrior and the knife and the man in the black boots who had kicked him.

The officer took a ring of keys from his desk and moved to unlock the cell door.

"I figured about as much," he said. "Just wanted to be sure by hearing you tell it." The door swung open. "You're a mighty lucky boy. If my deputy and a posse hadn't showed up when they did, I doubt there'd been enough pieces left of you to bother with the burying. Those Comanches had just finished butchering another fellow not far from where you were."

George stepped out of the cell, his legs still unsteady. He touched his throat, finding a small scab

where the Indian's knife had stuck him. Nobody needed to tell him how lucky he was.

He put a hand on his side. It ached about as badly as his head.

"The doc said you might have a cracked rib," the officer said. "Anyway, you're pretty bruised up. Probably happened when you were kicked."

The sheriff put the keys in the drawer and sat back down, his face blank. "Well, this kind of thing happens from time to time, doesn't it? And now that you're in Comanche, what are you planning to do?"

George looked around the room. A gun rack on the wall held several rifles, and hanging from nails were a couple of lariats and a hat.

"I came here to see about a job. I was told that a cattle drive might be forming close by."

The officer stroked his beard. "There's a herd here all right. About three miles north of town. It'll be pulling out on the trail in a couple of days or so. With your hurt side and that knot on your head, I don't see how you'd be much help to them. I doubt they'd be hiring a black button like you, anyway."

What if the sheriff was right? Where would he go then?

"I had a sack with me," George said. "There wasn't much in it. Just some clothes and a reata. And a Bible."

The sheriff searched under the papers on his desk and found a small, frayed black book. He held it out.

"Guess this is yours, then. My deputy said he found it flung open in a bush. That's all he and the posse found out there."

George took the book and wiped it off with his fingers.

"Do you read, boy?" The sheriff looked puzzled.

"No. The Bible belongs to my mother. She can't read either, but she and my papa always wanted me to learn."

There was an awkward silence and George felt the need to leave. He couldn't help but remember the story his father had told him about that other sheriff.

He took a few steps toward the front door and stopped. He was still shaky, but most of all, he was thirsty. He wished he could get a drink. But he knew white people didn't like for blacks to drink from their vessels.

"Is it all right for me to go?"

"You can leave, but I wouldn't if I was you. Jail food will be brought here in about fifteen minutes. Once your belly's full, you're back on your own."

SIX

A DOE RAN ACROSS the wagon road. George turned his head just in time to see the deer vanish into an oak thicket. He glanced up at the sun. There were still a few hours of daylight left. The sheriff had said the herd of cattle wasn't more than three miles from town. He should come upon it anytime now.

He pushed ahead, trying to ignore the nauseous feeling in his stomach. The stew he'd eaten at the jail had been good, but after days of nothing, he'd had too much of it. He could easily vomit it all up, though he wouldn't if he could help it. It might be tomorrow before he ate again. If he didn't get a cowboy job, it could be a lot longer than that.

At last, he heard the bawling of cattle. He climbed on top of a low knoll and found himself gazing at hundreds and hundreds of longhorns. Several riders circled the herd slowly. He was too far away to tell if Senor Valarde was among them.

George pulled out the straight pin holding his head bandage together and carefully removed the narrow strip of cloth. He touched the lump on his skull. It was large and it throbbed. It would be better to leave the wound covered, but if he was going to have any chance of getting a job, the trail boss must not know he was hurt.

With the bandage rolled up and stuffed in his pocket, he began to cross the open prairie, hoping he would find Senor Valarde. Their acquaintance might make a difference as to whether or not he'd be hired. Besides that, he really wanted to see him.

As he drew closer to the herd, one of the cowhands loped his horse toward him. The rider's white face was smooth and young beneath his wide-brimmed tan hat. He didn't look more than sixteen or so, about George's age.

The cowboy folded his hands over the saddle horn and spoke in a drawl. "You got business here, boy, or are you just passin' through?" His expression was stiff, and his eyes squinted, even though they were shaded from the sun by his hat. George stared up at him and answered slowly.

"Name's George, not 'boy.'"

"I'm Charley Tate, boy, and your name is whatever I say it is."

It was all George could do to control his temper and let the remark pass. "A friend of mine, Senor Valarde, told me he might be here. Do you know him?"

Charley seemed to consider the request. At last he spoke.

"He's here, all right. You just stay where you are. I don't want you walking around spooking the cattle."

The cowhand put his bay horse into a canter. George kept his eyes fastened on him as he rode off. Maybe he had been wrong about the black cowboys he had seen going past Rogers Prairie.

Soon Senor Valarde rode up on a small mouse-colored horse, and swung down from the saddle. He was so glad to see George that he threw his arms around him. The movement hurt George's side, but he didn't let it show.

At last Senor Valarde stepped back. "How's your mama and papa? Do they know where you are?"

"They're both fine. They made me come. We had some trouble after you left."

Sorrow showed in Senor Valarde's eyes. "I will take you to see the *ganadero*. I will speak for you, but I think he has already hired everyone he needs."

Valarde mounted his horse, and as George climbed up behind him, his side throbbed and the back of his head pounded. The gray horse jumped into a trot. Soon they came to a chuck wagon parked near the only shade tree on the far side of the herd. A canvas awning was attached to it, held up by two poles.

From beneath the awning stepped one of the tallest men George had ever seen, and probably the skinniest. He was somewhere near fifty years of age, with straw-colored hair and a drooping chestnut-colored mustache.

"You have some kind of problem, Valarde?"

"No, senor. No problem."

The vaquero motioned for the tall man to step back under the awning with him. George could see them talking, could see the tall man shaking his head, but he couldn't hear anything. Shortly they both walked back to George.

"I'm Jack Hayden," the trail boss said. "I understand you're looking for a job."

"Yes, sir. I work hard and I can do most anything. I can ride good and rope a little and"—George stumbled over the words—"and I can shoe horses about as good as anybody."

Hayden lowered his eyes, and George was certain the man was staring at his bare feet.

"I know I need boots, and a hat, too," George said. "As soon as I can earn some money, I'll buy them."

The trail boss shook his head. "How you dress is your business. Valarde told me you've come a long way to get here. To tell you the truth, I don't need you. But I need Valarde; and he says if I don't take you on, he will quit. So I'll try you out and give you a job helping the cook, keeping the remuda shod, and doing anything else I ask you to. Pay won't be much, but at least you'll have plenty to eat."

George felt his chest tighten up. He had hoped for the chance to become a cowboy. This job, though, was better than no job. And he didn't want Senor Valarde to quit because of him.

An unsteady feeling came over him, and he could no longer hold down the stew he'd eaten. He turned and ran a few steps from the men, and it all came

out. With each heave, his side ached and his head felt like it would split. Then, when his belly was finally empty, came the dry heaves.

At last he stood upright. Hayden held out a canteen. George couldn't even look at the man.

The trail boss uncorked the canteen and put it in George's hands. "What's wrong with you, boy? How long you been sick?"

George rinsed his mouth out and washed his face. "I'm not sick. Just ate too much in town, I guess." He handed the canteen back. "Thanks for the job, Mr. Hayden."

"Like I said, you can thank Valarde." Hayden turned and walked away.

SEVEN

S ENOR VALARDE held out a cup of something that
smelled like rotten eggs and vinegar mixed with
a half can of pepper. "Drink this. It will help you."

George made himself finish it in three gulps,
even though it tasted as bad as it smelled. He wiped
his mouth and looked at Valarde. "Mr. Hayden didn't
change his mind about me, did he?"

"No, but he wants for you to feel better before
you start working. Tell me what happened, George.
Who hit you on the head?"

George leaned his back against the tree trunk. He
spoke about the Indians and waking up in jail, and
about the sheriff.

He had no more than finished his story when a
rider burst into camp, shouting, "Mount up, waddies.
The remuda's gone and the wrangler is so drunk he
doesn't know the North Star from the moon."

Hayden rushed to the campfire. "You all heard Will. The bunch of you, saddle your night horses and let's get moving."

Valarde patted George on the shoulder. "I must go to help find the *caballos*. You rest. When I return, I will bring you something to eat."

George waited until the vaquero was out of sight, then used the tree to steady himself while he got to his feet. He did feel a bit light-headed, but just for a moment.

The remuda was the name for the horse herd the cowboys used for their mounts while trailing the longhorns. Without it, the cattle drive couldn't be made. He wanted to help look for the horses, but on foot, there was not much he could do.

He listened to the fading sound of hoofbeats as the riders rode quickly from camp. He walked to the empty campfire area, where he sat down on a log. Except for the low crackle of the fire and the occasional far-off howl of a lone coyote, the night was quiet.

His old life, the only one he had ever known, was gone. Riding with a herd of cattle had long been his dream. It would be the greatest thing that could ever happen to him. He had believed it with all his heart. But now, oddly, he felt let down and alone.

What was he doing here? he wondered.

Footsteps shuffled up behind him, and he turned to see a heavily wrinkled older man wearing a dirty white apron and holding out a plate of beans.

"It's plain that you're feeling better. When I saw you sitting over here by your lonesome, I figured you

just as well be doing something, like eating. You get any scrawnier and you'll have to put a post or two inside your overalls just to keep them up."

George managed a smile and took the plate. "Thanks."

"I'm Sandy Crebbs," the old man said, "and I'm the real boss of this outfit. Hayden thinks he is, but he's not. If it weren't for me, nobody would get anything to eat. Cattle wouldn't be taken nowhere at all. The hands would all up and quit. And then we'd see how Mr. Cock-a-doodle-doo aims to get his longhorns to the shipping yards at Abilene."

George nodded. "I guess everybody has to eat."

"Exactly." The cook shoved his sweat-stained gray hat farther back on his head. "You're one of the few that's smart enough to see the point of what I'm talking about. Why, if it weren't for me, everybody here would just up and die."

George sat back down and took a bite of hard crusty bread. "It sure is good."

"Well," Sandy said, "you just enjoy it, and be sure and remember where those vittles came from."

The cook turned and walked back toward the chuck wagon, continuing to talk as if someone else were alongside him.

George ate some more of the bread. He decided he liked Sandy. His skin color didn't seem to matter to the cook at all. He picked at the beans, but his stomach still wasn't ready to hold much. He stood up as Senor Valarde rode into the camp, leading a sorrel.

George went straight to him. "Is this the only horse you found?"

"No. This *caballo*, he came close to me, so I lassoed him. The other *caballos* are on the road to Comanche. They are grazing quietly. When someone comes to ride with me, we will go and bring them."

"I'll go with you."

The vaquero shook his head. "It is better for you to rest. Someone will come soon."

"I'm well enough. I know I am."

Senor Valarde shrugged and dismounted. Using his reata, he quickly fashioned a makeshift bridle for the sorrel and helped George swing up onto the horse's back.

IT WAS ALMOST midnight when they returned to camp, bringing in the remuda. They left the horses to graze near the herd, where the night punchers could keep an eye on them. George's side ached and his head had started pounding again. But he was glad he'd gone and had managed to be of some help.

Senor Valarde and George stepped off their horses. Jack Hayden approached from the campfire.

"George," Hayden said, "I've been thinking about you. You have sand, son. Hurt like you are, you still rode with Valarde and brought in the horses. I just got through firing my wrango for being drunk. I'll give you a crack at the job, if you want it. Pay's twenty-five dollars a month, and you'll have to help the cook with firewood and anything else he needs.

"Most important is the remuda. A cow outfit's no better than its horses. The remuda must be kept in good condition and ready to use at all times. You

don't handle the job and I'll cut you loose wherever we are to find your way home."

The trail boss stroked one side of his long mustache. "Well, you up for the job or not?"

Wrango. Twenty-five dollars a month. That seemed like more money than there was in the whole world. He was so excited he could hardly speak.

Hayden waved a hand. "Right now I want you to get some sleep. Startin' tomorrow, you're gonna need it."

EIGHT

SENOR VALARDE was teaching him about the horses. The man gestured at a small brown horse grazing on the right side of the remuda. "Look at that *caballo*, George. Even his mane and tail are brown. He always stays to the outside. Now, see that one?" The vaquero pointed toward the middle of the remuda.

There were eighty horses in the remuda and George had no idea which horse Valarde was talking about.

"That *caballo* is a little bit taller than the other one, and he is also brown. His mane is brown; but see his tail? It is darker. There is a black mark on his left hind foot. Because the other horses are in the way, we cannot see it; but it is there. That is how you have to know these horses. They look the same but they are different. They act differently. They think

differently. You must watch them and know them like you know yourself."

The task seemed impossible. There were too many horses. Besides knowing the way each one looked, he had to learn their names and in which of the cowboy's strings each horse belonged.

Valarde placed a hand on George's shoulder. "You watch them. You will learn them. If I were in the middle of one hundred other Mexican vaqueros, you would know me, wouldn't you? You will know each of the *caballos* in just that way."

The noon dinner triangle rang, and Valarde and George started toward the chuck wagon. The trail drive was supposed to begin the next morning, and Hayden had asked George to get with Sandy Crebbs sometime in the afternoon to find out what chores the cook expected him to perform during the drive.

A few cowhands were already at the wagon waiting their turn to have their plates filled. The short, stocky rider named Will, who had brought the news of the lost remuda the night before, winked at him. A smile tugged at the corners of his leathery face.

"I guess in a roundabout way, you sort of owe me, son."

George looked confused and Will continued.

"If I hadn't've told the boss about them missing horses last night, you wouldn't have the wrango job."

"I guess that's true enough." George took one of the plates.

"Well, all I'm sayin' is that you prob'ly want to repay me somehow, don't you?"

George shrugged. "I guess so. What did you have in mind?"

Senor Valarde motioned for George to get ahead of him in line. "Do not pay attention to that one, George. It is his job to report about the horses. Will is known for his joking. Two days ago he put a bull snake in the cook's stew pot."

"You shoulda seen that old man hop." Will slapped his knee. "That was one of my better ones."

Someone tapped George on the shoulder, and when he turned, he saw Charley Tate, glaring.

Charley stood a head taller than George, and his shoulders were wider. He folded his arms across his chest and spoke in a brittle voice. "You know better than to be up here, boy. You get on back to the end of the line, where you belong."

George could not believe what he heard. Then he wondered how he could have been so stupid. Stupid enough to think that being a cowboy on a cattle drive would somehow mean the color of his skin wouldn't matter anymore.

Senor Valarde stepped between them. "If you have something to say, Senor Tate, I think you will need to say it to me."

Charley sneered. "Figures. He's too ignorant to speak for himself."

George put a hand on Valarde's arm, staring coldly into Charley's eyes. Things were going to be different here. They *had* to be.

"I like it where I'm at," George said flatly.

Then Charley shoved him.

George's back hit the side of the wagon. He ignored the stab of pain and lunged forward, wrapping his arms around Charley's waist and carrying him several yards before forcing him to the ground with the weight of his own body.

George was no fighter. He had never been in a real fight in his life. But what he lacked in size and experience, he made up for in strength and determination. When Charley grabbed his arms, George twisted them away, reaching for the cowboy's neck.

Charley threw two short quick punches. The blows rocked George's head back, but he still held his hands on Charley's throat.

The cowhands were gathered around now, yelling and whooping. George heard none of it but just kept his hands around Charley's throat.

Charley gasped and kicked.

"It is enough, George." Senor Valarde grabbed one of George's arms, and Jack Hayden took the other, forcing him off of Charley.

Before him on the ground, Charley lay gulping air.

The cowhand made it to his knees. He gasped out his words. "I'll get you for this. I swear it."

NINE

DARK CLOUDS blocked the setting sun, and on occasion, the low rumble of thunder crossed the prairie.

It had been over a week since his fight with Charley. The tension in camp was always thick when he rode in with the horses. The cowhands nodded, but no one except Valarde, Will, or the cook actually spoke to him. Charley watched him carefully through narrowed eyes but, so far, had left him alone.

After the fight, Mr. Hayden had chewed them both out and warned them to stay away from each other if they couldn't learn to get along. George was glad, though, that most of what the boss had said was directed at Charley.

Hayden had told Charley that George had the same rights as anybody else in the outfit and that if he had a problem with that, he could get his war bag and move on. Charley didn't argue, but George was

wary of what he might do. Charley's pride had been injured, and sooner or later he was bound to try to make good on his threat.

George urged his small flea-bitten black horse into a lope. The horse the trail boss had assigned him was the ugliest one in the remuda, had the roughest gait, and was the clumsiest. Not one of the nine cowboys with the herd had chosen him for his string. Yet, in the week that had passed since they'd left Comanche, he had grown fond of the gelding. The horse had a big heart; and shown a little kindness and a light touch on the reins, he'd try his best to do whatever he was asked.

The eighty horses in the remuda veered away from George, moving in the direction of the chuck wagon. The horses knew that the wagon was their destination. At about this time every day, George took the remuda in for the cowhands to pick out their night horses. But the thunder and the scent of the coming rain had made the horses unusually restless.

George slowed his small black horse, returning to the rear of the remuda. He patted the horse's neck. "It's near supper time, Beggar. Maybe if Mr. Crebbs ain't lookin' too close, I'll be able to sneak you a biscuit."

The horse had an appetite for biscuits. After the first day on the trail, when George had given the horse a biscuit from his breakfast, he had always wanted more of them. He learned to smell the biscuits while they were cooking, and when he wasn't being ridden, he nosed around camp, getting in everybody's way, looking for a handout. So he had

earned the name Beggar. Sandy had threatened to put a dent the size of a frying pan in the horse's head if he didn't start staying away from the chuck wagon.

A cool breeze blew up, and George looked out at the approaching storm, seeing an occasional streak of lightning. He reached behind the cantle of the worn saddle the trail boss had loaned him and touched his yellow slicker to make sure it was still tied there.

He was glad to have it. It was the first one he'd ever owned. But he was even happier to have the lace-up boots on his feet, the felt hat on his head, and the bone-handled jackknife in his pocket.

Hayden was responsible for all of it. The evening before the herd left Comanche, the trail boss had given George a month's wages in advance and sent him and Senor Valarde into town to buy the things George would need for the trip.

Besides the boots, hat, knife, and slicker, he had bought a used bedroll and reata, a new pair of long underwear, a red bandanna, two pairs of wool socks, a pair of pants, a belt, and a corduroy shirt. He still had nearly three dollars in his pocket, which, up until he had received the advance, was more money than he'd seen at one time in his life.

Buying the boots had brought George the most pleasure, but wearing them was a different story. The boots were awkward and heavy, and they gave him blisters. It wasn't until the herd had crossed the Brazos River at Waco and the boots got wet that the leather shrank and they began to fit better.

George tiredly shifted his weight in the saddle, watching the remuda trot ahead of him. The work

was hard and the days long, but he felt fine now, and his side and back only ached from occasional sudden movements. His biggest problem since the trail drive had started was getting enough sleep.

Every morning the cook woke him well before dawn. His first chore was to gather and bring in the remuda. He had to have the remuda at camp by first daylight so the hands could pick out their morning horses. After that, he'd take the remuda back out to graze while he returned to eat breakfast, wash dishes, and help Sandy load the bedrolls and camp equipment into the wagon, then hitch up the team of mules before they all rode out.

The rest of the morning, George stayed with the remuda, letting the horses graze ahead of the herd. At noon he again drove the remuda into camp for the cowboys to choose fresh mounts. If water was nearby, he would carry it a pail at a time until the water barrel on the wagon was full, and he was in charge of keeping the rawhide cooney beneath the wagon full of wood or cow chips.

Afternoons were spent herding the horses along, much as he did in the mornings, then taking them into camp at dusk, as he was doing now.

It was the nighttime hours that had been giving him trouble. Worrying that if the horses were left unattended they would stray, he stayed out with the remuda until late, not getting more than two or three hours of sleep a night.

Senor Valarde had cautioned him about worrying so much, and even Mr. Hayden had told him he needed to start getting more rest.

Thunder clapped in the distance. The breeze stiffened, and in it was a sprinkling of rain. Using one hand and then the other to hold the reins, George managed to untie his slicker from the saddle and slip it on. Ahead, near the chuck wagon, Hayden and some of the hands, Axe, Juan, and Moss, were stretching out a single rope to form a temporary holding corral for the remuda. Another cowboy stepped up to help.

Charley Tate.

George kept Beggar back, watching the horses, trying to ignore Charley. The tall boy whispered something to Moss. They both laughed, and then Charley folded his arms and stared boldly at George.

George ignored him. The horses were skittish. If too many cowboys began swinging a lariat, it would unnecessarily excite them and could cause them to break out. Only one hand, Senor Valarde, was allowed to catch the horses. His skills were uncanny.

Valarde acted almost disinterested as he circled and mingled among the horses, effortlessly sending the loop of his reata around the neck of any mount the cowhands called for.

The rain began falling faster now, and George pulled the front of his hat down and raised the collar of his slicker. In moments the last horse needed was lassoed and the rope forming the corral was coiled up at both ends.

Jack Hayden called out his orders in a loud clear voice. "Supper will have to wait, boys. Everybody except the cook and wrango stays with the herd until

the weather clears. Don't crowd the cattle. Give them all the room they'll take. Sing to them. I doubt if we can get them to bed down on this wet ground, but we'll try."

Charley Tate brushed by Beggar, pushing a little too hard against the stirrup and George's foot.

George turned the horse around and was about to follow the remuda out of camp when Beggar lunged forward and then shot straight up in the air. George tightened his hold on the reins and readied for the next jump.

Beggar crow-hopped sideways and then stood in place, his whole body shivering. George stepped down and examined his rig. "What's the matter, fellow? What's gotten into you all of a sudden?"

He felt under the back of the saddle. A burr the size of his thumb fell out. George glanced around. Charley was gone, but George knew he was to blame. There was no time to do anything about it now. Hayden had given orders.

The horses in the remuda left camp of their own accord, moving at a trot across the prairie toward an oak-timbered ridge. Instinct told them that the thick stand of trees would provide shelter against the storm, but George couldn't allow them to go there.

He stepped up on Beggar and pulled him around, and with a hiss and the heels of his boots, put him into a gallop so he could get ahead of the remuda and turn it. In the woods, the horses could face danger from wolves, panthers, and bears. Besides, among the trees they could also easily stray without

George's being able to see where they were. Senor Valarde had instructed him to keep the horses out in the open if there was any way to do it.

By the time George had turned the remuda and brought the horses to a standstill, the rain was coming down in torrents. The horses huddled together with their rumps to the wind. What little dusk light there had been was now gone.

Out of the blackness a blinding flash of zigzag lightning forked down, turning the ground around them white. Beggar jumped and George pulled the reins tight and ducked his head, covering his eyes with his forearm.

Thunder crashed, reverberating and doubling and seeming to shake the whole earth.

The air smelled of burning sulphur. A dull phosphorescent light appeared as dancing balls of fire on the horses' ears. Fox fire. He knew because he'd heard a couple of the cowhands talking about it during supper one evening. They had said that fox fire sometimes also appeared on the horns of cattle during a lightning storm.

George stared into the black distance, and what he saw made his jaw drop. Out there were thousands of tiny fireballs eerily skipping and racing about on what had to be the horns of the cattle.

Suddenly the rain and wind stopped. The air grew warm and thick and difficult to breathe. George's skin tingled, and he noticed the fox fire on the cattle and horses glowed brighter.

All at once several streaks of lightning shot down, lighting up the prairie. George could plainly see the

cattle, the chuck wagon, and even a few of the cowboys.

Then there was a deafening clap of thunder, splitting and crashing and shaking everything in its wake. The heavens opened and rain and hail began falling so hard and fast they stung George's shoulders right through his slicker.

He bent forward, trying to protect his bare hands with his body. Beggar danced back and forth, and George yanked the reins, pulling the horse's head up to stop him.

Another sound came. It was like thunder but lower in tone, and it seemed to be coming from the ground instead of the sky. The mighty rumble was mixed with loud clacking noises.

George turned in the saddle to look in the direction of the herd. The night blackness had returned, and all he could see were thousands of dim fiery lights moving swiftly to the north. There could be just one reason for the sea of rushing fox fire. The cattle had stampeded. Their long horns clacked as they slammed together.

The neigh of a horse and Beggar's excited answer drew George's attention back to the remuda. He couldn't see the horses, but the fox fire on their ears told him where they were. They, like the cattle, had bolted from the blast of chain lightning and were running.

He gave Beggar slack in the reins, and the horse broke into a hard gallop after the remuda. More lightning flashed. Rain and hail pelted George's face and hands.

He clenched his teeth. Not only was there the danger of being struck by lightning but Beggar could easily stumble or step into a prairie-dog hole. At the breakneck speed the horse was going, George knew he'd be thrown from the saddle.

For a moment he considered reining the horse to a safer speed, a lope or a trot, but he couldn't bring himself to do it. Every cowboy in the outfit was no doubt riding as fast as he could to catch up with the herd. They all faced the same dangers he did. A sobering thought came to him. The success of the trail drive could very well depend on what he did.

He leaned forward in the saddle, tucking his chin against his chest so that his hat brim would catch more of the rain. He dug his heels into Beggar's sides and hissed, urging the horse to move faster.

Beggar veered sharply to the left, stumbled but didn't go down, then just as quickly straightened out again.

At last the night grew quiet. The storm blew over as quickly as it had come, and he reined Beggar to a stop. He peered into the darkness but could see nothing.

He patted the horse's rain- and sweat-soaked neck. An owl hooted, the sound echoing in the stillness. Staying in the saddle, George listened intently, trying to catch any noise that would tell him where the remuda was. The last time he'd seen the fox fire at their ears, he was riding right behind them. But now, with the passing of the storm, the fiery lights were gone.

Beggar raised his head and whinnied. A horse answered, and George was surprised by how close it was. He walked Beggar slowly toward the sound, not wanting to frighten the horses if they were grazing.

He saw the form of one horse and then the vague outline of others. He continued on until he was sure there were enough to give the cowboys new mounts. Then he swung down to stretch and give Beggar a rest.

He leaned his head back and looked up at the sky, trying to find the Big Dipper. Since nobody in the outfit had a watch, all the cowboys used the turning of the Dipper to tell time at night. Senor Valarde had made a point of teaching him how to do it, too.

But tonight no stars were visible anywhere.

TEN

THE LATE MORNING sun beat down. Mr. Hayden walked past George and stopped at the head of the freshly dug grave. His eyes searched the faces of the cowboys gathered around.

"Boys," he said, "I'm no preacher and we can't hold much of a church service out here, but I want you to know this. Moss was as good a man as I ever rode with. He was honest, dependable, and it wasn't in him to shrink back from any task that lay ahead.

"Last night he rode in front of the herd and turned the cattle just before they hit the banks of the Red River. His horse stumbled, and the move cost Moss his life. But if he hadn't done it, we'd have lost half the herd, and maybe all of it. Moss died right. He went out the way I want to go when my number is drawn. May the good Lord give rest to his soul."

George hadn't known Moss all that well. The young cowboy was one of Charley Tate's friends and

had kept his distance. But George knew that if things had gone differently, it might have been *his* mangled body Will had found this morning.

The cowhands put their hats back on. They were reluctant to leave the grave, but slowly, one by one, they left to return to their work.

Charley Tate was the last to go. He closed his eyes, looked up at the sky, and then walked back to his horse without a word.

Hayden rode up beside George. "We're goin' to cross the Red today, George," the boss said. "I know you're worn out. We all are, and so are the cattle. They're dry and thirsty, and this afternoon while the sun is at their backs is a good time to swim them. It will be big swimming. The river is flowing over the willows, and we can't wait for the water to go down. If it rains tonight, the flooding will be so heavy we might not get the cattle across for another week.

"I want you to take the horses across in front of the herd just like you did on the Brazos. Except this will be different. You be careful. The Brazos didn't have half the water we're fixing to cross. The river is swift, and there'll be suck holes and undercurrents. If you get into trouble, slide out of your saddle and hold on to the saddle horn, or your horse's mane or tail, and don't turn loose for anything."

George could tell that the trail boss really was concerned. He nodded. "I'll be careful."

IT WAS MIDAFTERNOON before the herd of longhorns was allowed near the river and crowded into position for the crossing. Because of their thirst, holding the

cattle and keeping them in a compact bunch had been difficult. Several times George had left the grazing remuda and helped, finding that the busier he kept, the less time he spent thinking about what had happened to Moss.

At last the remuda was in place in front of the herd. Like the cowboys, George had stripped to his long underwear, tying his clothes behind the cantle of the saddle and leaving his hat in the chuck wagon. The trail boss waved to signal that all was ready and it was time for him to start the horses across.

"*Yaah,*" George yelled, slapping the coiled reata against his knee and causing Beggar to move forward.

The lead horses balked at the river's edge. George focused his attention on a blaze-faced red roan named Chief. The horse had been the first to take the water on the Brazos, and George believed if he could push him a little, he might be the first to jump into the water here.

Riding slowly through the horses, George managed to get within a few feet of the roan. He hissed and raised the coiled reata, shaking it. Chief pushed past the other horses and reached the water's edge. George crowded Beggar closer, and the roan pawed nervously at the wet, sandy riverbank. Chief reared, fighting the air with his front feet, and then he plunged in.

George whipped Beggar around and galloped behind the remuda. He yelled and raced Beggar back and forth, driving the band of horses into the river after Chief. Soon all of the horses were swimming, their heads held high.

At last it was George's turn to start across, but he stopped Beggar on the bank, watching the muddy, rushing flow. It was much easier to put the remuda into the river than it was to make himself go in.

He heard whistles and looked behind to see that the cattle were coming. They were being squeezed into a narrow column by the cowboys on each side.

There was no more time to hesitate. George gave Beggar slack in the reins and kicked his sides. The horse lowered his head and danced sideways a few steps, then snorted and leaped into the air as if he were trying to cross the whole river in a single jump.

The splash was loud. Water sprayed everywhere. George was soaked, and he felt the tug of the current against his legs and feet.

Beggar floundered, and for a moment George thought he would surely go down. But the animal kept his nose just above the surface, and soon his body leveled out and his head emerged.

He gave the horse more rein. Reins were useless when a horse was swimming, and Senor Valarde had told him that pulling on them could cause a horse to drown. If a direction had to be changed, it could only be done by splashing water on one side or the other of the horse's face.

The remuda ahead was doing fine. George could see that Chief was still in the lead, and it wouldn't be long before the horse reached the far side. He glanced behind. A dozen or more steers were in the water, their high horns looking like floating rocking chairs.

George relaxed a little. Though the river was

threatening, the cool water felt refreshing and Beggar wasn't having any more trouble swimming.

The cowboys called out encouragement to the cattle. They whistled in low calm tones and urged them forward. Riders entered the river, staying on the downstream side of the herd to keep the cattle from drifting with the current. It was a pretty sight, George thought, and everything was going smoothly, just as it had on the Brazos.

Chief reached solid ground and scrambled up the far bank. In minutes all of the horses were safely across, and the odd feeling of riding on air rushed away as Beggar's front feet touched ground. When he reached the crest of the riverbank, George saw that the remuda hadn't traveled far before stopping to graze. He turned Beggar back around to watch the cattle coming across.

Now there were hundreds of floating rocking chairs in the river. The lead steers were a little more than halfway across and swimming straight. It looked as if crossing the Red wasn't going to be much trouble at all.

Then something upstream caught his eye. He stared as it floated closer. It was a partially submerged tree with a trunk the size of a horse.

"Look out!" he yelled, pointing at the tree. But the cowboys in the river were busy with their work and didn't see or hear him. Maybe it really didn't matter. There wasn't a thing any of them could do about it.

The tree drew closer. Some of the cattle saw it

and veered sharply downstream. One of the cowboys was in their path.

Will. The mounted cowboy was frantically waving a coiled lariat and yelling in an effort to turn the cattle back. It was no use. The steers didn't find Will nearly as frightening as they did the tree. They passed by him so close he could have reached out and touched them.

More and more of the cattle turned downstream, until there was a solid wall of brown hides and ivory horns all heading in the wrong direction. The cowboys were helpless to stop them.

Now the tree was gliding straight toward Will. The cowboy slid from his saddle on the down-flow side. George couldn't see him anymore but guessed that he was holding on to his horse's mane.

Just before the massive tangle of tree branches was about to crash into Will's horse, the animal panicked and began to struggle. The horse lunged up in the water, turned sideways, and then went under.

The tree floated past and the water's surface was unbroken. There was no sign of Will or the horse.

George jumped Beggar back into the river. It would take a long time to reach the spot. *Too long.* But he had to try.

"No, Charley!" someone yelled from up the river. "Keep out of the middle of 'em."

George looked to his left and saw that fifty or more cattle had locked themselves into a spiral, circling into each other in an ever-tightening corkscrew. Standing on top of one of the steer's backs was

Charley Tate. He held on to its horns to balance himself while trying to reach down and break apart the tangled, frightened animals.

"Get out, Charley!" a voice boomed. The trail boss swung a rope and swam his horse near the edge of the milling cattle.

George looked back to the spot where he had last seen Will. It was now covered by the horns and heads of cattle. Everything had happened so fast. He'd never get to Will now.

He splashed water on the side of Beggar's head and turned him toward the bank. The horse had no more than straightened out again when Hayden shouted at him.

"Catch him, George! Catch him."

He jerked his head around. Hayden was near the milling cattle, waving his hat. But Charley Tate was no longer on top of the longhorns. He was thrashing about in the river, trying desperately to swim as the current rushed around him.

There was little time. George took the coiled reata from his saddle horn and shook out a loop. Then the thought came. *Why should I help him?*

He shook his head. He had to at least try.

Beggar was facing the wrong way for the throw, but in the water, there was no way to quickly turn him. Instead, George pivoted himself around in the saddle so he was facing the horse's backside.

The river had drawn Charley closer but not close enough. Senor Valarde had spent many hours teaching George to rope. *The loop, it is a rock. Throw it past your ear like you would throw a rock.*

George whirled the lasso just as Charley's head went under the water. He swung the loop faster and faster. One of Charley's arms lashed up and George threw the rope. Water splashed and George felt a heavy tug.

He had him.

Quickly the weight strained against his muscles and became almost too great to hold. He twisted around in the saddle and slipped the dally loop over the saddle horn.

Then Beggar began to struggle. The pull of Charley coupled with the burden of George was too much.

George shot a glance toward the riverbank. It wasn't far. Behind him Charley was now holding the reata with both hands, and his head was above the water.

George pushed on the saddle swells and stood so that his feet were in the saddle seat. Then he dived into the water.

The river current grabbed him. He closed his eyes, directing all the energy he could muster into his arms and legs. At the surface he took a breath, then turned his head for another and instead took in a mouthful of water.

He pushed his arms and legs faster and faster. His lungs felt like they might explode and he knew his strength would not hold for long.

At last his cupped hands caught mud. His knees found it, too, and he crawled onto the riverbank. He opened his eyes and then closed them again, panting, fighting for enough air.

Beggar stepped briskly past him, stopped, and shook himself. The reata was still attached to the saddle horn, and at its other end, Charley Tate was lying on the ground, removing the lasso from his wrist.

Charley turned his head and coughed. Water spewed from his mouth, and he coughed again and again. When his breathing eased, his eyes narrowed and he looked at George. For a long while the two stared at each other.

George pushed himself to a sitting position and deliberately shifted his attention to the river. The cattle mill had broken up, and the group of steers now in the water was crossing in a straight, uniform line.

Hayden rode toward them along the bank. George started to rise to his feet.

"Keep your seat, George," Hayden said. "If anybody ever deserved a rest, it would be you." The boss nodded at Charley. "You all right?"

"I'm fine." Charley rubbed at the rope burn on his wrist.

The boss swiped at a mosquito on his ear. "I want the both of you to stay here and rest awhile. The cattle are movin' smooth now. We lost some, maybe more downriver, but I don't think it'll be too bad. We'll be stayin' here a couple of days, ridin' the riverbanks, roundin' up strays. Tomorrow we'll build a raft and float the chuck wagon across."

The trail boss started to turn his mount, but George stopped him.

"Mr. Hayden." George pulled himself to his feet. "It's about Will. I saw him—saw him and his horse go down in the river. They never came back up again."

The creases in Hayden's face grew deep and his lips tightened to a thin line. He stared past George and Charley, downriver to the west. Then he spurred his horse into a lope, calling over his shoulder. "When the cattle are across, we'll ride the riverbanks looking for him."

George leaned against Beggar and coiled his reata.

Charley crawled to his knees, still shaky. He stared up at George. "Why'd you pull me out?"

George looked down and met the cold blue eyes. "I don't know. I really don't. I guess because the boss ordered me to."

Charley coughed till his face began to turn red. Finally he spoke. "You coulda missed."

"Could have. But I didn't." George hooked his reata over the saddle horn. He took Beggar's reins and started toward the remuda.

Behind him he could hear Charley's choking cough.

ELEVEN

F OR THE THIRD time in as many days, Will was
telling the story of his escape from death in the
river.

"Let me tell you fellows how it was. There I was
a-swimming my horse in the middle of that old river,
as pretty as you please, when I saw this big tree
coming along, heading straight for me. Well, those
horned floating steaks saw it, too, and they com-
menced to turning with the current and swimming
right on past me like I wasn't even there. I was
a-swinging my rope and hollering, and doing everything I could think of to turn them back, and all the
time that big old tree just kept right on coming."

George fingered the edges of his mother's Bible
and grinned at Senor Valarde, who was seated on the
other side of the campfire. The last time, Will had
told how Hayden had found him wrapped around a
willow tree near the bank, holding a turtle that had

its teeth clamped solid to one of his fingers. He wondered what ending the old cowhand would put on the story this time.

"We've already heard all about it," Axe complained, his dark mustache drooping. The middle-aged puncher stood, shaking his headful of long, wavy black hair and throwing the coffee grounds from his tin cup into the fire.

"Don't any of you have a new story to tell tonight?" he asked. "Or are your lives so dad-blamed boring that you haven't ever seen or done anything except fall off your horse into a river, or trail along behind some old poor cow?"

Will lay back on the bare ground, cupping the back of his head in his hands. "Well, if you got something more excitin', Axe, you just go ahead and tell us. 'Course it'd have to be something more entertaining than me fighting three miles of river water, dang near drowning, and then having my hand nearly ate off by some hard-shelled varmint."

"All right then, I'll do just that." Axe shoved his thumbs into his front pockets. "You all know that I wasn't always a saddle tramp working for a two-bit cow outfit. Why, I once was my own boss, delivering a herd of horses clear to Nebraska. It was a cold, stormy night, and rather than sleep out in the open, I stopped by one of the soddys and asked if I could stay until morning. That settler welcomed me straight off and fed my horse. Then he took me inside to meet his wife and five younguns.

"That house was neat as a pin. But they only had one bed. It was disappointin', but I was prepared to

find me a spot somewhere on the dirt floor when it came time for sleepin'.

"After talking awhile, the three youngest went to sleep on the bed. The woman then carried those little ones to a corner and laid 'em on a blanket. Next, the two oldest kids got on the bed, and as soon as they were asleep, she did the same thing with them."

Axe stopped talking and looked his audience over as if he was making sure he had everyone's attention before continuing on.

"Well finally," he said, "after talking to them folks a while longer, they insisted that I get up on the bed while they slept with the kids. Being the gentleman I am, of course I was against such an arrangement, but they wouldn't hear of nothing else. So I lay down on that fine bed and went right to sleep.

"The next morning, I'll be dogged if I wasn't lying in the corner with them kids, and that man and his wife were lying on that soft bed. Before I left I handed them five dollars. They didn't want but fifty cents, but I told them that any woman who could take me off a bed as if I was a child and put me on the floor without waking me deserved that much and more, too, if I'd have had it."

"We've all heard that story a dozen times, too, Axe." Charley Tate stepped up to the fire. He noticed the Bible in George's lap. "You know how to read that book?"

George's chin came up. "No. But I aim to learn— someday."

Charley rubbed the back of his neck. "It so happens that I can cipher letters some."

George studied the boy's face, trying to see if this was another trick. Slowly he held out the Bible.

The young cowhand opened it and knelt beside the dim firelight. "In . . . in the be . . . beginning, God made the hea . . . vens and the earth."

He stopped and looked up. George nodded and Charley kept reading. George marveled at the words that tumbled out of Charley's mouth from the marks on the paper.

Charley stopped again and moved closer to George. "This here word says 'in.' It has two letters. See 'em? You call this one *i* and that one *n*. Put together, they make a word."

George ran his finger down the page. He stopped at every *i* and *n* and said them out loud.

Charley nodded. "I 'spect you'll be readin' before too long."

Sandy Crebbs stepped up and set a big iron pot in George's lap. "Before you get too almighty big for your britches learning how to read and all, you might try learning how to wash dishes. You went off and left that pot so greasy inside I could fill the hub of a wagon wheel with it.

"Now you go on and get it cleaned up, and when you're done, there's a stump for you to bust up into kindling for the morning's fire."

George set the pot on the ground beside him and took the Bible from Charley's outstretched hand. "Maybe you could show me later?"

Charley nodded. "I'll be around."

TWELVE

B Y THE LIGHT of a coal-oil lantern hanging on the wagon tongue, George used his jackknife to shave off a few slices from a bar of lye soap. Then, adding a little water to the soap he put in the pot, he began to scrub with a brush.

He tried to keep his mind on his work instead of on the letters in the Bible and the change in Charley—which he didn't fully trust. But if they could continue to get along, it would make things easier. Abilene was still a long ways off.

After cleaning and rinsing the pot, George found and chopped up the stump Sandy had told him about. To try to make the cook happy again, he then went to the chuck box at the rear of the wagon. He took the coffee grinder down from a shelf and started grinding coffee beans a handful at a time. He was nearly finished with a small sackful when he stopped for a moment. The camp was quiet.

Too quiet.

George looked toward the campfire. The trail hands were on their feet. In the dim fringe of the firelight stood three Indians wearing long breechcloths and buckskin leggings. They were naked from the waist up.

George left his work to get closer. Just close enough that he could tell what was going on.

He stopped a few paces behind the other cowhands and listened as Hayden spoke to the visitors in a voice that was unusually stern.

"Why are you here?"

One of the Indians wore a necklace made of seashells. He pointed at his chest with a bundle of small sticks in his hand. Then he pointed at the ground. "My land. You"—the Indian gestured at Hayden—"pay."

The Indian knelt, laying the sticks on the ground, spacing them carefully. When he was finished, he swept his hand over the sticks. "Many *wohaw.* You pay."

Hayden reached down and picked up all of the sticks except one. He pointed at it. "I will give you one *wohaw.* One cow. No more."

The Indian shook his head.

Hayden turned slightly, pitching the sticks into the fire. He held up a finger. "One."

Again the Indian shook his head. He held up his hands with palms out and all of his fingers extended. "Many *wohaw.* You pay."

"No," the trail boss answered, making some type of motion with his hands that George couldn't see.

The Indian and trail boss stood, still staring at each other. At last the Indian wheeled sharply on his heels and, with his two companions, disappeared into the night.

"Boss," Axe said, breaking the silence, "those are Comanche just as sure as I'm standing here. Lord help us if a big war party is with them and they're hid out there somewhere."

Senor Valarde shook his head. "They are not Comanche. They are too tall and there was no fringe on their leggings or moccasins. They are Kiowa or perhaps Wichita, but they are not Comanche."

"All right, boys," the trail boss said. "Listen up. The time for rest is over. Tonight these Indians may try and stampede the herd. I want every hand except the cook in the saddle and packing shooting irons. Charley, you stay with George and the remuda. If they come, they're sure to try to take the horses."

George started toward the picket line that had been set up just north of the chuck wagon, wondering why the boss had ordered him and Charley to work together. Maybe, he considered, Hayden had seen them by the fire and decided that the trouble between them was over.

Beggar snorted and smelled George's hand when he reached him. All of the cowboys' night horses were tied to the picket line, and although George had hated to do it, the last three nights he'd kept Beggar tied there, too, to keep him from nosing around camp and getting into trouble with the cook.

Another thing George had started doing differently since crossing the Red River was that now he

went to sleep at night. He had finally quit worrying about the remuda so much. He couldn't continue to go without sleep all the way to Abilene. And if the horses did run off like they had during the stampede, all he had to do was go find them again.

Charley reached the picket line as George was swinging a saddle onto Beggar.

"Can you shoot?" he asked.

"A rifle or shotgun, but I don't have one." George pulled the latigo strap snug and tied it off.

"It's probably just as well," Charley said, untying a bay horse from the picket line that was already bridled and saddled. "If there is a big Comanche war party out there, what few men and guns we have won't make much difference. I just wish Mr. Cock-a-doodle-doo would have given those Indians a few beeves and let it go at that. Depending on how many of them there are, he could wind up losing the whole herd and most of us with it."

George put his foot into a stirrup. The memory of the Indian sitting on him and holding a knife to his throat made a cold shiver travel up his spine.

Other cowboys were untying their horses. Charley rode past. "You coming?"

"Ah, yeah." George hoped the Indians he'd seen in camp didn't return tonight. And like Charley, he was wishing Hayden had tried harder to meet their demands.

THIRTEEN

Dawn broke with a fiery red eastern sky. Much to everyone's relief the night had passed without a hint of Indian trouble. The cowboys had eaten a quick breakfast of biscuits and salt pork and were already on their day horses and getting into position for the day's drive.

George gazed over at the line of cattle stretched across the prairie. The morning task of rousing the cattle and getting them ready to be moved always amazed him. No one needed to be told what to do. The two point riders took their positions at the head of the herd, the two swing riders rode about a third of the way back from them, and the two flank riders stayed near the rear. The unlucky cowboys behind the herd rode drag.

Of all the positions, drag was the most disagreeable. Unless a strong wind happened to be blowing in the same direction the herd was going, there was

no way to get out of the thick dust. And spending a day swinging a rope and prodding straggling cattle was hard, tiresome work.

To keep any one hand from having to ride drag too often, every cowboy except the point riders rotated positions daily. A swing rider who was on the right side of the herd today would be on the left side tomorrow. Then, for two days he'd ride flank before it was his turn to ride drag. After a couple of days of pushing weak and sore-footed cattle from the rear, he'd ride flank again, working his way back up toward the swing position.

The herd always looked like a huge mass of confusion, with steers going here and there after they'd left their bed ground in the morning and before they were squeezed and strung out by the cowboys into a long thin line. But most of them somehow wound up in the same positions they'd been in the last time the herd was moved. And the same brindle steer, with the widest set of horns George had ever seen on a longhorn, was always in the lead.

The trail hands were ready for the day's drive to begin and were awaiting the signal from Hayden. Charley, who had been with George and the remuda all night, was riding flank on the right side of the herd.

Now Hayden was loping his horse toward three Indians who were approaching the herd. Behind the braves were three women and a child, on horseback. One of the women held something in her arms. George thought it might be a baby.

Soon the trail boss rode back to the herd and,

with the help of Senor Valarde, roped a small steer and dragged it to the Indians. The three braves used their knives to slit the steer's throat, and the women were quickly off of their horses, slicing the carcass down the middle and cutting it into pieces. Hayden then signaled for the drive to begin by waving his hat in the direction the herd was to go, and he and Valarde loped their horses back to the herd.

"Look at them," said the cook. Sandy had stepped up beside George. "The Indians are so hungry they're eating that steer raw. Kind of pitiful, isn't it? And to think that some of these lazy bowlegged cowpunchers go to grumbling about the least little old thing. Why, they ought to have to starve awhile like those Indians and then they'd see how lucky they are to have me cookin' for them."

"Yes, sir," George said, keeping his eyes on the Indians. He was glad Hayden had given them the steer. It was plain that the Indians weren't much of a threat to anyone. He hadn't had to do it.

Sandy walked toward the wagon, talking as he went. "You going to sit there all day, George, or help me get this rolling cookshack moving? Don't just stand around like a lizard on a rock enjoying the sunshine."

George threw a glance toward the remuda. The horses were grazing quietly. He took the short spade in his hands and began shoving dirt onto the coals of the campfire. Sandy went right on talking.

GEORGE SWUNG his reata once over his head and released it. The loop settled neatly over a bluebonnet

blossom, and he yanked the slack. He'd been roping flowers all morning as he followed the remuda, and he was getting better and better.

He coiled the reata and placed it over the saddle horn. Senor Valarde had ridden with him for a while and told him he was getting almost as good as himself. George knew that wasn't true. But he was glad to hear him say it. It reminded him of old times back on the ranch.

He sighed, remembering an evening last summer when his family and Senor Valarde had gone fishing together. It was one of the few times in George's life that they'd had time to spend together when they weren't working. The day was warm, and he had dozed off under the shade of a tree. Heavy tugs on his cottonwood-branch pole woke him, and he scrambled to his feet shouting.

"I got one!" he'd called. "I got a big one."

The fish turned out to be the end of his father's line, which had been purposely tied to George's. His father had laughed and laughed, saying he was certain that it was a very smart turtle that had done it.

He thought about his father's crooked smile and his mother's gentle touch. A shadow came over the land, and George glanced up at the small cloud that covered the sun. It was close to noon, and Hayden, who was riding ahead of the cattle, would soon give the signal for the herd to stop. While the cattle grazed, the cowboys would eat their dinner.

Beggar stepped out on his own, wanting to keep up with the other horses. George sat back in the saddle, removed his feet from the stirrups, and

stretched his legs. As much as he loved to ride, twelve to fifteen hours a day of it was tiresome.

Farther along, a bright white object in the tall grass caught his eye. He swung off Beggar for a better look. He knelt to part the thick grass with his hand, and a human skull stared up at him. He took off his hat and started to wave it at the cowboys with the herd, then changed his mind. Whoever it was had been dead a long time.

Who could this have been? He wondered how the person had died. Why hadn't there been a burial? Maybe there had been, and coyotes or wolves had dug up the grave. But just the skull alone made no sense. Somewhere close by, there had to be a skeleton, or at least a few bones.

George walked slowly around the site, leading Beggar as he went. Beneath a small mesquite bush, he noticed something odd—a light-colored oval rock attached to a wooden handle by what appeared to be strips of rawhide. He reached for it. A buzzing noise came from the bush, and he jerked his hand back.

He saw the flash of the striking rattlesnake and felt the snake's fangs hit the palm of his hand.

He jumped backward into Beggar, scaring the horse and causing him to lunge sideways, almost ripping the reins from his hand.

The snake's rattle grew louder, angrier, and George scrambled to get farther away from it.

Already, a burning sensation shot through his hand, and he stopped, raising it close to his face. The two fang puncture-marks were clear, each showing a speck of blood.

Back in Rogers Prairie he'd heard about a girl who had died from a rattlesnake bite. And at church there was a man who had lost part of his leg because he'd been bitten on the ankle.

He swung on top of Beggar and put the horse into a hard gallop. By the time he reached the wagon and slid the horse to a stop, he was weak, short of breath, and starting to feel sick to his stomach.

Sandy, who stood at the rear of the chuck wagon busily preparing the noon meal, met George as he stepped down from his horse.

"Just what do you think you're doing, running that crow-bait horse in here like that and throwing dust all over ever'thing? Maybe you like dirt in your stew, but the rest of us don't care for it. I aim to throw a whole handful of it on your plate, and maybe a few rocks to go with it. Maybe next time you'll learn not to—"

George shoved out his hand and took an unsteady step toward the cook, cutting him off. "I got bit—"

Sandy grabbed the hand. The fang marks had darkened and the hand was swollen. He pulled George to the fold-out table beneath the chuck box. The table was cluttered with plates, cups, and utensils, and Sandy sent it all crashing to the ground with one swipe of his arm.

"Kneel down there and hold the back of your hand flat against the wood. Keep your hand open, and no matter what I do to you, or how bad it hurts, don't move or jerk, or I'm liable to cut too deep and take that hand of yours clear off."

There was the clap of hooves as someone rode into camp.

"Hurry on over here." Sandy's voice echoed in George's ears as if it came from inside an empty barrel. "George got bit by a rattler. Hold his arm still."

Senor Valarde's large, callused hands clamped George's arm and wrist to the table. George closed his eyes as Sandy took a knife and cut deep gashes, crisscrossing each of the fang marks on his palm.

George shook against the pain. Finally he felt the pressure on his wrist release. His arm was lowered from the table and he opened his eyes to see that Senor Valarde had his mouth over the snakebite wound. Then his friend raised his head, his lips and mouth covered with blood. He spit to the side, then again put his mouth on the palm of George's hand.

Everything began to move in circles. The flat blue sky, the wagon, the cook, Valarde with his bloody chin and lips. It all began to spin.

FOURTEEN

W HEN HE OPENED his eyes, he looked up into the darkness. The stars above were bright. He had been awake before. Maybe two or three times before. One time was in the daylight, and Sandy had fed him some broth.

He touched the hand that had been bitten by the snake, finding that it was still wrapped. He tried to move his fingers against the bandage, but the stabbing pain made him stop.

A cowhand was singing in the distance, trying to soothe the cattle and keep them quiet and bedded down. George was familiar with the tune and could make out every word.

> "Rock of ages, cleft for me.
> Let me hide myself in Thee.
> Let the water and the blood,
> from Thy wounded side which flowed . . ."

The song reminded him of his mother. He could

see her singing it as she went about her work in the kitchen. His throat tightened. He hoped she was all right. How long had he been gone? A month? Two months? How much farther to Kansas and Abilene? A bright fiery light shot across the sky, and George wiped his eyes so he could see better. It had to be a falling star.

At home, in Rogers Prairie, he'd spent many summer nights lying on the ground in front of the cabin and gazing at the night sky. The stars fascinated him, and he wondered why it was that some of them fell and others did not. That, and how come sometimes there was a moon, or at least part of one, and other times there wasn't?

The Big Dipper was clear, and George noticed that it hadn't turned very much, so it couldn't have been dark for long.

He put his good hand on the wagon bed for support and slowly raised up. Through the dense foliage he saw the yellow glow of flickering firelight. Then he saw a different light, the light of a bobbing lantern coming toward him.

Sandy Crebbs climbed the spokes of the wagon wheel and held the lantern over the side boards. George could see Charley standing beside Sandy, on the ground.

"Well, I'll be." Sandy grinned. "How long have you been sitting there like a possum in a tree? I was just here a little bit ago and you were sound asleep."

"Just . . . just got up."

"You hungry? You have to be. You haven't eaten hardly anything in four days. Can you eat regular

vittles? Before sundown we killed one of those straggling, sore-footed grass eaters that was causing the drag riders to swear so much. I made the best son-of-a-gun stew out of him you'll ever eat. You think you can take some? Sure would be good for you, if you could."

Charley put his foot on one of the wheel spokes and stepped up so that his head was over the side boards, too.

"And there's the best sinkers to go with that stew that you ever tasted. If he hadn't've put raisins in them, they'd be so light the gnats and mosquitos would've already carried them all off."

George smiled. The biscuits might really be good, but he knew that Charley was just trying to stay on Sandy's good side.

"I'm hungry enough to eat a steer, horns, hide, and all." He managed to balance himself against the wagon side and rise to his knees. "It'll just take me a minute or two to get down from here."

"Oh, no you don't." Sandy stepped down from the wheel, taking the light of the lantern with him.

"I haven't done all your work and mine, too, and then nursed you like a buttermilk calf just to have you go traipsing around here getting sick again. You stay right there and I'll bring you some grub and coffee. But don't you go to getting the idea that I aim to fool with you much longer. Just a little old rattlesnake bite, and you haven't done a lick of work to help me ever since." Sandy turned to walk away. He yelled over his shoulder, "Valarde is watching the remuda. I told him I'd let him know if you woke up."

Charley climbed into the wagon and sat down. "You had us all pretty worried. For a while there, no one knew if you were going to pull through or not." The gentle breeze felt good on George's neck. "Where are we? How much farther is it to Abilene?"

"I can't say for sure because I've never been there. But the talk is that we'll be reaching the South Canadian River in a couple more days. Another day or two, providing we don't have any trouble, and we'll cross the North Canadian and be getting close to the Cimarron. According to Hayden, that puts us way over halfway there."

Charley took his hat off and set it in his lap. "I wish you coulda seen the country just this side of the Red River. That's the prettiest land I ever saw. High rolling prairie with knee-high grass, and the trail was skirted with blackjack oak woods. We went up on a big flat mesa and from there could see Monument Rock, nearly fifteen miles away."

"'Monument Rock'?"

"Yeah. It's two piles of boulders, each of them about twice as high as a man. They are set a ways apart from each other. Sandy said some of the early trail drivers stacked those boulders there to mark where the trail was. Cowboys that have come through have carved their initials and their brands on those rocks. I put my initials there, and I put yours, too, except it was just a *G* because I didn't know your last name. What is your last name, anyway?"

George turned his head. Since he had been born a slave, he had no last name of his own.

Shoeboy, he started to mutter, but stopped himself.

"McJunkin," he blurted out. He didn't like that name because it belonged to the slaveholder. But it was better than nothing, better than Shoeboy.

"Well," Charley said. "After Abilene, if we go back to Texas the same way we came, we'll stop at those rocks and add an *M* to the *G.*"

"That'd be fine," George said, wondering what was taking Sandy so long. He was hungry, but because of his dry throat, he wanted a few sips of hot coffee more than anything else.

"Is Beggar all right?" he asked.

"He's fine. No one has rode him. The remuda is trail broke now. You've done a real good job with 'em. They ain't much trouble. Sometimes, because there's just enough of us to hold the positions with the cattle, we just let the horses follow along with the wagon and nobody much watches them."

George remembered seeing the blood on Valarde's lips from trying to suck the snake poison out of his hand. The memory came back of when he got bit.

"I found a skull, Charley. A man's skull, or I guess it could have been a woman's. Close to it, there was some kind of an Indian club beneath a bush. It was a smooth, kind of long round rock that was wrapped up with strips of rawhide and tied to a short handle. When I started to pick it up, that's when the snake got me. I didn't know it was there until it was too late."

"Wonder who it could have been?" Charley ran his fingers around the edge of his hat brim. "Was the skull old looking?"

"Yeah. Whoever it was died years ago."

Shouts came from the direction of the campfire. Charley shoved his hat on and sprang out of the wagon. "Come on. Something's happening and we're going to miss it."

Charley ran on, and George, using his good hand, climbed out of the wagon as quickly as he could. By the time he reached the campfire, he was short of breath and his legs had a strange tingling sensation in them.

Several of the cowhands, and Sandy, too, were gathered a short distance from the fire. Closer to it stood Axe and one of the night punchers, Juan. Juan was a small young man who was always quiet and kept mostly to himself. George wondered what had caused him to abandon his post and ride into camp.

Both Axe and Juan were dusty, and Juan's shirt was torn. Axe towered over the smaller man. He took a step backward, then ducked his head and dived for Juan's middle. The vaquero sidestepped the move, sending Axe sprawling to the ground.

The cowhands howled and cheered. Axe quickly rose, brandishing a pistol. Juan pulled out a knife.

Now the hands were silent, and rapid hoofbeats sounded as Hayden approached on his horse.

"Drop it!" he demanded, sliding off his mount. "The both of you."

The two men stood motionless, glaring at each other.

"I mean what I say," the boss continued. "Whatever the trouble is between you, it's going to have to

wait. The cattle come first, and I need every hand I have. Juan, get back to the herd. Whatever your argument is about, it'll wait till we get to Abilene. Then it's none of my business what you do. Put your gun up, Axe."

Axe hesitantly let the hammer down on his pistol and holstered it. The knife that had been in Juan's hand was gone. The vaquero turned and walked away.

"All right, boys." Hayden took a step and turned so that he was speaking to everyone. "We'll let that be the end of it. I don't want to hear any more about it. You're all wanting some excitement, and as soon as we get to Abilene you can have your fill. But first we have to get there."

FIFTEEN

GEORGE THREW an armload of firewood beneath the chuck wagon, then got to his knees and bent over to shove it, a stick at a time, into the rawhide cooney. Finally he wiped the sweat from his brow with his bandanna and glanced at the afternoon sun. Two hours or better of daylight remained, and his work for the day was done.

The cooney was full of wood and buffalo chips. He'd filled the water barrel and helped Sandy repair a broken spoke on a wagon wheel, and he'd also replaced a missing shoe on one of the mules. The wagon was unloaded, and although there wasn't a cloud in the sky, he'd set up a canvas awning over the chuck box, just in case it rained. At dusk he'd have to bring the remuda in for the hands to get their night horses, but until then, he was done. He hoped Charley was through herding the cattle, so they'd have time for a long reading lesson.

They'd set up camp alongside the Cimarron River, and he could make out several ducks swimming near the middle. A fish jumped and splashed among them, and the ducks dived beneath the surface, popping back up one or two at a time, like cork fishing bobbers.

He raised his eyes from the water to the yellow, empty plains beyond. He was glad that Mr. Hayden had decided to make an early camp today and swim the cattle across the river tomorrow. Otherwise, it would have been dark before the last of the cattle were across and camp would have been made on the other side, probably without benefit of the bedrolls or the chuck wagon and provisions in it.

Besides, if crossing the Cimarron went as well as crossing the South and North Canadian Rivers, the herd was still likely to travel ten or twelve miles tomorrow, about as far as they usually went.

George swiped at a mosquito that had lit on his right hand, leaving a streak of blood. He inspected the knife gashes Sandy had made in his palm and saw that the scabs had broken, probably from gathering the wood.

Senor Valarde had continued to take care of the remuda for several days after George had recovered from the snakebite. The old vaquero had tried not to let it show, but George could tell that he had been very worried. George had tried several times to thank him for saving his life, but Valarde only waved his hand and said, "*De nada*. It is nothing."

Someone moved behind him. He had been so preoccupied with his thoughts, he hadn't heard anyone

come into camp. He turned and saw Charley holding his fingers to his lips.

"Hurry up and get on your horse. There's a herd of buffalo nearby and Hayden wants us to chase them away from the herd."

George hurried to the picket line and saddled Beggar. His reading lesson would have to wait. Only twice during the trip had he caught a glimpse of buffalo—both times from too far away to tell much about them.

Charley spurred his horse into a gallop, and George followed him close behind. They hadn't gone far at all until the buffalo were in plain sight farther to the south. He reined Beggar into a canter, not wanting to wind the horse too soon, and Charley slowed down, too.

As they moved closer to the shaggy brownish black animals, George's heart beat hard. They were beautiful. And they were huge. He could remember the cowboys saying that a really big buffalo bull could weigh as much as three thousand pounds and be as long as twelve feet. Buffalo cows were much smaller, though, weighing eight or nine hundred pounds, about the same as an average four- to eight-year-old longhorn steer.

Soon, several of the buffalo became aware of the two riders and began to trot off. Charley, now riding alongside George, shook out his lariat.

"Let's catch one, George," he half yelled above the horse's hoofbeats. "I've heard of others doing it, and there isn't any reason why we can't catch a young one, if we can both get our loops around his

horns. Sandy can butcher him and we'll have ourselves buffalo steak for dinner."

George didn't answer at first. For one thing, he didn't want to bother the herd of buffalo any more than they needed to, and for another, his roping Charley's arm that day in the river and sending his loop over prairie flowers along the trail were a whole lot different from catching a running buffalo and tying him solid to the saddle horn.

But Charley would not understand his excuses. He might take them as a sign of weakness or cowardice.

"Maybe we better not," George tried. "The boss might chew us out for it."

They had drawn up close to the buffalo now, and the entire herd was running. Charley spurred his horse faster and began to swing his rope.

"Come on, George. Hayden won't care. They're getting away!"

George allowed Beggar more slack in the reins and dug his heels into the horse's sides. He removed his reata from around the saddle horn and swung the loop out to the side, spinning it a couple of times to get it the right size. If Charley managed to get his rope on a buffalo, he was bound to need help.

Dust boiled thick from the hooves of the running buffalo. A cow darted in front of them, and George saw Charley make a throw.

It was all wrong. As George released his own loop from his right hand, he knew it was wrong. This was no calf. This was a full-grown buffalo cow.

Charley's loop slapped the buffalo's head and neck and slid off, just as George's settled smoothly

around her horns. George quickly dallied a few wraps around the saddle horn and pulled the reins for Beggar to stop.

The horse slowed, and a terrific jolt knocked George backward. He was soaring through the air. The saddle was still beneath him, but Beggar was not.

He hit the ground hard, still sitting straight up in the saddle but being dragged rapidly. Through the dust, he could see the buffalo cow running ahead, pulling the saddle along by the reata. He tried to unwrap his dally, but the wraps were stuck and wouldn't budge. The ground rushed past him in a blur, pulling and scraping his legs.

He wanted to turn loose of the saddle horn and just fall out of the saddle. But that would mean he'd probably never see the saddle again, and it belonged to Hayden.

He reached into his pants pocket and with some difficulty retrieved his jackknife. He managed to get the blade open and, with one swing, sliced the reata in two. The saddle stopped so abruptly, it threw him headlong, rolling end over end across the prairie grass.

For a good long moment, he was stunned. He lay there gasping for breath. Charley reined his horse up and slid down.

"You all right? Are you hurt?" Charley hovered above him. "I never saw anything like that in my whole life. I thought that buffalo was going to drag you clear to Montana."

George sat up, closed the blade of his knife, and

put it into his pocket. His pants, on both sides, were ripped below the knee.

Charley offered his hand. "Can you stand? Will your legs hold?"

"I think so." George stood up and rubbed his eyes to get the dust out. The buffalo were still running, in the distance now, just a dusty dark blur racing across the prairie.

He looked around for his saddle. The sight of the cut end of his reata hanging from the horn made him angry, and he wished he hadn't gotten into all this. He shouldn't have listened to Charley; he shouldn't have thrown the loop.

"Where's Beggar?" he finally asked. "Is he all right?"

"Sure . . . sure he is," Charley said quietly. "When you and your saddle came off, it scared him pretty bad and he hightailed it back toward camp, dragging the reins along behind him."

George inspected the saddle. Other than the front fenders and stirrup leathers being scratched up pretty badly, it was undamaged. The cinch hung from the off-billet strap, so he checked the latigo, finding it busted.

"Look, George!"

A few hundred yards away, four shirtless Indians quietly sat on their horses, watching them.

Charley climbed onto his horse. "Hurry!" he whispered. "Leave the saddle and get on. We gotta get out of here."

George was still angry and not at all sure that

they needed to be alarmed. The last time he'd seen Indians they'd turned out to be nothing but a poor, pitiful starving family who just wanted some beef to eat.

He tossed the saddle into Charley's lap. "I'm not leaving it. If those braves wanted to kill us, they'd probably have already done it." George swung up onto the rear of the horse. "Just try to ignore them."

But Charley barely waited until George was on before he spurred the horse into a gallop.

The Indians let out a couple of yells, and in an instant, they, too, were running their horses. Running them straight for Charley and George.

Charley shifted the saddle he was holding to the side, as if he was about to toss it off. George grabbed it by the horn, at the same time wrapping his other arm around Charley's waist to keep his balance.

The bay ran faster and faster, but it was no use. Handicapped by the weight of two riders, there was no way the animal could outrun the Indians' ponies.

One of the braves held a rifle out from his side and another held a bow. They were getting closer.

The Indians split up, two to the right and two to the left. Soon they were riding even with George and Charley, yelling and waving their weapons.

The brave closest to them ducked to the side of his horse. None of his body showed but the calf of his leg hooked over the animal's backbone. Then he hung beneath the neck of the horse, his arms and hands wrapped around it. He released an arm and leg, and finally held on by just one arm around the horse's neck.

To George's left the Indian who had the rifle was sitting on his horse backward, not even holding the reins, while his brown-and-white paint horse sped on. The other one was leaning so far off his horse that his hand was touching the top of the grass and he was catching prairie flowers as he went by. He rose upright and threw a handful of them into the air. George was sure the Indian laughed.

Comanche. These Indians had to be Comanche, the famous horsemen of the plains. But they were also known for their fighting abilities and their dislike for intruders on land they claimed as their own. They could have already killed them easily, but instead, they were just showing off.

A gunshot boomed, and George looked over Charley's shoulder toward the cattle herd. Two riders, about seventy-five yards away, were coming fast. George could tell that the lead rider was Senor Valarde, and judging from the buckskin color of the other horse, Hayden was not far behind.

The four Indians crossed directly in front of the bay and rode off, heading south.

Charley slowed the horse to a canter, stopping when Hayden and Valarde met them.

"What's going on?" the boss demanded. "We saw Beggar come into camp empty, so we knew something was wrong."

The bay was sweating and blowing hard. George slid off and set the saddle on the ground.

Charley answered. "We chased the buffalo away from the herd, but it was my dumb idea to rope one and I kind of talked George into it. I missed my throw,

but George didn't, and that buffalo took him and his saddle off quicker than a man can blink. George managed to cut loose, and that's when we saw the Indians. At first, they just watched us; but when we left in a hurry, they did, too, chasing after us."

Hayden glared.

"Boss," Charley continued, "those were Comanche. You never saw such trick riding as they did. One of them had a rifle, and they had us just as dead as could be. I don't know why they let us go. Seemed like they were just wanting to play. After you shot— well, you saw the rest."

Hayden stared at George with his jaws set tight. "I thought you had more sense than to listen to the likes of him." He aimed a thumb at Charley.

George looked at his feet, unable to meet the eyes of Hayden or Valarde.

THE SUN HAD almost set when the group reached camp and George swung down from Charley's horse. Axe and Juan were eating supper by the campfire, sitting on the same log; and George was glad to see that whatever the trouble between them had been about, it was over.

"George," Valarde called, "the next time you want to rope something so big, make sure the horse you are riding is bigger." He winked and rode to the picket line.

Charley held up the saddle. "I'll fix your latigo if you want. You ought to take my horse to bring in the remuda. By the time you get Beggar saddled and ready, you'll be just about out of daylight."

Hayden spoke. "Listen up, boys. We may be having some more Indian trouble, and it's going to be another long night. Everyone stays with the herd, except the cook and wrango.

"Charley, I want you to stay with George and the remuda again. No more foolishness out of you, or those Comanche are liable to have your scalp the next time."

The boss led his horse toward the chuck wagon, and George mounted Charley's bay. The horse was worn out, but it wouldn't take much effort to bring in the remuda.

A short distance from camp, and close to the river, George found the horses grazing peacefully. But his thoughts weren't on the remuda. He was thinking about the buffalo he'd seen, the reata he'd lost, and how close he and Charley had come to losing their lives.

The four Indians' actions still didn't make any sense. Were they really gone or would they be back tonight? And if they did return, would they bring other warriors with them?

He held the bay at a trot, swinging around behind the remuda and staying close to the foliage along the river's edge.

The bay stopped and snorted, holding his ears erect, signaling that something was wrong. A man wearing a broad-brimmed felt hat and riding a coal black horse stepped from the dense shadows of the trees.

The dusk light was dim, but George could see the man's face clearly. It was flat, small-nosed, and snow

white. It was the same face that had sometimes haunted George's dreams since he'd awakened to find himself locked inside a jail cell in the town of Comanche. His mouth went dry.

George had to force his eyes to shift from the man's face to the black boot in the stirrup. The boot had a tall top, and barely visible on the side of the spur were two golden crosses.

The man spoke, his voice holding a faint Spanish accent. "I am just passing through, boy. Do you think your trail master and your cook would be hospitable to a stranger at their fire?"

George was unable to answer. He just raised his arm and pointed in the direction of camp.

SIXTEEN

WHEN HE WAS calmed down enough to get back to camp, the night darkness was nearly full. A slight breeze blew, and he could see the hint of a coming moon in the east.

George quietly hurried to a spot where he could see the area around the campfire clearly while staying hidden among the trees along the river. He would have to get word to Hayden that this rider was trouble. It could be a coincidence that their visitor and the Comanche had shown up on the same day, but he doubted it.

The white-faced man and Mr. Hayden were seated now, alone, by the fire. The man had a plate of food in one hand and was gesturing with the other as he talked. George started back toward the picket line.

Because of George's new clothes and hat, the man apparently hadn't recognized him, but he'd try not to let their visitor see him again.

George spotted Sandy by the chuck box, cutting steaks off a hindquarter of beef, and edged up to him. The old cook drove the point of his butcher knife into the table and began wiping his hands on his dirt- and food-stained apron.

"There's a little stew left by the fire, George, and I saved you a piece of dried-apple pie. You'd better eat quick, though, and hurry on back to the horses.

"Dad-blamed Indians, anyhow. They like as not won't do any more than the last bunch did. Just make everybody lose a bunch of sleep and cause a bunch of worry for nothin'."

"I've got to talk to Mr. Hayden, Sandy. It's about the man he's with. Could you think up an excuse to bring him over here?"

"Well, just what is it that you think you know about this feller?" Sandy ran a hand over the stubble of white beard on his face. "Why, I knew that fellow was trouble when he rode in here and I first saw those black beady eyes of his. And did you ever see skin so white as that? It'll nearly cause a fellow to go blind."

"Could you just tell Mr. Hayden I'm at the picket line?" George asked, knowing he was getting a little short with the cook. "Tell him my horse is lame and I want him to have a look. Then maybe you could keep our visitor busy by talking to him or giving him some more to eat."

"Of course I could do it," Sandy said. Then he started going on about how no one told him anything and how he was the real boss of the outfit.

Finally George just turned and walked toward Beggar to wait.

Within a few minutes, the boss approached.

The man ducked his tall body under the picket line. "I hear you have a crippled horse on your hands, George. Lead him on over to the wagon so we can get the lantern and have a better look."

"No, sir." George stepped closer, speaking just above a whisper. "You remember when you first saw me and I was sick and had a knot on my head? I had been caught by some Indians, and that man you're talkin' to was with them. He's still wearing the same spurs he wore then, and he's the one that kicked me. I don't know for certain, but he might be with those Indians we saw today, and they could be after the herd."

"You're sure? There's no way you could be mistaken?"

"I'm sure."

There was silence between them. The sounds of the crickets and frogs along the river were loud and constant.

At last Hayden spoke. "This fellow you're talking about calls himself Rapheal Mancito, and there's nothing I'd like better than to give him back some of what he gave you. But that wouldn't help us any. It would just tell him that we know something about him, and when I let him go, he'd spend all of his time figuring out ways to make it rough on us.

"From what you've told me, it might be that he's a Comanchero. If he is running with Comanche, it's

likely they'll try for the remuda instead of the cattle. Horses are easier to handle and trade, and he's already been asking questions about them."

The boss pushed his hat up on his forehead. "I want you to get what hobbles we have out of the wagon, and you and Charley start putting them on the horses. I'll send Axe out with ropes and gunnysacks and anything else he can find that could be used to hold a horse's forelegs together. You probably won't get much more than half of them hobbled, but that will have to do.

"Then I want you to push the remuda farther out from the cattle and wagon than usual, and keep them close to the river. Stake Buck out with them. As soon as Mancito leaves camp, I'll be out to join you."

"But Buck is your night horse," George answered. "He's the best horse in the outfit. You don't want to take a chance on losing him, do you?"

"No." Hayden smiled. "But a good-looking horse is always admired by a horse thief. After I get through telling Mancito all about him, he's going to think old Buck is made of pure gold."

MAYBE IT WOULD be a quiet night, after all. George stretched his legs out in front of him, trying to ease the cramps. He and Charley had been crouched behind this tree for what must have been five hours. More than anything, he wanted to stand up. But Hayden's instructions were for Charley, Axe, Senor Valarde, and himself to stay hidden and keep a careful watch.

He yawned and looked up at the sky, wondering if the night was ever going to end. The moon was

now in the west. Its brightness wouldn't allow him to see the stars of the Big Dipper, but dawn couldn't be too far away.

He glanced at Charley, who lay beside him with his revolver in one outstretched hand, breathing slow, regular breaths. He thought maybe he should wake him, but what difference did it make if he slept? From the looks of things, Sandy had been right. All that was going to happen tonight was that everyone was going to lose sleep over nothing.

The horses in the remuda were clearly visible on the moonlit plain. Most of them had eaten their fill and were quiet. Close to them, standing alone at the end of his stake rope, was the boss's buckskin night horse, bait for the trap that had been set for Mancito. Hayden had hidden himself in the brush by the river, directly across from the horse.

Over somewhere on George's left, Axe and Valarde were tucked away in the bushes with rifles, watching the remuda. George hadn't seen them or the boss since they had all left their saddled horses tied in a stand of willows by the river.

One of the horses in the remuda whinnied, and several others moved about, leaping forward in their hobbles. George stiffened. Whenever there was anything unusual around, the horses always knew it first.

Then he heard the booming of gunfire from the direction of the river. George was now on his knees, and Charley hopped up, too, standing in a low crouch. Fire belched from the muzzle of Charley's pistol.

"No, Charley." George grabbed his arm. He hadn't seen anything and didn't see how Charley could have, either. "You'll hit the horses."

More shots boomed, from both the left and the right. The remuda horses jumped and reared, and those that weren't hobbled ran in circles. The outline of a horse and rider raced past, and Charley fired his gun again. The shot had no visible effect.

Gunshots continued to roar around them for another minute or so and then suddenly stopped.

The stench of the gunpowder hung in the air from Charley's two shots. The silence was eerie. They remained stone still until they heard the bellow of Hayden's voice asking if they were all right.

"We're all right," George yelled.

Axe called out from the distance. "Doing just fine here, too, boss. I think maybe Valarde hit a couple of them."

A low moaning came from somewhere near the spot where Buck was staked. The groans sounded almost like the muffled bellow of a cow or calf, but they weren't. They were *human.*

"I . . . I am hurt. I have helped you. Please . . . please help me."

Mancito. The sound of his voice made George even more tense.

"Stay where you're at, boys," Hayden hollered. "Don't move until I tell you."

"Who do you think that is?" Charley asked, as he reloaded his gun.

George hadn't told Charley about Mancito, and he didn't feel like talking much now, but he quietly

started the story from when he first saw Mancito and kept going until Hayden called out again.

"The rest of you boys come on out. Looks like we have a hanging to tend to."

A hanging.

George stepped from his hiding place among the trees. He was remembering when he was five or maybe six years old. He and his mother and father were on their way back to their cabin after a day of picking Master McJunkin's cotton.

A big elm tree stood beside the path, and they had almost passed it before George saw a man hanging from a high limb with a rope around his neck. A black man, with his head cocked to the side and his tongue sticking out the corner of his mouth.

George's mother had quickly covered his eyes with her hands and rushed him on so he couldn't look anymore. But he would never forget.

WHEN HE AND Charley reached the remuda, Mr. Hayden and Axe were shoving the figure of a man up onto the top of Buck's back. Valarde was holding the horse.

The man raised his head to speak, his white face shining starkly, covered with a greasy sweat.

"No, you cannot do this thing," Mancito said, his voice hoarse and his breath strained. "I . . . I am hurt. Badly wounded. I only came because I heard the firing of guns and . . . and I wished to be of service to you."

But the boss would hear none of it. "We're Texans," he said. "And Texans hang horse thieves."

Mancito slumped forward on the horse.

"Valarde," Hayden said, coiling up the stake rope, "lead Buck to the nearest tree and let's get on with it."

George tried to make what was happening right in his mind. This man had come here to steal the horses, that was clear. And he probably would have killed George back near Comanche if the posse hadn't shown up. But now he was helpless and doubled over with a bullet in his gut. Somehow hanging him didn't seem right.

The brightly glowing moon was sinking below the horizon. To the east was the gray coming of dawn.

Hayden threw half of the stake rope over the limb of a large tree, then positioned the loop at the end of it around Mancito's neck.

The next few minutes seemed to stretch into hours. At last, at the sound of the boss's voice, George opened his eyes.

"If it hadn't been for you telling me about him," Hayden said, "we'd probably have lost the remuda. I'll pull his boots off now. Between the gold on his spurs and the Colt I took from him, you should be able to get enough money to buy you a real nice saddle in Abilene."

George didn't answer.

"Go on and bring our saddle horses up. The day's just starting, and by the end of it, we'll have crossed the Cimarron. It won't be long until we're in Kansas."

SEVENTEEN

A FEW DAYS LATER George was looking back at the miles of grassy plains and the winding trickle of green that was the Arkansas River. The herd had crossed the river just hours earlier, right after dawn, and everything had gone much smoother there than the crossing of the Cimarron River. That task had taken a full day longer than Hayden had expected.

The trouble hadn't been so much the water, but quicksand along the edges of the river. Over forty steers, along with a few horses, had become bogged down in it. Bone weary from lack of sleep, everyone had worked with ropes and pulleys for two long days, dragging the animals out of the sucking mud.

One of the horses, a line-backed dun, had broken a leg and had to be shot. And after trying everything they could think of to free seven of the steers, they'd finally given up. To end the animals' suffering, Hayden had ordered them destroyed, too.

George turned his attention up ahead. The horses in the remuda traveled at a slow walk, snatching tufts of grass where they could. They were so used to keeping pace with the chuck wagon and the cattle that he rarely had to do anything except follow.

At least a hundred times he'd recalled the night that Rapheal Mancito had been hanged. Since that night, there had been another disturbing incident.

Before reaching the Arkansas River, the trail drive had crossed a dry creek, and there they had come upon the bleaching bones of dozens of people. Hayden had said they were the bones of Indians— Wichita—and that they'd died from a cholera epidemic. The skeletons of the small children and babies had bothered George the most.

The sound of Sandy striking the dinner triangle rang out across the prairie, signaling that the noon meal was ready. All at once every horse in the remuda held its head up and ears erect, and they all started to move in the direction of the chuck wagon.

The remuda was soon within the confines of the rope corral that was held waist high by four cowhands. George dismounted, wrapping the reins around Beggar's neck so the horse could graze without stepping on them.

A sudden gust of wind kicked up the dirt around him, and George grabbed for his hat, pulling it down tighter. Up until now the day had been calm and the air hot and sticky. A few clouds dotted the sky. One in the east appeared particularly dark and heavy.

George looked to the north, where the herd would be heading this afternoon. The land was rolling and

held a few narrow draws. A long furrow had been plowed in the ground, and farther on, faintly visible against a bluff, was what he guessed to be another sod house.

Hayden and the cowboys called the houses soddys, and they called the people living in them sodbusters, nesters, grangers, or homesteaders. The homes were built out of lengths of cut sod stacked like bricks. But most of the ones George had seen were really not much more than dugouts—square holes in the ground, or on the side of a bluff—with timbers covered by dirt for a roof.

The closer the herd came to Abilene, the more soddys he'd seen and the more furrows that had been plowed in the ground. The furrows were the homesteaders' one-hundred-and-sixty-acre property boundaries.

Because the Kansas plains held little firewood, the people living on them were forced to burn buffalo or cow chips for fuel, and even those were in short supply. To replenish their stock, several settlers along the trail had asked Hayden to bed down the herd on their land.

In one case, about a week ago, two men had nearly come to blows over whose property the herd would spend the night on. To settle the dispute, Hayden had driven the herd across a furrow separating the land so that about half of the cattle were on each side.

The land was given to the settlers by the government. All a homesteader had to do to own it was to stake out an unclaimed plot, live on it for five years,

and make improvements. The soil was rich and black, and nearly every homestead they'd passed had crops of corn sprouting up.

When George found out how easy it was to own the land, he shared an idea with Senor Valarde. Someday they would all come back here. This was the sort of place his parents needed. With hard work, he, Senor Valarde, and his parents could build a home to be proud of and a farm that would supply all of their needs.

He could see it so clearly. The house would of course be made of prairie sod. But it would be much larger than the other soddys he'd seen, and the roof would be built out of thick logs they would cut along a river. And instead of just planting small fields of corn here and there like the other settlers, they'd plow all of their land. When the corn sprouted, their home would be surrounded by one hundred and sixty acres of green fields. After the corn was harvested and sold, they would all go to town and his mother would buy whatever she wanted. They'd get windows for the house and maybe even enough plank lumber to build a real floor.

George shook his head. *A dream.* That's all the notion was and might ever be.

EIGHTEEN

THE LAST LEG of the journey was over. Hayden had been right when he told the crew they would be in Abilene in less than two weeks.

George could feel the tension in Beggar as a steam-belching, wheel-pounding mass of iron passed by on the railroad tracks. The horse snorted and shied backward, and George held the reins tight, staring at the steel monster.

Several wooden railroad cars rolled by filled with bawling cattle. When the train had passed, Sandy shouted at the mule team and slapped the reins. The chuck wagon creaked and bobbled as it crossed the tracks.

Hayden had ordered Axe, Charley, Valarde, and George to accompany him into town to load up on supplies and make arrangements about the cattle. When they were finished, the rest of the hands would be allowed to come in.

For nearly three months George had looked forward to seeing the city. Now Abilene lay before him and he could hardly take it all in. It was the biggest town he had ever seen. They passed the stockyard and its rows and rows of large wooden corrals filled with cattle. And across a creek, there were a dozen or so log cabins, each roofed with sod.

The main street was crowded with people, horses, buggies, and wagons. Buildings lined it, many of them so new that sap still oozed from the pine boards. One structure stood three stories high, with rows of windows at each level and fancy scalloped woodwork along the front edge of the roof.

Sandy stopped the wagon, and George and the others tied their horses to the same hitching rail.

The boss stepped onto the boardwalk. "You boys wait here. I'll go have a little talk with the cattle buyers."

All around, people bustled past and clustered near the storefronts. Many of them were cowboys who had left their herds to graze the prairie land outside Abilene, the same as Hayden had. Other men wore suits, though, and strange-looking hats with tall tops and hardly any brim.

A group of ladies crossed the street, and George couldn't help but stare at them with their long flowing dresses made out of expensive fabric and trimmed with lace.

Charley drew closer. "What do you want to do first?" he asked. "I think we should buy us a new set of clothes. Ours are so thin and ripped and full of holes they aren't even worth saving. Then we'll get

us something to eat. Eggs, that's what I want. It's been so long since I had them, I can't remember what they taste like. After that we'll just go from place to place looking at everything there is to see."

"Sure." George nodded, still taking in the sight of the busy crowd and the steady hum of voices all around them. "Eggs sound good to me."

In a few minutes Hayden returned. "You boys come on up and get your money. I know you're itching to spend it. Sandy and I will take care of the supplies. If I don't see you before, I'll see you back at the herd by dark. Don't be late. The other hands are waiting for their turn to come to town, too."

AN HOUR OR SO later, George strode out of the dry-goods store. He was proud of his new flannel shirt and brown duck pants. He touched the brim of his new hat and smiled.

Senor Valarde was waiting for him on the steps. "You look good, I think." He rubbed his chin. "Perhaps a little older."

"Aren't you going to wear your new duds?" George pointed to the wrapped parcel under Valarde's arm.

"Soon, but not today. I will save them until these will no longer do."

They heard Charley clear his throat. He stood at the end of the rail, wearing black striped pants and a shiny red shirt.

George shook his head. "Now, don't you look like a dandy? If I didn't know better, I'd think you were rich and owned half the town."

Charley hooked his thumbs in his waistband. "I kinda feel like maybe I do. Come on. Let's go see what all I own."

"Wait for me." Axe stepped out of the store, holding a piece of paper. "Look what I found. One of you boys tell me what it says."

George stood next to Charley and studied the flyer. He recognized one of the words and thought he might know another, but that didn't help much.

"What does it say?" he asked.

Charley put his finger under the first word. "That one says, 'Elect,' and this one, 'Ulysses,' which I never would've figured out except I've heard his name before. The whole thing says, "Elect Ulysses S. Grant for President."

George noticed a sign across the street, tacked to the exterior of a building. "LAND," he read. "That sign says LAND . . . LAND OFF—"

"LAND OFFICE." Charley half-pulled him down the street. "That's where they buy and sell land. It's not for us. Let's find us a place that cooks food. I'm starving."

"Amen." Axe jogged to catch up with them.

George looked back. "You coming, Senor Valarde?"

"First I am going to speak to the people inside that building. I won't be long. You go and find your eggs."

"You don't have to tell me twice." Charley continued to pull George down the street.

The aroma of cooking meat came from an open door ahead, and Charley stopped. "This smells like my kind of place."

The room was smoky and filled with people. George followed his friends, moving sideways between the many tables.

When they passed near a stocky man with a blond mustache, the stranger kicked his chair back and stood. He began to shout. "Darkies ain't allowed in here, boy. You ought to know better than to think you can just waltz in here and sit down and eat with the white folks."

The words stung and George's face burned. Everything flooded back, all of the hate he had known in Rogers Prairie. He had been foolish to have forgotten, to think that anything had changed.

Charley pushed between them. "Leave him alone. He's with me and we're not bothering anyone."

George backed up a step, the shock he'd felt fast changing to anger. "I've been on the trail from Texas for a long time, and my money is just as good as anybody's, but I sure don't want to spend any of it here."

When George walked out the door, he could hear Axe and Charley tell the man the same thing. Outside in the street, Charley spoke first.

"That's tellin' 'em, George. To heck with him. I didn't want to eat in that greasy hash house, anyhow."

"Look." Axe pointed at another building. "That place is bound to have food. There's a big iron fork and spoon on the door. Let's go try our luck."

"You two go on ahead," George said. "I'm going to see if Senor Valarde is still at the land office."

"Ah, come on, George," Charley insisted. "The three of us can take care of any ol' sodbuster who wants to shoot off his mouth."

"I know we can. You fellows go save me a seat. I'll be along."

George watched them cross the street, and then he almost walked into Hayden and Valarde before he realized they were standing in front of him.

"George." Senor Valarde grinned broadly. "I have good news. I have been to the land office, and there is still much land for homesteading. You should send word to your mother and father."

Hayden frowned. "But I thought you said you might take me up on my offer, Valarde."

"What offer?" George asked.

"I told Valarde that I just made a deal to take a herd of horses to New Mexico. He said he might be interested in working for me again."

George chewed his lip. "You should take the job, Senor Valarde. The land will wait."

"I was hoping you would come, too, George," said Hayden.

George didn't know what to do. He wanted to return to Texas, even if it was just for a day or two, so he could tell his folks about all he had seen and done, and especially about the land for homesteading. But it wasn't every day that a man like Hayden asked you to come back to work for him. In fact, it might not be so easy to get another job.

"I showed Rapheal Mancito's Colt and spurs to the blacksmith," Hayden went on. "He's got a real nice saddle he wants you to take a look at when you have time."

Valarde put his hand on George's shoulder. "Send word to your mother and father, my friend. Charley

will help you write out the words, and your mama will get someone in Rogers Prairie to read it for her. Perhaps if we give the land office money, they will hold a good place for them. We can join them later, after the drive. Then we will have even more money to buy seed and livestock."

"What do you say, George?" Hayden raised one eyebrow. "I need a wrango—somebody who's good with horses. Someone I can trust."

George felt as if his chest would burst. "Let's go see the blacksmith. I want a look at that saddle. I'm going to ride it clear to New Mexico."

EPILOGUE

GEORGE MCJUNKIN took the job driving a large herd of horses west. This trip would eventually take him to the eastern part of present-day New Mexico, where he worked for several years breaking and training horses.

During this time, George learned to play the guitar and violin. He also taught roping and riding skills to boys in exchange for lessons in reading and writing, managing to finish all of the school textbooks through the fourth grade.

As the years passed, George began to collect rocks and fossils and learned all he could about them. He read everything he could get his hands on and was given an encyclopedia and a book about the stars. For hours he would lie on his back under the night sky, trying to locate and name the stars. And using information from his encyclopedia, he built a rain gauge

and a miniature windmill for measuring wind speed.

In his fifties, George became foreman of the Crowfoot, an eight-thousand-acre ranch near the town of Folsom, New Mexico. It was here, in 1908, that he made a spectacular discovery.

A heavy rain had fallen, causing a devastating flood. Soon afterward, George was out riding. He came to a familiar arroyo that had been only a few feet deep before the flood. Now it was much deeper and the fence that crossed the arroyo would no longer hold cattle.

While he was thinking about a way to repair the fence, something peculiar caught his eye. He dismounted and walked down into the ravine, finding a large bone. Around it were many other bones.

At first George thought they had to have come from a buffalo. Yet the more he puzzled over his find, the more he realized that something was amiss. The bones had been buried too deep, and they were too big.

In the coming weeks and months, George returned to wonder over the site many times. He found so many bones there that he named it the Bone Pit. But no one he questioned about it could tell him any more than he knew, though a few said they would like to someday travel to the ranch and have a look.

Years went by, and George's health began to fail. On January 22, 1922, he died without knowing the monumental importance of his discovery.

A few years later scientists from across the country would travel to McJunkin's Bone Pit. They

renamed it the Folsom Site and marveled at a spear point sticking between two prehistoric bison ribs.

Because of George McJunkin's find, scientists were able to prove that humans had lived in North America for at least ten thousand years, much longer than previously thought.

SELECTED GLOSSARY

Foreign terms are in *italics*.

caballo	horse
cantle	back of the saddle seat
chuck box	storage box for food staples
cooney	cowhide tied under the chuck wagon for storage
cowpunchers	another term for cowhands; sometimes called punchers
dally	to wrap the rope around the saddle horn; also used to refer to the dally loop
dally loop	first wrap of a dally
fox fire	phosphorescent light sometimes seen on the horn tips of cattle and the ears of horses during stormy weather
ganado	cattle

ganadero	cattleman
horse string	group of horses attached to a particular cowboy
latigo	leather strap that attaches the saddle rigging to the cinch
off-billet	strap on off-side of saddle for the cinch buckle
reata	braided rope made of rawhide
remuda	horses of a trail outfit
rig	saddle and attachments; sometimes used to describe a cowboy's belongings or the gunbelt and guns he wears. Also refers to almost any kind of vehicle.
rowels	rotating disk of a spur, sometimes with sharp points
soddy	house made from sod bricks
vaquero	Mexican cowboy
waddies	cowboys
war bag	cowboy's bag for his personal possessions
wohaw	cattle

BIBLIOGRAPHY

Adams, Andy. *The Log of a Cowboy*. Reprint, Bison, Nebr.: University of Nebraska Press, 1964.

Adams, Ramon F. *The Old-Time Cowhand*. Reprint, Bison, Nebr.: University of Nebraska Press, 1989.

Dobie, J. Frank. *The Longhorns*. Reprint, Austin, Tex.: University of Texas Press, 1994.

Durham, Philip, and Everett L. Jones. *The Negro Cowboys*. Reprint, Bison, Nebr.: University of Nebraska Press, 1983.

Folsom, Franklin. *Black Cowboy: The Life and Legend of George McJunkin*. Niwot, Colo.: R. Rinehart Publishers, 1992.

Gard, Wayne. *The Chisholm Trail*. Reprint, Norman, Okla.: University of Oklahoma Press, 1988.

Haley, J. Evetts. *Charles Goodnight: Cowman and Plainsman*. Norman, Okla.: University of Oklahoma Press, 1949.

Hunter, Marvin J., ed. and comp. *The Trail Drivers of Texas*. Reprint, Austin, Tex.: University of Texas Press, 1992.

Wallace, Ernest, and E. Adamson Hoebel. *The Comanches: Lords of the South Plains*. Norman, Okla.: University of Oklahoma Press, 1986.